First Edition

Editing by Krista Dapkey and Chris Hall

Cover art by Anna Volkin

 Created with Vellum

Forgery, Love, and Other Lies

ART OF LOVE

CHARLIE LANE

For Brian, my favorite person to experience art with.

One

M*ay 1822*

The strange man had stood on the opposite side of the street from Frampton & Son's Jewelers every day for the last fortnight, watching, never inching closer, as if he stood still to have his portrait painted. Now, his hands were stuffed into pockets and his shoulders hunched up around his neck, almost shoving off the beaver hat pulled low over his brow. A large rust-red scarf swallowed his neck and lower face, obscuring his features entirely. All days he looked the same—a cold, dark, featureless column with a blade of danger about him, a shadow of mystery.

The wind howled, and safe inside Frampton & Son's Jewelers, Fiona Frampton pulled her shawl close, and backed away from the winter chill frosting the glass of the shop window. A deeper chill ran through her because of the man. Who was he? Why did he watch? Did he plan to rob them?

Was he a runner? Did Papa have a long-lost son with an unknown first wife who'd come to claim his place as the *son* in Frampton & Son's? It would be nice, if quite the shock, to find herself in possession of a brother. Her older sister, Posey, would certainly not be amused. *She* was the "son" in Frampton and Son's after all, if one disregarded gender. No one could cut gems like her. No one knew wires and settings and paste and goldsmithing—Fiona shook her head and chuckled, turning from the window.

The cold man outside was no long-lost brother, and Mama would beg her to please focus.

Fiona did not wish to focus, though. Better to let her mind wander toward much-needed distractions from—she heaved a sigh—life.

Life as in her many mistakes.

Life as in the missing Dowager Lady Balantine.

Life as in Fiona's paintings.

Fiona's—she slammed a portcullis down on the subsequent words. She wouldn't even think it. Thinking it put it too closely to her lips, her tongue, and those words were ones she would take to her grave.

Hopefully.

Anyway, she would never do what she'd done again. It had been moment of weakness. Ten moments of weakness, to be precise, and they had been necessary. Not a horrid number of unforgivable sins for the three and twenty years she'd been on this earth. But ... never again. She scrubbed the thoughts from her mind till not even a speck of them remained and turned to her sister.

Posey stood at the front of the shop, speaking with a customer; as the face of Frampton's, she dressed appropriately, managing to appear fashionable and a touch out of reach. All of London thought her a mere shopgirl, a dutiful spinster daughter who helped her papa keep his doors open while he and a proper male apprentice sweated away in the back, making the wares they sold. All of London had it wrong. The apprentice was more of a delivery boy, and Posey completed at least half of the commissions these days, knew all her father's tricks of the trade.

But a woman jeweler? They kept that fact a secret.

The woman Posey currently spoke with, a countess who often patronized the shop, smiled and left a small box on the counter, never knowing the hands she left her jewelry with would do more than store those gems in the safe.

Posey opened the box, studied its contents. A bracelet or necklace. Perhaps a full parure. In her green silk gown and with her white-blonde hair styled in an elegant coiffure, a simple diamond drop necklace at her throat, she looked more like a lady about to dance the night away in a ballroom than a jeweler's apprentice.

Pride washed over Fiona, and she let herself float along in the warm ocean of it. *Her family*. Everything she did for them, and for the shop. In the only way she knew how. In the only way they'd enabled her to.

Fiona looked up and smiled as she snapped the lid of the jewelry case closed. "A victory. Lady Albion brought the emeralds to us for repair instead of to Mr. Foggy." She sniffed. "That upstart."

"He's a complete sham." And the reason their shop had not fared so well in the last several years. And the reason Fiona needed to, finally, tell her parents her true desires and abandon painting in pursuit of jewelry design instead.

Perhaps she possessed greater technical skill with brush and paint, but she'd never liked it. The act of painting had never sent a spark of joy through her. Paintings merely told stories from the safety of a sheltered room. Jewelry lived the story, glittering from the wrist of a debutante about to meet the man who would become her husband, stolen from a reticule by a masked highwayman, handed down from father to son, inherited, lost, loved. Jewelry experienced life, and Fiona designed pieces with those moments in mind—necklaces and earbobs for when you wanted to fall in love or when you needed to mourn, the perfect shapes and colors for every emotion.

All of it, though, lifeless in her sketchbook because her parents wanted at least one acceptable child, one daughter whose desires and talents did not laugh in the face of society's expectations for women.

Fiona gave a bitter laugh. If they only knew what she'd done with her painting lessons.

Hopefully they would never know.

"Foggy knows nothing about gems and gold," Posey grumbled. "Not even after five years of doing business in them." She clutched the jewelry case tight and disappeared into the workroom at the back of the shop just as Daniel, their fake apprentice, stepped out.

"Can I walk you and Miss Frampton home, Miss Fiona?" he asked, stuffing arms into his coat, his floppy yellow hair falling into his eyes. He delivered jewelry and ran errands and sat in the back of the shop when he was not busy elsewhere, to give the impression he was Papa's apprentice, not Posey.

"No thank you, Daniel." She needed to speak with her sister alone, and the walk home was the best time for that. "'Tis but a short jaunt. We'll fare fine."

"You Pa won't approve."

She winked. "I'll tell him you walked us." It would not be her first lie.

He grunted, rolling his eyes. "If you insist. Don't get abducted, miss. Or killed."

"I swear it."

Daniel strode out the door, leaving her alone with the glittering wares they could not sell as quickly as they'd like. As quickly as they *needed* some months. If they would give her own designs a chance, perhaps ...

Fiona strolled through the cases in the front of the shop, tidying up and checking locks. Mr. Foggy did not know gems, nor did he seem to understand very well how to set them without the entire piece falling to bits within a year. But he did understand color. And shape. And depth. And how it all worked together to create something people could not look away from. He understood fashion and what people wanted, and how what people wanted constantly changed. Fiona knew that because she often could not look away from the pieces he'd created. She disdained Foggy. All Framptons did. But she admired him, too.

Perhaps one day ladies would flock to Frampton's for one of Fiona's designs. No "perhaps." No. One day soon. A promise. A vow. Her future. First, she must convince her parents to let both daughters go rogue.

The sounds of the safe unlocking, opening, then closing and locking preceded Posey's reappearance, stuffing her arms into a pelisse. She reached for her fur-lined bonnet as Fiona donned her own outerwear, and together they stepped into the cold and locked the door behind them.

The strange man still stood across the street.

Fiona nodded toward him as she and Posey started home "Do you see him? He's been there every day for the last fortnight."

Posey craned her neck to look over her shoulder.

"Don't!" Fiona ducked. "Don't look like that! You'll draw his attention."

Posey turned back around, a bonnet-hidden scowl thinning her lips. "If he's been outside the shop for a fortnight, I'd say we already have his attention. I don't like it. Why didn't you tell me sooner?"

"I thought you'd notice." Why hadn't she noticed when

Fiona, the least of the Framptons, had? "And then I kept meaning to tell you, but"—she quivered her fingers away from her—"you know my thoughts. Always lost in the wind."

Posey rolled her eyes. "Of course. You're like a crow with a shiny bauble. Except your baubles are thoughts. A shinier one comes along, and all else is forgotten. Does Papa know? About the man?"

"I can't say. Should we contact a constable?"

"I should say so. We'll tell Papa just in case. Perhaps we can talk to some of the lads at the tavern to see if they'll watch over the shop tonight."

"An excellent idea." But Fiona's stomach still twisted. She should have told someone sooner. As usual, with the exception of Mr. Foggy, she remained her family's biggest downfall.

That. Word. The one she'd been trying to ignore jumped about her mind, and she shoved it down with a heavy fist of optimism.

Hopefully, the dowager would reappear, having gone for a jaunt on the Continent. She'd done so before. But never this long. At least Fiona's paintings remained safe, locked up in Lady Balantine's personal, secret gallery.

Worry still assaulted Fiona. She could not arm herself against it no matter how strong and sharp the mental portcullis she used to block it out. Because every time she closed her eyes, she remembered Lady Balantine was missing, and then she wondered if she'd taken the paintings with her, though why she would do such a thing, Fiona could never say.

But what if she had, placing them in watertight trunks for the journey across the channel and using a second coach once she arrived in France? Perhaps she'd have them unloaded at every stop and set up in a private room so she could dine while viewing them. Anyone could view them at that point—a maid bringing more tea, the innkeeper ... *anyone.* They'd say, "Where'd you get those Rubens, my lady?" and then they'd take a closer look and know. They'd *know*. Or perhaps a high-wayman would discover her art-loaded coach one day in the Spanish countryside, realize their worth, if not their lack of authenticity, and steal them. And as soon as he tried to sell them, he'd know ... everyone would know, and Fiona would find herself a criminal.

Wasn't she already a criminal? Bother. Ethics confounded her. If only the dowager baroness would respond to Fiona's letters.

A short, brisk walk brought them home, and their shivering drained away in the warmth of the townhouse foyer. Laughter echoed down the hall.

"They're playing cards again." Posey untied her bonnet and piled it on a small circular table with her pelisse. Fiona did the same, and they found their parents glaring at one another across a small table set before the fire.

"Your father's a cheat, girls." Their mother spoke without breaking her hold on their father's gaze.

Papa grinned, wide and merry. "I must resort to cheating because you're so good with numbers my dear. It's hardly cheating, if you ask me. It's leveling the playing field."

Fiona and Posey plopped into seats nearby. The glow that warmed her inside and out came not from the fire. Being with her family always made the world's difficulties fade away.

"You must put away your cards," Posey said, "for we have news of a troubling nature."

Their mother's face cleared of all emotion, and she tilted her head in the way that meant she was listening. Their father's face did the opposite. He seemed to scrunch into himself in order to keep a volley of emotions from exploding out of him, and his eyebrows narrowed toward one another.

"Troubling?" she said, "Tell us now."

Posey sat tall, her hands folded in her lap, looking every inch the titled lady she'd never been and never would be.

"Fiona has observed these past few weeks a man standing outside the shop."

Papa scratched his head above his ear, making the still-thick white hair there stand out. "Hm."

Mama patted his arm. "Many men stand outside the shop."

"The same man," Fiona said. "Day in and day out."

"Do you think we should call the constable?" Posey asked.

"Absolutely," Mama said.

"Best to be safe. Though one hopes it does not come to violence." Papa turned to Fiona, a single brow lifted. "Why didn't you tell us of this sooner?"

Fiona tangled her hands in the skirts, unable to meet her father's eyes. He was a sweet man who preferred the glittering world of jewels and golden wires to anything else. He'd have stuck his nose into his designs and never once noticed Foggy stealing their clientele, ruining their business, had Mama not taken control, taken over the books, and allowed Posey to work the front of the shop. And secretly the back of it.

But Fiona, she took after Papa, after all—too much daydreaming—so she wasn't allowed to help. "At first I did not realize it was the same man every day. Then once I determined that it was, I knew I must tell you, but something or other always blew it right out of my head. An idea for a painting or an angry customer. Or I'd remember only after I was tucked in bed and everyone else asleep." Everyone groaned. "I am terribly sorry," Fiona muttered.

Unlike her mother and Posey, she had never excelled at practical things. Her mind would always flit away with ideas, stories, concepts for brooches with green trees and moons high above. Oh, or perhaps a … a geometric bracelet design. Brown diamonds cut in squares, boxy and sharp but glittering—London on some lady's wrist. Yes, and—

And there she was again—distracted.

"I am sorry," she mumbled. "I will do better."

Papa reached over and patted her hand. "No harm done."

"Too true," Mama added. "We are well aware of the limitations on your abilities. Large creative soul, little brain box." She chuckled.

Fiona did not.

Mama's head bobbed up and down. "If the fellow means ill, we must strike before he does. Papa and I will handle it all. You concentrate on your paintings, Fiona. Lady Abernathy asked about them the other day. She'd like a little watercolor for her parlor. Thinks you're quite talented."

Fiona offered a smile, hoping it didn't tremble. "Of course, Mama. I'll try." That had been her opportunity to tell him what she wanted. Not watercolors. Not even close. She must seize the moment! "Papa?"

"Yes, m'dear?" He blinked at her.

"I would like to help with the shop. I've a few finished designs you could look at, and—"

"Oh, no, no, no. That would never do." His mouth, at least, offered the rejection with a sympathetic slant.

Mama patted Fiona's hand. "Darling, we must show our clientele that we are as sophisticated as they, our daughter just as accomplished. Besides, you must not worry yourself with the shop. Posey and Papa and Daniel are capable without you. Perhaps we should move your art materials here. It seems to have been a distraction to allow you to paint in the workroom."

"No!" Fiona threw up her hands. She loved being in the shop every day, loved seeing the different pieces that came in for fixing, loved seeing Papa's designs, tweaking them when he was not looking, making them better, hearing the praise for the pieces she'd tweaked when it floated faint from the front of the shop to the back. "No. It is no distraction at all. I merely wished to ... help in some substantial way."

Papa patted her on the head. "There is no need, Fee."

"You were made for softer things, darling," Mama added. "Painting is work enough."

Did they think to marry her off to a peer's son? She wouldn't. Unless she loved him. But not even then if he didn't understand her desires, if he didn't see her and love her back and let her follow her own path. She would only escape from her childhood home to her marriage bed if it came with the promise of a different life, one where she wasn't Fiona of the big soul and little brain.

She could convince her family of the quality and stoutness of her mind if she showed them the right drawing, her most brilliant design. Right? A bit of inspiration would solve everything. If she could but grasp it, she could help her family in a less dangerous way. And she must help. She couldn't sit behind an easel all day long while they did all the work.

She hated that—feeling useless, having no skill that could keep her family safe and warm and well fed, having a small brain box, as her mother had reminded her.

She *would* find inspiration. And yet her body did not seem convinced. She almost couldn't breathe. Her chest squeezed tighter than an ill-fitting corset. She compelled herself to calm down. No use swooning over something that had not happened.

Mama clapped her hands. "Let us do what needs to be done and not worry about it. Papa can find some willing men at the tavern to guard the shop tonight."

"Just what I said." Posey tapped the arm of their mother's chair, her hand pale against the dark oak.

Papa patted Posey's hand. "Sharp as a whip. Just like your mother."

"Come, let's eat." Mama smiled as if nothing in the world were wrong. "We were waiting only for your arrival."

Their father stood and took up position behind Mama's chair. "Asparagus soup tonight, m'dears."

Groans all around.

"I helped. It's a recipe of my own invention." He grinned despite the increasing volume of the groaning.

Mama sighed. "Cook has made some lovely bread, though, so we'll not starve."

They had two servants—a cook and a maid whose work mostly consisted of helping Mama. She had not been able to walk since her accident five and ten years previous, and sometimes had terrible headaches. But Lillian had been gone of late, visiting her sick mother across London, and so Papa had been staying home to take care of his wife.

He helped her out of the room, and Posey and Fiona followed. As they passed through the hall toward the small room where they ate their dinner, a knock sounded at the door.

Fiona jumped then stilled, a premonition skittering up her spine. No one ever called on them at this hour.

"A visitor?" Mama asked. "This late at night?"

"Is it Lady Crestmore?" Papa asked.

Few visited their little home except for the Duchess of Crestmore, Mama's friend.

Fiona shook her head. "She'd never be so careless as to call unannounced at so late an hour."

"It can't be Lillian," Posey said, a question in her tone. "She's not due to return until tomorrow."

Another knock echoed in the hall, and the front door shook with the force of the caller's fist.

Another premonition skittered up her spine. But Fiona strode to the door. If something horrid was about to happen, she'd not run from it. "Silly to just stand here and look at the door. It won't open itself." She flung it wide.

There, standing before her, a man in a greatcoat, his shoulders shrugged up into his ears, his beaver hat pulled low. She knew that coat, knew that hat, and the familiarity of them, of the blade of danger about the man standing on their doorstep, knocked the breath from her body.

He lifted a hand, pushed the hat back on his head, and she finally saw his features. Dark eyes, sharp jaw shadowed with scruff, black hair a tad too long, a mouth thinned with ... anger. All the demons of hell lashed out in his eyes, and he trained that fiery gaze on her.

She stumbled backward with a gasp, and he stepped over the threshold. The wind caught the candlelight, made it dance with the shadows.

"I've come to speak with Mr. Frampton." His gaze snapped away from her to her father. "And I'd like to do so now."

Fiona reached for the wall behind her, needing something to lean against as her legs had become less than useful.

"Me?" Papa asked, and his voice faltered just a bit.

The falter gave Fiona strength. She surged toward the stranger. "You were not invited into this house, and you will certainly not order us about." She placed her hands on her hips and made herself as tall as she could, but she was tiny even to a shorter man, and this man towered high above her.

He didn't even look at her. "I have business with your father, and I'd like to meet with him." He flashed her a polite smile full of needles and knives. "Please."

Papa put himself between them. "Very well, then." He gestured for the stranger to follow him into the parlor they had all so recently exited. "Meet, we shall."

"Who is that rude man?" Posey asked.

Fiona clutched her hands in her skirts and shut the howling wind outside with a slam of the door. "That is the man who's been watching us."

"What business could he have with your father, I

wonder?" Mama looked at the parlor door as if wishing to see through it could make it so. Her hands clutched the arms of her bath chair so her knuckles shone white, and the blanket she had tossed across her lap slid partly onto the floor.

Fiona righted it. She could not guess the answer to her mother's question, but that shiver that had twice traveled up and down her spine returned once more. Whatever he'd come to say, it would not be good.

Two

⟶

When Lord Lysander Bromley set out to learn the identity of the man who had forged his father's most valuable paintings, he'd not expected the man to be a jeweler. When he'd set out to speak with the man, he'd not expected to have to corner him at home, and when he'd set out to do the cornering, he'd not expected to have to first defeat a tiny, female, fire-breathing dragon with large green eyes.

But he'd had to do all those things, and on perhaps ten hours of sleep in the last week, too.

The parlor Mr. Frampton, financially strapped jeweler to the *ton*, led him to glowed bright and unexpectedly cozy. Mr. Frampton himself appeared unexpectedly harmless. His white hair was still thick and pulled into a queue at the back of his neck. His eyes, green like the dragon's, held curiosity, welcome, and exhaustion in equal measure. Hardly at all like the wicked, thieving forger of art Zander had expected.

Cards still lay scattered about the table before the fire, as if the family had only recently vacated the room, and Mr.

Frampton, who sat in one of the chairs, gestured for Zander to join him.

He did, his fingers sliding over the cards and lifting one, studying it as he gathered his thoughts. He should need no time to gather, having gathered them a fortnight ago when he'd discovered the address belonging to the forger. Even before he had that key fact, he'd known what he would say when he discovered the man.

Tell me where the Baroness Balantine is. Give me any information you have on the six rare Rubens paintings you've copied over the last five years. Or I'll call the constable.

An empty threat. How could Zander notify the authorities when he was as guilty in the whole affair as the man sitting before him? He had, after all, rented the original paintings, which had belonged to his father, to the dowager, who had paid for and arranged for the copies to be made. And the copies had been made expressly so Zander could fool his father into thinking the originals safe and in his possession.

If Mr. Frampton was a forger, Zander was a thief.

But he'd gotten a good penny and a good laugh out of it at the time and had been plagued by very little guilt. His father had ruined his family with his ostentatious spending on all things art, had drained their coffers to fill their galleries. If Zander could fill those coffers back up a bit by renting the very art his father so revered and fool the old man in the bargain ... an excellent deal indeed.

But his father must not have been fooled after all. He'd left his six children rare works of art as their only inheritance. Rubens. The very paintings, in fact, Zander had replaced with copies in the last half decade. The old man had known. Must have. And now the family needed those paintings, needed to replace the useful income provided by renting them out with the ostentatious profits they would acquire once sold. But they had no idea where they were.

Lady Balantine had disappeared, taking her art collection into the unknown oblivion with her.

Yes, Zander had known well for weeks what he would say when he finally stood before the art forger.

But all the … unexpected … elements of this evening, of the past fortnight, had stolen those organized words away. Where to start? How to go on when casting the accusations he had planned at such a nice-looking man as sat before him?

"Well?" Mr. Frampton said. "You barge into my home, interrupt my dinner, and make demands. You can at least give me your name, sir."

"I am Mr. Lysander Bromley, art procurer and curator of personal art collections, and you are Mr. Frampton, jeweler."

"I am."

Zander licked his lips, waiting for further response. When none came, he said, "I hear you like Rubens." He tapped the edge of the card on the table.

"The painter?" Mr. Frampton scratched his head. "I suppose. A fine artist, but I prefer jewels to paint."

Zander flattened his palm over the card on the table and leaned forward. "You suppose? A man who copies Rubens's genius as if it were his own cannot but feel passionate about him."

Frampton's brow furrowed for a moment, then he broke into laughter, falling back into the chair and making it wobble a bit, his hand covering his belly. "Ah. You're not here for me if you're after a painter. You've come for Fiona." He cupped his hand and leaned toward the door. "Fiona!"

Zander straightened. Fiona? What had a Fiona to do with the most talented forger Zander had ever seen?

The parlor door flew open, and the tiny green-eyed dragon stood in its frame, her chin high, those eyes wary, her gaze flying over her father's frame as if she expected Zander had done the man some injury. One of the daughters, the one with dark-blonde hair. That one day the sun had shone in the street outside the jewelry shop, her hair had turned, almost, pure yellow, but now in the firelight and shadows, it seemed burnished bronze. She had full pink lips and a sharp nose. Likely the rest of her sharp as well. Two other women, likely her sister and mother, stood beside her, both with blonde hair of various shades and blue eyes.

"Are you well, Papa?" the green-eyed woman asked.

"Fine. Just fine. Now I've solved his riddles." Mr. Frampton chuckled and tilted his head toward the woman. "There she is. We're quite proud of our Fiona."

"I'm afraid I've entirely no idea what's happening," Zander admitted. "I'm looking for the painter in this house."

"That is me." The chit stared at him as if he were the daft one, her mouth a thin line, her head tilted. "If you are looking for a painter, I am who you are looking for."

"Impossible." She hardly looked the nefarious or crafty type. She looked as if she wore her every emotion on her skin and in her eyes. This one would have no secrets.

The dragon's mouth dropped open. "Pardon me? Do you suggest a woman cannot be a master painter?"

He held his arms out wide. "Not at all. I know better than that." And his mother would wail herself into a fit if she heard him suggest otherwise. The entire ordeal would likely burst his eardrums. "It is merely that you do not seem the type."

She snapped her mouth shut and crossed her arms beneath her breasts. "Oh? And what type is that?"

He grinned. He'd been in a foul mood when he'd arrived here, but this little dragon made him want to laugh, lifted his spirits a bit. So determined, so spiky. "Do you wish to be the type who forges paintings?"

Her eyes grew so wide so slowly he would not have noticed it except for the fact that the rest of her had stopped moving entirely. Not even her breast rose and fell to signal breathing.

The color drained from her face, and then like a wind shivering the leaves in a tree, her body began to tremble.

Then she fainted.

"Hell." The curse clipped out from beneath Zander's teeth, and he dove for the girl.

But not fast enough. She'd become a puddle of wool and limbs on the floor. Her father and the standing woman, likely to be her sister, dove for her, too. Frampton knelt, and the sister sat, pulling the girl's head into her lap and tapping her pale cheeks with the flats of her fingers.

"Fee, oh Fee, wake up." The sister's hands fluttered about the girl's breast.

Zander pushed them away. "Let me lift her, put her on the settee."

The sister wrapped her arms around the fainted girl and glared at him. Another dragon. Sigh. He'd stumbled into a cave of them, it seemed. "I do not know who you are, sir. You shall not touch her."

She truly wished him to waste time with pleasantries? He only just kept his eyes from rolling back in his head as he bowed low, exaggerating his elegance. "Lord Lysander at your service. I'm an art curator. I'm not going to hurt her. I intend only to make her—and you I might add—more comfortable."

The woman growled. Growled? Perhaps he should have expected a forger to have a feral family. Or a forger to have been nurtured in a feral family. He studied the soft lines of the fainted woman's face. Was she really who he sought?

"Will you allow me to assist her?" he asked, checking his nails as if he did not care.

The sister's gaze glued to him, she scurried away, and he replaced her lap with his arms before the green-eyed dragon's head could hit the hard floor. A feather, she was, and he lifted her with ease. He'd seen her often over the past fortnight as he'd stood outside their shop in the wind and rain, waiting for an opportunity. He'd seen both women more often than he'd seen the father. Another frustration, that. He'd hoped to speak to the man on his way home, but when he visited the shop, he had a daughter on his arm, or two, and Zander had never had a chance to speak to the man alone.

Zander would wait no longer. He crept closer than ever to finding Lady Balantine, finding the paintings, his family's inheritance, and getting it back. Paying for his past mistakes. He wouldn't let a family of women looking on stop him from getting the information he'd come to collect. If they did not know about their patriarch's nefarious activities, they were about to find out.

He laid the dragon on the small blue settee in the corner of the room away from the fire. A bit too cold here, but the color seemed to be returning to her cheeks. She'd best stay unconscious if she didn't want another shock.

"Does anyone have smelling salts?" he asked.

The family pushed past him to crowd around the fallen girl. Woman, really. A discovery he could not help but make as he'd carried her across the room. Such a sweet innocent face when those raging eyes were not open and accusing—slightly rounded cheeks and a pert little nose and chin. A wide, pink mouth, the bottom lip plumper than the top. And hair the color that shifted from one yellow hue to the next.

A hand touched his wrist, and he looked down.

The woman in the bath chair looked up at him, entirely composed. "You must leave. You've upset my family enough for an evening."

"I'll not leave without the information I've come for, without answers to my questions." He couldn't. He'd been searching too long to back down now, even with the soft stern eyes of this woman boring into him, promising pain if he hurt her family.

"Then ask them and be gone." She had the type of

commanding presence one did not dismiss, seemed capable to her very bones.

"Very well." He'd not intended to speak of this in front of Mr. Frampton's wife and children, but they would be unlikely to allow him a private conversation with the fainted woman, and she might be who he really needed. He'd have to do this here. Now. "I have come to talk to Mr. Frampton about Lady Balantine, about the Rubens paintings he copied for her. Or perhaps I've come to speak to your daughter, Mr. Frampton."

Mr. Frampton shook his head and wrung his hands. "What you're saying makes no sense. Forgery?"

The fainted woman's eye ticked. A wince? Maybe not so fainted, the brazen chit.

"I tracked down a footman who used to work at Lady Balantine's London address. He tells me she had correspondence with you, with your shop. He also tells me this correspondence regards the painting-shaped packages that would arrive from that location, delivered by a young boy who lives nearby." Though now he studied the Miss Frampton currently prostrate on the settee ... perhaps it hadn't been a young boy delivering packages, but a small woman cleverly disguised.

Hell, he shouldn't smile. Not now. But he did so enjoy a ridiculous scheme.

"We know no dowager," Mrs. Frampton said. "Nor boy. Nor anything about packages that were painting shaped or otherwise. My husband and I know parures and gems."

"Gold, silver, wire, paste," Mr. Frampton added. "I am a man of fashion not forgery."

"Precisely." The softest glance traveled between husband and wife as Mrs. Frampton nodded. "You can hold my husband's art in the palm of your hand, not hang it on a wall. And since you have no ability to speak sense or believe me when I speak sense, I ask you to leave."

Mrs. Frampton did not tremble, but Zander did. He

couldn't leave. Not now when he was so close. He felt like a leaf clinging to a branch in late autumn. The smallest breeze, a breath, could send him swaying to the earth. Like the young woman fainted on the settee. *Fake* fainted. Sure of it now.

Something like despair almost drowned him in a wave that stole his breath and his sense, and he choked out, "The dowager has my inheritance, and if I do not find her—" He forced his mouth shut, refusing to continue voicing a truth he never should have given up.

He looked at each face staring wide-eyed at him. The angry father, the curious mother, the vengeful sister. He peered, just a moment, at the face of the likely-not-truly-unconscious dragon, her pale-blue eyelids fluttering. Crafty, she was. He'd have to retreat and join the fray another day. Once he'd had time to think and hours to sleep.

He'd wanted only, since his father's death, to undo the wrongs he'd done, find his family's paintings—the real ones, not the copies hanging in the gallery at home—sell them for mountains of money, and help his brothers restore the family coffers. And reputation. But he'd failed once more.

He'd not fail in the end, though, because he'd not give up. Let the girl deal with her family, with the revelations he'd set in their midst, then he'd be back. For her. Because he believed the father when he said he was no forger. And he believed the unspoken words of a woman who fake fainted when faced with her sins.

"I am sorry to have caused you distress," he said. "It seems my informant did not understand, and I apologize for disrupting your evening." He could be crafty as well. Let them think he would give up then attack again when they—she—felt safe. He bowed and strode for the door.

"Wait!"

He stopped, one foot hovering over the floorboards in the hallway. He shifted that hovering foot back into the room and peered in the direction of the settee. The young woman sat bolt upright, her hands twisting her skirt in her lap. Not at all unconscious and clearly aware of the recent events. Ha. He knew it. Crafty minx.

"I cannot tell you much," she said, "but I can tell you what I know. You are looking for a forger, and"—she took a deep, steadying breath—"I am she."

Three

The word she'd been avoiding, tried to lock up safely, had slipped into the world and still reverberated around her. No one else seemed to hear its ringing, but she did.

Forgery.

Her secret. Her sin. Now a secret no longer.

The man who'd lifted her as if she weighed no more than a doll stared at her with eyes so dark a gray they bordered on black and a touch of amusement about him despite his quite recent brush with some deep emotion that had sounded very like despair on his mobile lips. He looked like a man used to smiling and getting his way. And when he'd held her in his arms, he'd felt like a man used to working hard, putting muscle and bone to the test.

He strolled back into the room, his gait the deceptive loping of a jungle predator. "Were you even unconscious, Miss Frampton?"

She gasped, affronted. Pretending to be at least.

He had the right of it. She had very much *not* swooned. Not a bit. She'd needed time to think, and her body had responded to that need with action—wise or not, it had not cared. She'd pretended to swoon and commenced thinking. He came looking for her. And for every horrid reason. The man standing before her may as well have stepped out of her nightmares to make known all her sins, and he was unfairly, devastatingly gorgeous. A fact she would ignore moving forward, because he had orchestrated her complete ruination.

To be fair, *she* had orchestrated her own ruination.

There existed only one course of action—lay her sins on the table and pay the price. She might not have decided to do so had his voice not wavered. Had she not heard in his few words what she felt in her own heart—desperation.

"My fainting spell is neither here nor there," she said.

"You're right." He prowled closer. "Tell me, Miss Frampton, how you became a forger of fine art?"

She closed her eyes and inhaled. What a weight, what a disaster. The paintings *gone*, he'd said. Gone, as she'd feared. Not a story she'd concocted with her overeager imagination. The truth. She wanted nothing more than to sink into the floor and never return, but she forced herself to open her eyes and face her curiously silent family. Her father's mouth gaped open in a shocked O, and her mother's gaze grew glassy, thoughtful. No shock there? How odd.

When she met Posey's blank gaze, her sister said, "It's not true. You've not forged a single thing. What an absurd idea."

Fiona licked her lips. "I have, though. I've—*ahem*—forged quite a few paintings." Among other things.

Lord Lysander stepped closer, looming over her, his face a mask, unreadable. "Which ones?" The question in his voice—suspicion. He did not yet believe her.

And she wished it weren't true.

She stood to better face him, to end his looming. Didn't quite work. She came only up to his shoulders. Perhaps if she went on tiptoe, she could tap the top of her head on his chin.

"The Rubens only, since those are the only ones that matter to you, Lord Lysander, are, in no particular order, a few unfinished sketches, *A Landscape with a Shepherd and His Flock*, and—"

"Enough." His jaw ticked. "*You* are who I'm looking for?" He turned and paced toward the fire, the long, muscled length of his arms angled behind his back, his hands clasped, tossing a string of mutterings into the flames. "A woman? But why not? Mother always said. Ha. Wouldn't she like this. Yes, then, a woman. But so young and—" He turned to them sharply. "Where is Lady Balantine? Tell me anything you know of her."

Fiona wrapped a hand around her wrist, the tendons there tight against her fingers, tight like the rest of her body. And tired, too. But she'd not sleep tonight. When he left, the true conversation began.

"I wish I could tell you," she said. "I wish I knew myself. You think I have not been plagued with worry since her disappearance? She"—Fiona swallowed hard, hoping to wet her throat to better push the words out—"she was a source of income for me, and now that's gone."

Forgery had been her only option, the only way she'd been able to help, covertly of course, because no one would even consider for more than a moment the idea that she could help *at all*. But she could. She had a brain, despite what everyone thought. What she didn't have was any skill beyond what they'd paid for—painting, technical perfection, and the ability to copy the old masters. It's what one did when learning— copy. Only one was not supposed to do it as well as she could. Nor should one learn from rather shady baronesses how to make a painting look older than it was. And one should especially not sell what they'd copied.

She'd not done all that in ignorance. She'd known the laws, the risks, and she'd taken them, earned her keep, and kept her family fed ... with the only skill they'd allowed her to culti-

25

vate. Fiona's palms broke into a sweat, and she wiped them on her skirts. "I thought the paintings were safe. Lady Balantine assured me they would not be sold."

"They were not for the dowager, and they never hung in her house," Lord Lysander said. "They were for me and have been at the center of my father's art collection since you finished them and shipped them off to Lady Balantine."

Fiona stumbled backward. Her legs hit the settee, and she toppled to its cushions.

As if they were connected through a tattered cord, his body jerked forward as she fell.

"Careful," he said.

Her family swarmed her. Posey sat beside her, and her father stood closer. Her mother sat up taller. Fiona did not deserve their protection. She'd been trying to save them, but she'd quite possibly, ruined them all. Hopefully Newgate was not as horrid as she'd heard. But perhaps they would not imprison her. No. She could very well hang at the end of a rope. She wrapped her hand around her throat, and the world fuzzed a bit at the edges.

Posey's arm tight around her shoulders. "Fee."

Lord Lysander stepped closer, his face large, consuming, in her vision. "Going to faint for real this time?" The long line of his mouth tipped up at one corner. Was he ... amused? At a time like this?

That snapped her right out of it. "No! You must believe me, Lord Lysander. She assured me she would not sell them, that they were for her own delight. I ... I did not mean to fool you. Or anyone. How much did you pay for them?" Oh, merciful heavens. How much had he paid for copies? She'd have to pay it all back, no matter how large the sum. She really might swoon.

"No." Lord Lysander's semi-smile melted as he stood. "*She* paid *me*. For the use of the paintings, for permission to make the copies. But when I saw how perfect the forgeries were, I offered to let her keep the originals. If she paid me a bit more. Still too low a price for the value of the works."

Hope and relief—twin roses—bloomed in her breast. "What did you do with the copies?"

"They are at my brother's country seat. Safe." He sighed. "I am not here to demand a pound of flesh, Miss Frampton. I merely want answers. And, if possible, the original paintings so I can sell them for what they're truly worth. Do you have them? Or know where they are?"

"No, of course not," Fiona admitted.

"The copies." Papa's voice shook. "You'll return them to us?"

Lord Lysander nodded. "Once I find the originals."

"And you'll not report her?" Mama asked.

"I have no desire to ruin your little forger's life. I merely want the originals back. You have nothing to fear from me. I am, after all, the orchestrator of the entire debacle." His voice was hoarse with self-censure.

She turned to her father, touching his cold hand for a moment, but he did not return the embrace. She reached then for her mother but pulled her hand away before skin could comfort skin. Something in her mother's sharp eyes spoke of knowing, understanding, memory. Only once had Mama asked Fiona how she'd procured such large sums of money, and the weak answer Fiona had provided—that she'd sold her paintings, which wasn't truly a lie—buzzed in the air between them now. Had she suspected something? Had she lied to Papa for Fiona?

"I must say I am relieved, Lord Lysander, to hear you will keep this information safe," her mother said. "But ... Fiona ... why?"

Safe? Were they? From Lord Lysander perhaps, but Fiona had copied more than just the Rubens. Eight more to be

27

precise. And it could be that those circumstances were not as she believed, either. She would likely never be safe again.

She closed her eyes and spoke into the darkness. "Mr. Foggy stole all of our clientele. And then your accident. And then your chair broke, and then ..." And so many, many *and thens*. "I felt helpless. I've only ever been good at one thing."

"Painting," Lord Lysander drawled. "You're damn good at that, Miss Frampton."

Fiona glared at him. Now was not the time. And she cared for that skill only insofar as it paid for what her family needed.

He held his hands up, palms flat, and backed away. "My apologies. For the compliment."

Fiona twisted to face her father behind her. "There were so many times I felt helpless to contribute during all our worries. And then Lady Balantine came by the shop. She saw one of the paintings you keep in the showroom, and when I admitted I had painted it, she said I had great talent. Said she wanted to be my patron." She'd thought the woman sincere. She'd said she only wanted to have copies so she could view her favorite paintings at home as often as she pleased. She'd promised not to sell them, that the owner had given her permission to make copies for her personal use. They were to be destroyed at her death. All the right things to assuage Fiona's guilt, her fears. "So, she became my patron. Your new chair, Mama. The last work I completed for her provided it. And rent for the shop, the two before that helped there. And—"

"No more. I am ... I am all astonishment." Papa spoke low but the words were bricks, large weights that punctuated the end of the conversation better than any exclamation point. She'd never wanted him to know, never wanted him to feel shame for her, for himself.

She grabbed for his hands, held them fast between her own. "It is not your fault, Papa. I have—"

"Quiet." His voice shook, an ocean of disappointment in

the single word. "You've taken the valuable education we provided for you and used it for … this? For *this*!" He raised his gaze to Lord Lysander. "Is that all you've come here to say? If so, you may leave now."

Lord Lysander huffed a laugh. "I came here to say much more, actually. I had thought to find some conniving devil. Thought perhaps you'd—oh, I don't know—duped the old dowager like some criminal mastermind. And I thought"—he laughed again, this time a harsh bark—"I had planned to bring you to justice and find the missing paintings." He snapped his chin toward his shoulder. "What a fool I was. There's nothing here but a series of foolish mistakes much like my own." His gaze settled on Fiona, connecting them, one desperate fool to another. "I'll be taking my leave. Good evening." He strode for the door, pausing to slip a hand into his coat and slap a calling card on a table. "If you hear from Lady Balantine, please let me know." Then he disappeared into the hallway.

And Fiona could breathe again. The harbinger of her doom had gone for good.

But the destruction he'd wrought, she'd wrought, remained. And there went her lungs' ability to function once more. She stood on numb legs and found herself somehow before the fire. Was it warm? She could hardly tell.

"I could have provided for us, Fiona," Papa said from behind her. "What you've done is … it is a crime. You could hang."

She dropped her face into her hands. Her lungs, tight from disuse, exploded in an inhale so ragged it must have ripped her throat open. It ripped open her tears, and she wet her palms with sorrow.

"He will not tell anyone," Mama said. "I believe him."

"But how many others might know?" Papa yelled. "Why, Fiona?"

Because she'd wanted—needed—to help. Papa could not

see past the glittering of jewels, and the family had been sinking. She was not like Posey—good with customers. Nor was she business minded, like Mama. Fiona had only her paintbrushes, a talent that had always cost the family more than it had provided. She'd needed lessons and paper and canvas and paints and brushes and ... and no way to pay her family back for something she'd never really wanted to begin with.

Until she'd met the dowager.

"I am sorry, Papa, Mama. I—"

"Not good enough." Father's words were soft but threatened to shatter the windows nonetheless. "Do you understand the danger of a situation such as this?"

Silence welled up thick around them with his last word.

Then the swish of Posey's skirts as she circled her father and settled a soft glare on him. "Papa, we must all settle down. Let us go into dinner."

"What are we to do?" Papa demanded.

"Survive, as always," Mama said. The gaze she rested on Fiona wasn't full of rage like Papa's. It brimmed over with sympathy, understanding. She knew, after all, the disaster their books had been in before she'd taken them over, and she'd notasked Fiona any questions about her sold paintings, which ones she'd sold or who to.

"Let us eat," Posey said. "Every trouble feels worse on an empty stomach."

Her face still buried in her hands, Fiona heard only the sounds of crackling flames and shuffling footsteps, the sound of the bath chair wheeling across rug and wood as Posey ushered them all out of the room.

Then a warm hand alighted on Fiona's shoulder. "You are right, Fee." Mama's hand squeezed. "We *were* in trouble. I know the shop's books better than your father. You should not have done what you did. Surely your father did not believe us to be *so* desperate but ... you were right. Because we *were* that desperate. At times." The warmth of her mother's hand disappeared.

She meant to comfort, but Fiona might never know comfort again. She dropped into the chair next to the abandoned cards by the fire and finally dropped her hands to her lap to stare into the flames.

She was a fool. She knew that then and she knew it now, and her father's words—*what do we do now?*—rang in her head. If she wasn't such a fool, perhaps she could figure it out. Solving the mess that might see her hang remained her only means of redemption.

She knew quite well what to do now, as clear as where to put a line on a canvas when copying a master.

Adopt a version of Lord Lysander's plan—find the dowager, find the originals, then beg for the copies, and burn them. But how?

Four

Fiona woke up tired and hungry, hollow and sick. An illness of her own making. She'd been determined to give up painting altogether, to focus her creative energy on jewelry design, but she couldn't now. Not yet. Not until she'd put the mystery of the missing dowager to rest, not until Fiona's missing copies were found.

So, as the first hint of sunlight crept yellow and slow into her room, she slung her feet to the floor, threw open the wardrobe, and dressed. And when she heard Posey walking around on the other side of the thin wall that divided their chambers, she ran the few steps to her sister's room and knocked on her door. It swung open with a shocking *swoosh* almost immediately, and Fiona fell inside.

"Good morning." Fully dressed in a muslin day gown but for shoes, Posey rubbed a fist in her eye and yawned the last word.

Fiona snorted. "Hardly good. Don't let the sun fool you. But I'm determined to make it better." She waltzed over to the window and stood sentinel, a general preparing for battle. London had no idea of her war waging, though. It drifted silent and lonely down below, the streets gray and empty. What sort of jewelry did one wear out on a day like this one? Perhaps a lady just stepping out, her cloak hood pulled low, her face turned down to prevent being recognized, wore only eardrops. Pearls that mirrored the morning fog. Her story would have a jubilant ending. But Fiona's ...

Fiona turned her back on the outside world. "I *shall* make it better."

"Ah. How so? Wait." She rummaged in her wardrobe. "Let me put my boots on just in case."

Fiona clasped her hands behind her back. "You'll need them."

"Where are we going, then? We must be back in time to open the shop."

"We are going to visit the duke."

Posey stilled, one arm frozen halfway into her pelisse. "Are we? And why is that?"

"Because he knows everyone, and I need to know more about this Lord Lysander." She slipped her hand into her pocket and pulled forth the calling card the man had left last night, wrinkled and dirty and not containing his name. "The card belongs to a Mrs. Blake. There's an address, and I intend to visit it today. But first, I want to know all there is to know about the horrid man."

They stepped into the early morning sunshine outside the townhouse arm in arm, and Fiona pulled her sister tight to her side, a warm strength, no matter what happened. They crossed a street, rushing their steps and clinging to their bonnets at the very last to avoid a careening carriage.

Fiona pulled her sister even tighter when they'd caught their breath and calmed their racing hearts. "I *am* sorry." Soft words to be lost in the morning wind.

"I know. I wish you'd told me so I could have convinced you not to do it," Posey said. "At the same time, thank you. I did not know how to survive once everyone ran away to that old fraud Foggy."

Fraud. Fiona's steps hitched.

Posey helped steady her, squeezed her hand. "Is that a sensitive word? Should I refrain from using it?"

"No. I am a fraud. Why aren't you mad at me?"

Posey shrugged. "Papa is mad enough at you for an entire church choir's worth of people. You need someone to lean on. And my shoulder is quite broad."

Fiona laughed. *Imagine that. Laughter on a day like today.*

"I am scared, though," Posey admitted, her fingers threading with Fiona's, squeezing.

All laughter gone, victim of a quick death to Posey's guillotine admission. "I'm scared too."

"The duke will help."

Fiona could not find the strength to answer, and Posey's statement needed no response, so she simply quickened her steps, and soon they found themselves knocking on the duke's front door. They were likely the only ladies without titles who were allowed to do so. But if Archer Halston, Duke of Crestmore heard they'd entered through the servant's entrance, the responsible party in his household would lose their employment. It had happened before. Poor Harold the footman.

The door swung open, revealing the butler, Mr. Quill. "Good morning, girls. Come in, come in. What an unexpected surprise."

"Are your joints any better today, Quill?" Posey asked. "And is His Grace at home?"

"No and yes, Miss Frampton."

"I am sorry, Quill." Posey patted the butler's shoulder. "I wish it were the other way around."

"May we speak with him, Quill?" Fiona peeked up the stairs she knew led to his study.

The relationship between the Framptons and the Duke of

Crestmore, as well as his widowed mother, was an odd one by the ton's standards, a scandalous one, even, not to be borne. A duke and his duchess mother close as family with jewelers? Unpardonable. Except everyone seemed to have pardoned them. Mostly. The Framptons never thought themselves above their station because of it, and that seemed to appease most. Besides, no one liked to anger a duchess and a duke, and suggesting her favorite conversational partner was unsuitable would have angered her indeed. There were no two women as mad about and as knowledgeable about gems as the duchess and Mama. A perfect friendship but for station, one that had flourished despite differences of class.

So much so that Quill led them upstairs and right into the duke's study.

The duke lifted his head at the intrusion, his frown exploding into a grin. "Thank God you're both here. I'm drowning in numbers and need a break. Catch." He tossed something into the air. Posey snatched it without blinking, gave it one glance, found it to be a now-mangled scone, and took a bite. "Well done, you," the duke said, his grin going quite lopsided.

Posey finished off the scone then frowned at her soiled gloves. "You've ruined them."

"Me?" The duke scoffed.

"You threw the pastry."

"You could have let it hit the floor."

"Its trajectory was perfectly arched toward my head." She cut him a look his cook would likely find useful in the kitchen, so sharp it was. Then she sauntered farther into the room and leaned the side of her hip against his desk. She picked at her gloves, removing them, instead of looking at him. "We're not here for games, Crestmore. Fiona has a question to ask you."

The unusual ice in Posey's voice told Fiona how to move forward. Carefully and with secrecy they did not usually follow around this man. Was her anger really so piqued over a pastry?

Fiona swallowed hard and hovered in the doorway.

Archer steepled his fingers and braced his elbows on the top of his desk. "What is it, Fiona?" They'd grown up together during their mother's weekly chats and had not bothered with formal names in some years. As they never met in public— except sometimes at the shop where he *Miss Frampton'd* them and they *Your Grace'd* him—it did not matter.

"Do you know a Lord Lysander?" Fiona asked. "Mr. Lysander Bromley?"

Archer leaned into his chair, closing his eyes and folding his arms over his taut abdomen. "Hmm. Bromley. There's a family with that surname I know of. A marquess who died this year. I remember because his son took his place in the house this season." He opened his eyes. "The man, the new marquess, has four brothers. So Lord Lysander is logically one of those."

A marquess's son. She had no trouble believing that. "And do you know a Mrs. Blake?"

Archer quirked his lips to one side and then to the other, lifting his gaze to the ceiling and tapping one finger on his waistcoat. He lowered his gaze to Fiona. "No. I am sorry. I do not know that name. Though ..."

Fiona lurched farther into the room. "Yes?"

"There is a family with that surname. An earl. Could be this Mrs. Blake belongs to them. Or not." He shrugged. "I am sorry not to be able to offer better help."

"You've offered as good help as you can," Posey said, her gaze softening. "Thank you, Your Grace."

"Thank you, *Archer*." The duke frowned and rose to his feet, a slow, almost menacing growth of inches that resulted in a body coiled taut like a spring.

Posey raised an eyebrow, and Fiona knew the conversation,

argument really, that would soon grow around them. Best to avoid it.

She turned sharp and headed for the door. "Thank you so much, Archer. You've been a wonderful help, as I knew you would be."

Posey followed. "Good day, Your Grace."

Archer circled the desk and chased after them. "Where are you going?"

"To visit Mrs. Blake," Fiona said. And hopefully discover Lord Lysander. She didn't want to divulge that bit, though. The duke's strides caught up with them quickly, and he had that take-charge look about him she's always found particularly annoying. The price of being friends with the posh, though.

"I'll come with you," he said.

Posey stopped, one foot in the hallway, and turned to him sharply, green skirts swishing between their bodies. "And why do you think you'll do that?"

He turned to her, slowly, arms crossing over his chest, a single supercilious eyebrow raising into a wayward brown curl that drooped over his forehead. "Because I recognize a scheme when I see one, and I'll not allow the two of you to traipse off alone after someone you don't know." He threw his arms wide, leaning slightly toward Posey. "You won't even tell me why you wish to meet this Mrs. Blake or what business you have asking after Lord Lysander. You will not skip into danger when I can protect you."

Posey lifted her own haughty brow.

Oh dear. Fiona took a step backward. Best to stay out of explosions. "Please do not ask us to say more. Please, Archer. You are like a brother to me, and—"

"If you felt brotherly toward me, Fee, you would let me help you more than a Debrett's publication could." He rocked back on his heels, his gaze still trained on Posey.

37

She wanted to trust him, but how could she? A duke. If he had any knowledge of her crimes, he might end up in high waters, too.

"We can't," she said, her voice small.

"I am sorry, Archer." Posey reached for him. "I wish we could." She let her arm fall.

He straightened his jacket, and set a line for the front door. "Very well then, tell me nothing. But I'm still coming. I'll stay in the coach. Be there if you need me. In the dark." His voice a grumble. "But there. Just in case."

Fiona sagged in relief, and Posey linked their arms, dragged her after the duke.

"You know why we cannot tell him the details he desires," Fiona said.

"Yes." Posey's voice a flower folding in on itself as light stole away from the sky. "I know."

This was the outcome of her poor choices—she hurt all those she loved most.

Fiona squeezed her sister's hand. "We cannot implicate him in any way. He cannot know."

"I know," Posey repeated, harder now, two words close to tipping from annoyance into anger.

"I'm sorry."

"I know." She patted Fiona's hand. "No more apologies."

Archer opened the front door of the townhouse and flooded the hall with sunlight. They followed him onto the street.

"I'll have my coach readied," he called.

"No," Posey snapped, "a hack will do."

He wrinkled his nose but did not argue.

"You must truly dislike numbers to be shadowing us this morning," Fiona said as they stepped into line with him. "And into a public conveyance as well."

He cast a glance right past her to her sister, his eyes hard yet soft at the same time. He grunted, hailed a hack, and soon, they were crowded into the odiferous interior, each of them leaning into their own corner, sinking into their own shadows.

She'd given the driver the address on the rumpled calling card, and they rumbled that way much too quickly. Would Lord Lysander be there with this Mrs. Blake? And would he want the information she hoped to share with him? Would he share what he knew with her? The thought of sharing anything with that horse's arse made her want to stay in the hack, no matter how pungent. But she would do it because she would do anything for her family, and it was the only thing she knew to do to salvage this shipwreck of a situation.

Five

When the orange glow of sunrise rolled across Zander's face, he was already awake, thinking. Nothing else to do but think—of a solution, of his next move, of the dowager and where the hell she'd run off to.

Some thoughts, he tried to avoid—the very real possibility something nefarious had happened to the woman, a thousand nefarious scenarios, the Frampton family and their shock last night, the role he'd played in that, the green-eyed dragon who liked to fake a swoon and did so with skill. He laughed. Couldn't help it. Who faked a swoon? Forger. Fake swooner. What else could the lady do? She had great talent. Clear as day, that. Likely even Rubens couldn't paint in his own style as well as she could. Not that it mattered. Her talent didn't matter in the least to his investigation.

He groaned. Between his thoughts and those he avoided, his brain had quite turned to mush. And he was scheduled to leave London in a few hours, to hie to Scotland and procure a family heirloom of some sort for a family who had no heirlooms but needed them to gain the status they craved like a starving man craves food.

He rolled out of bed and stood at the window, watching the sky turn pink then yellow before he turned with a sigh and dropped into a chair near the cold grate, his arms falling heavy to either side, the knuckles of one hand wrapping the top of the table. He hunched forward with a grunt, massaging the bridge of his nose. Another day, another work of priceless art to procure for the highest bidder. Priceless? Ha. Everything and everyone had a price, especially art. When he'd learned that lesson years ago, he'd found a vocation that suited him better than the church ever had. Just because your parents are friendly with the Archbishop of Canterbury does not mean you'll suit that line of work.

Zander much preferred buying and selling, finding the newly rich but title poor and helping them fill their hallways with those signs of cultured class they were not supposed to have access to, helping them climb the social ladder just as his own family, titled and ancient, nose dived into financial ruin.

He fumbled on the table next to him until he felt the time and habit-smoothed edges of the old wedge of broken glass he'd left there last night. He picked it up and tapped it against the tabletop, creating a rhythm to think to.

He'd head to Scotland. Had to. A Manchester Midas had promised him enough money to help his brother fix the roof of the family manor if he delivered that damn family heirloom. But he could stop at the dowager's London townhome once more before leaving town, see if he could discover another clue or jog the memory of some neighbor. Or perhaps she will have returned. He rolled his eyes, tapped the bottle-green stained glass. Not likely, that. Too bad he was headed north. Her country home lay to the west, and he'd not be able to spare time to visit in such an out-of-the-way locale. He'd annoyed her solicitor quite enough and worried the next time he stepped foot on the premises, the man might have him shot.

Tap, tap, tap.

Knock, knock, knock.

"Come in," he said to whoever stood out in the hall. Maggie, likely. This was his sister's home. Hopefully she'd not brought her husband, Tobias Blake with her to make ridiculous comments and think himself funny indeed. Zander felt too sour for quips.

The door eased open, and Maggie appeared. "Good morning, Zander." She had the same brown hair as her brothers but more neatly kept. Even in a proper morning gown, she looked a little imp and always had. Their father had named her Magnificent, and Zander and his brothers had always considered the name rather apt. They doted on her.

But why the wariness? She did not usually succumb to such emotions.

"What have you done?" he asked.

"Now, don't overreact." She swung the door wider and looked to her right. His youngest brother Theo stood there, hands in greatcoat pockets, seriousness etched into every line of his face. As usual.

"Not him," Zander moaned. "Go away."

"No." Theo stepped into the room. "I'm as curious to know what happened last night. Maggie wrote to say that you came home looking like death, refused dinner, came up here, and cried."

Zander scoffed. "I certainly did not cry." Might have felt like it, though. For a moment or two.

Maggie shut the door, closing them all in between the four cozy walls. "I certainly said nothing of the sort. No fibs, Theo. But do tell, Zander. We have a right to know. Did you finally speak with the forger?"

Zander let his head fall back onto the chair with a groan,

and he flatted the glass on the table with his palm. "Yes. A disaster. It's not the man, the jeweler, Mr. Frampton."

"It's not?" Maggie said.

"Who is it, then?" Theo demanded.

Zander dropped his chin to his chest and started up the tapping again. "The man's daughter. Miss. Fiona. Frampton."

Maggie gasped. "Delightful!"

"Delightful?" Zander lifted, heavy, to his feet. "The family had no clue of the girl's criminal activities, and I'm the one who told them. And apparently, she forges art only to earn enough blunt to provide her sick mother with the care she needs. The girl knows nothing of the dowager or the location of the originals." Zander had not failed to note the similarities in their reasoning, and he felt about her actions the way he felt about his own. He understood the desperation and felt keenly the foolishness.

He cringed and opened a box on the mantel to drop the glass inside where it tinkled against a handful of other worthless trinkets. He reached inside and felt around, grabbed a random object, and pulled out a rusted copper button. He tossed it in the air and snatched it.

"Sounds familiar," Theo drawled.

Zander made a lazy pass by his brother, tossed the button again, snatched it again, and popped it into his pocket.

Theo wrinkled his nose. "Are you wearing yesterday's clothes? Did you even change out of them before going to bed?"

Zander shrugged, ducked his head, and sniffed. Hell. He needed a bath. "Hardly the point here, dear brother. The point is that we've hit a wall, fallen off a cliff, are lost at sea with no stars to guide us. Our inheritances have disappeared."

Maggie dropped onto his bed and fell backward. "They were gone years ago when you sold them, Zander."

"Not sold. Rented. It was an excellent scheme."

43

Theo propped a shoulder on the nearest wall and crossed his legs at the ankle. "Until it wasn't."

"Don't tell Raph," Zander said. "I'd like to have some other direction with this problem before he knows."

Maggie snapped upright. "I certainly don't wish to be the one to ruin his marital bliss. I've never seen him so happy."

Yes, Raph was damn near ecstatic. Still poor, still running himself ragged to fix the estate, to make it profitable once more, but in love and happy. And Zander had almost ruined it. Raph had almost abandoned the woman he loved for the financial safety of marriage to an heiress because Zander had told him the truth—the inheritance he'd worked so hard to earn, those priceless paintings he thought would save them all when they sold them—copies.

Thankfully he'd seen reason, listened to his heart, and won back the woman he loved.

But Zander had been less than useful in that regard. In any regard. Even when he thought he'd been acting incredibly useful—renting and copying the Rubens—he hadn't been.

He hissed a curse. "Don't tell Raph, Theo. Don't make me beg."

Theo held up his hands, palms out. "Take a bath and I won't tell anyone anything."

"Gladly." Zander sank back down into his chair, slipping his hand into his pocket to rub his thumb along the smooth curve of the copper button. "I'm off to Scotland today. I can't put the trip off a moment longer. Mr. Cullsby in Manchester grows more agitated by the day. His epistles practically scream."

"No, don't." Maggie scowled at him. "You've barely slept recently, and with this disappointment, you'll not be focused. You'll fall from your horse, and then who will find the paintings?"

"Don't you mean 'and then who will be my favorite brother?'" Zander asked.

"Why don't you quit this nonsense?" Theo tapped his boot, annoyed. As usual.

If Zander weren't so tired, he'd bristle. But he couldn't even summon a *humph*. His eyes were heavy, his fingers floating, already, into dreamland. "What nonsense, Theo, do you mean?" he managed to ask.

"Buying artwork of cultural significance for the highest bidders! For people who do not care about its meaning, about the artist, about anything but what others will think of them because they own it."

"Prig," Zander snorted. "Art isn't only for the refined." He tried to snort again, couldn't find the power to do so. "You should know, Mr. Satirist."

"A very weak insult, Zander," Maggie said, slipping to the floor, "if that was your intent. Theo is proud of his work."

"Is he?" He tipped his chin to look at his brother. "Are you? You don't use your real name to publish."

"If I did that, every peer in the realm would be on my doorstep, pistol in hand, to shoot me point-blank in the gut."

Zander bobbed his head to the side. "Actually, Theo, that's an excellent point. Don't use your name. I'd rather not attend another funeral so soon after the last." He sighed. "I'm too tired to spar with either of you at the moment. Will you please leave so I can bathe and—" He'd been tired for ages, only felt a glimmer of energy once recently, when the young Miss Frampton had fake-fainted. Hadn't been tempted to laughter so much in ... he could not remember how long. Laughter! In such circumstances. Should have been impossible.

A knock on the door.

"Hell. What now? If it's that husband of yours, Maggie, I'm sending him away."

"You're in his home, Zander. He'll send *you* away."

Zander made a growling noise deep in his throat that turned into a long groan. "Come in!"

It was the butler, who looked to Maggie as soon as the door swung open. "My lady, there are two young women here to speak with you. Are you at home?"

Maggie frowned. "Did they provide their names?"

"Miss Frampton and Miss Fiona Frampton."

The energy of the rising sun filled him to the brim, and he snapped to his feet. Theo and Maggie straightened, too, looking to him for guidance. He was, after all, the only one of them who had any acquaintance with the Frampton sisters. He gave Maggie a nod.

"Show them to the back parlor, Barnett, and have Mrs. Patricks bring in tea."

The butler bowed low and left, and Maggie ran.

"I need a more formal frock," she muttered, racing down the hallway.

Theo lumbered toward the stairs. "I admit to curiosity, but I'll be leaving now. I've an appointment with the last of *Father's artists*." No mistaking the disdain dripping from those words. Their father's will stipulated that they continue to patronize three of the artists he had supported while he'd live. Theo had been working since his death to find the artists new patrons so they did not bleed from the family hundreds of pounds a year.

"Two down, one to go," Zander said, leaning on the doorframe. Theo had placed a sculptor fellow with a rich Italian patron a few months ago, and he'd waved a painter off to Scotland last week.

"Hopefully none after this morning." Theo grimaced. "She has a house, Zander. Father bought the woman a house on top of presenting her with a yearly stipend."

"A whole damn *house*?"

"Thankfully, he did not put it in her name. Raph owns it."

"Was she ... Father's ..."

"Mistress? God no. I can't imagine that. He hardly ever came to town. Couldn't stand to leave Mother. And this woman's not a by-blow, either. Raph's solicitor says she's an earl's daughter. Hardly matters, though. She's a leech on our resources, and she must be removed."

"Poetic, brother." Zander sank low in his seat. "And sympathetic."

Theo grunted, waved, and left. "Take a bath."

Zander lifted an arm, sniffed again, and choked. Yes. Very well. A quick bath before facing the Framptons. Facing the dragon. Why in hell were they here? Hadn't he made a hash of their lives last night? And their realities, in turn, making a hash of his? Perhaps that's why they were here, to bring down some sort of biblical vengeance on his head. He'd revealed the girl's nefarious secrets to her entire family.

He likely deserved vengeance.

In less than half an hour, he ran down the stairs and shoved open the door to the back parlor. And stopped dead in his tracks at the happy laughter of the three women in the room.

"Making fast friends, are we?" He sauntered inside, chose a chair far from the others, and stretched his legs out before him, adopting a pose he hoped spoke of nonchalance.

The Frampton sisters sat around a small round table with Maggie, who had changed into a more formal gown faster, apparently, than a winning horse at Ascot. The sister who was not the art forger sat straight as a fire poker, her gaze full of ice, and the sister who was the forger looked ready to bounce from her seat. If the one was cool composure, the other was ecstatic activity.

Maggie held a teacup in her lap and glared at him. "Miss

Frampton, Miss Fiona Frampton, I hope you will excuse my brother's poor manners. He's a bit sleep deprived at the moment."

He yawned. For effect. "Sleep deprived and curious. Tell me, Miss Fiona, have you received news from the dowager in the few hours we've been parted? Or did you remember something of import to my search?"

Ah—there it was—that barely contained energy bouncing her out of her chair. "*Our* search, Lord Lysander."

"Our? I hardly think—"

"Then catch up, sir, as I've done nothing but think last night. And this morning. In bed, breaking my fast, on the ride over here, standing on your doorstep. Think, think, think. And here is the conclusion I've come to. The both of us have insight into the dowager's life but from different perspectives. We should work together to—"

"That's why I left my card with you last night." He slammed to his feet, her energy coursing across the room and making him feel the necessity of movement, banishing his exhaustion. "So you could send polite word if some bit of information crossed your little nose, not—"

"Not a particularly bright idea, Lord Lysander."

"Hell, woman!" A laugh exploded out of him, her sauciness the gunpowder and the spark that made it go boom. "Will you insult me twice before I've even broken my fast?" He grinned, couldn't be grumpy about it, about her.

She tilted her head to the side. "You've not eaten yet? Hm. That's your fault, is it not? Not mine. You could be facing insults with a full stomach."

Well damn him, she had a point. He strode to the table resting like an island of sanity in the middle of a female ocean of madness and almost cried with relief when he saw a pile of scones. He snatched one up and bit off half of it. She wanted to help, did she? And in an active way, it seemed. But how would she do that? He was a known member of the art world with contacts—shady and legitimate—and people who owed him favors. He routinely traveled the length of England in search of expensive pieces and thus needed no justification for his presence anywhere he pleased.

She was a jeweler's daughter. As much as she amused him, she'd likely get in the way. And he could not let her tag along. That would lead only to whispers, questions about their connection to one another, pressure, even, to do the proper and make a legal connection he did not wish.

"Well, Lord Lysander," Miss Frampton barked. "What is our next step?"

He wagged the remaining half of his scone in Miss Fiona's wide-eyed, fresh face. "Not all the scones in the world could fortify me against this, against your concentrated attack. But I'm ready to prevail nonetheless. I understand your desire to help, but hear me well when I say it is not the proper way to go about things. Send me information if it comes your way, but there is no *our* about this investigation."

"And why not, Zander?" Maggie looked at him as she often looked at a sketch she was working on, a pattern to be woven on the silk her husband made and sold for a pretty penny. Her usually bright eyes were hard, and her mouth thin, both signs the gears in that head of hers were clicking, clicking, clicking. "Why will you not let her help? The matter impacts her as much as it does you, us."

Zander shoved the rest of the scone in his mouth and paced back and forth across the room, chewing. "Let's see." Scone bits flew in all directions. "First, she's an art forger. Second, who knows what nefarious plots have the dowager tied up who knows where. Little Miss Forger Frampton might get hurt if she sticks her nose where it does not belong." He did not truly believe the dowager had been abducted for her art collection, but perhaps it would keep the dangerously intrepid miss at bay.

"Pardon me, sir." The sister's voice was like winter that had come too soon, killing every bit of green in the land. "You will desist from your insulting language."

He stopped pacing. "But she can insult me?"

Miss Fiona stood, smoothing her skirt with hands that shook just slightly, and faced him with a face calmer than her trembling fingers. "Let us put insults aside, Lord Lysander. We share a problem, and I would like to be part of the solution."

She was brushing aside their animosity in order to establish a partnership. But what good would a partnership do? His need for an excellent artist had long passed. The girl knew nothing. He must stride on alone. He came to stand before her in two long steps and held his palms out, offering the only thing he had for her—rejection. She smelled of wind and paper, a curiously fresh combination that soothed him, made the boundless energy coiling through his veins slow a bit, made him think of resting because the perfect place to rest might be just within reach ... It was a slow sort of tiredness, a peace, not the rocking exhaustion he'd felt of late.

He cringed. He could at least be kind. "Miss Fiona. I apologize for my unpardonable manners. I have not been myself of late."

She nodded. "Understandable with the stress of the dowager's disappearance. I, too, have been out of sorts."

"But I cannot let you involve yourself further. It seems to me you should duck your head low, give up painting entirely, and pray to God no one but me ever discovers what you can do. What you have done." He took a step back. "I've a trip to prepare for."

"Something to do with the dowager?"

Partially. "No. Work."

"You work? You're a marquess's brother."

He shrugged. "A *poor* marquess's brother. Good day, Miss Fiona." He bowed then flicked a gaze toward the sister. "Miss Frampton." He reached into his trouser pocket as his feet slapped against the worn hallway planks. He'd put an old locket there before leaving his bedchamber. Or half of one, the hinges ripped open, and the front half hidden. What picture had a long-ago owner put in there once? Likely it had been more valuable to them than the metal that encased it.

But not more valuable than the missing Rubens were to Zander. Selling them would be a new start for their family, would undo much of the damage their father had done. His mother had even agreed to give them the paintings without the will's single stipulation—that they create a work of art first. A worthless concession now that they could not sell the paintings at all. They didn't have them, and it would be a crime to sell the forgeries.

Zander had to find the originals. Not only to help his family's finances, but because he needed to right his wrong, to return to his family the stability his father had taken from them. That Zander had stolen from them, too, when he'd stolen the originals and replaced them with fakes.

And now the joke was not on dear old Papa but on his brothers and sister who'd counted on their inheritances to make the way forward easier. He'd robbed them of that, enraged his brother Raph, and proven himself a burden. When he'd only ever wanted to be, like his older brother, a savior for those he loved most.

Six

The emerald between Fiona's finger and thumb glittered as she set it into its golden home, completing the leaf Mr. Foggy had designed and crafted. Designed well and crafted poorly. As usual. One more emerald to set and the brooch would be fixed. She looked behind her at Papa snoozing by the fire. He'd gotten up from the worktable mid job and plopped down in that chair, leaving the piece unfinished. And Fiona had wandered away from her easel once the snoring had started, abandoned the vapid painting of the still life posed before her, and picked up the broken brooch.

Her father would find it completed when he awoke and think he'd done it and simply didn't remember doing it. And Fiona would keep her silence gladly by imagining the benefits of such a deception.

Perhaps the woman who owned the brooch would be so grateful it had been fixed with such expertise, she'd switch her custom, make Frampton's her jewelry home. Then she'd tell all of her tonnish lady friends, who would turn their backs on Foggy and march themselves down to the Frampton's door, wringing their hands, begging Posey and Fiona for high-quality settings. Then, knowing he had finally met defeat at the hands of two young women (she could ignore the fact no one was supposed to know women essentially ran Frampton's in her own imagination), Foggy would shutter his doors and leave London, tears wetting his cheek. *Then—*

"Fiona!" Posey swung into the backroom of the shop, only her hand wrapped tight around the doorframe stopping her trajectory. "One of the boys you've bribed is here with news."

Fiona's tools clattered to the table as she popped to her feet. "Excellent. I'll speak to him in the side alley." They could not converse inside the shop. The fancy ladies of the ton would not approve of riffraff like Tommy and his friends loitering there, even if they'd been given permission to do so. A hypocrisy after sailing through a duke's front door, but a necessary one. The Framptons had to maintain a façade of gentility, even when they clung to its very edges only. Especially then.

Posey disappeared, and Fiona donned her pelisse and bonnet. She glanced at her Papa, snoring in an armchair. Best not to bother him. He'd been silent with her since Lord Lysander had forced her to spill her secrets. She did not blame him, though the silence felt fragile, as if any wrong move might shatter it, sending glass shards into her skin to burrow down deep, to cut her everywhere.

She held her breath as she left the workroom and entered the alley through the shop's back door.

Tommy waited for her, his cap pulled down low. He leaned on a wall, hands shoved into pockets, and he whistled a song she knew to be crude.

"Good afternoon, Tom," she said as the door closed behind her.

He looked up. "The fella's back in town, Miss Fee."

She inhaled sharply. She'd guessed as much. She'd

promised Tommy and his little band of ruffians new coats and shoes if they kept a watch of several residences. Everywhere Lord Lysander frequented, including his sister's townhouse, and one of his brother's rented rooms. She'd also asked them to watch after the dowager's townhouse. But this was the first she'd heard back from any of the boys about any activities since she'd set them to this business a little over a fortnight ago.

"Thank you, Tom," she said carefully. "And where did you discover him?"

"Arrivin' at his brother's rooms. And then leavin' again. Fella looks like death on legs. A strong wind might knock 'im over. Do you mind if I have a look in his pockets if he falls, Miss Fee?"

"You will do no such thing. What do you mean he was leaving? Do you know where he went?"

Tommy nodded, his wide grin revealing a missing tooth. "Followed 'im, didn't I? All the way to the old lady's place. It will just be a quick look. Won't take nothin'. Pockets are small, after all."

"The size of his pockets is not the point, Tom. The point is you will too do more than look. Why else look at all? Do you mean the dowager?"

"That's the one. The one who's not there. The one wot's missin'. And looking only can be fun, Miss Fee. Swells like 'im don't miss a few pence from their pockets now and then."

Swells like him needed pence as much as she did. "No."

He kicked a rock.

"Kicking rocks will not change my mind."

He kicked another. "Good thanks I get for standin' out in the cold all day looking after your gentleman."

"Go ask Posey for something warm to eat. Is that thanks enough, you pickpocket?"

He did a jig and rubbed his belly.

Fiona crossed an arm under her breasts and rested the other elbow atop her hand to chew on her nails as she thought. She'd need coats now. And shoes. But the duke would help her if she asked, and the emerald brooch she'd just been fixing would pay well. In truth, they'd not been so pinched in the pockets for a year or so now. Things were better.

She paced.

"What do you want me ta do, Miss Fee?" Tommy asked. "Or can I go see Miss Posey now?"

She stopped and patted his shoulder. "Only stay warm in the new coats I'll secure you. Thank you."

He tipped his hat to her and ran, his feet slapping against the pavement of the wet alley.

"No picking pockets, either, Tom!" A hollow reminder. A boy, or woman, had to do what they must in order to eat.

He raised a hand in salute. Hardly a reassurance. Kindred souls, they were. She turned and leaned her forehead on the cool wood of the door. What to do? Only one thing to do.

She cracked the door and cried out, "Posey!"

"Yes?" her sister responded, equally loud.

"I'm going ... to find something to eat."

"Wait. Pardon? Fiona, what—"

Fiona closed the door and ran. Posey would likely not believe her, might give chase, which was only one reason to make haste. The other—Fiona could not know how long Lord Lysander would be at the dowager's house. She must catch him. If he'd discovered anything in the interval between their last encounter and today, she needed to know.

So she flew, her arms pumping, her lungs screaming, and her mind racing as fast as her feet. Finding out information on her own had proved deuced difficult. She had access to many of the dowager's friends, but she could not ask them outright about the woman because that would create a connection between them that might prove dangerous later. If—when?—her activities had been discovered by someone other than the curious circumspect Bromleys. Curiously circumspect? Perhaps not. They had a stake in the risks as well as she. Lord Lysander may deny it, they were chained to the same fiasco, and that meant they should help one another.

The row of terrace houses the dowager resided in appeared around the corner, and Fiona slowed her stride, tried to catch her breath. She'd need to be quiet. No great gasps or choking on air allowed because … because what?

She cringed even as she doubled over, bracing her hands on her knees. Because she meant to break into the home, and that required stealth.

"Horrid … idea." She panted between words, taking in great gulps of air, then she straightened with a "*Whew!*" and set her steps to a much more placid pace toward her goal. Going round the back would be best, slipping in under cover of the mews. And then what? Where would he be? In the alley as well? Skulking about the mews, too? She stepped into the shadows behind the row of terraces. No one. Not even the jingle of a horse's harness broke the dark silence. She pressed on toward the door she knew would belong to the dowager and tried the handle. Vain to hope it was—

"Open?" she whispered. Had Lord Lysander picked the lock? He seemed just the sort to be able to do so. "*Humph.*" What was he doing inside, though?

The interior of the house was as dark as the alley and musty, and she stood for several moments, arms outstretched, as her eyes became accustomed to the dark. When she could see enough to move forward without risk of collision, she did so, finally finding the bright entryway since sunlight flooded through the fanlights above the door.

Now, where did he hide?

Something fell in a room down the hall, and she heard the

dull thud of something hard hitting carpet. She whirled with a gasp. What if ... what if it was not Lord Lysander inside? What if someone far more nefarious awaited her, and Lord Lysander had left as soon as he'd found the baroness still missing?

She clenched her fists in her skirts and backed up until her shoulder blades hit the door. She'd done something stupid again, hadn't she?

"Bollocks," a man said from a room down the hall in a voice she began to find familiar.

She set her steps toward the room and flung the door open. And found Lord Lysander. Just as tall and straight and strong looking as she remembered him from the two times they'd spoken, from the two weeks he'd watched her from across the street. Watched her father, really. But he'd felt like her ominous stranger, and even though she had the truth of the matter now, he felt even more hers than ever. His hands sat at his slim hips, drawing his trousers tight against his thighs, and his dark, wavy hair slicked back from his forehead.

He seemed like a cravat pin with an onyx stone at the top, sucking all the light from the room. He did not sparkle like a diamond or draw the eye like an emerald. But he had a sheen about him all the same, beckoning the viewer closer because closer was where the hidden depths and beauty lay if you looked long enough.

"Why are you looking at me like that?" he demanded.

"You, sir, gave me a fright," she said, hands on hips, because she couldn't very well tell him she'd been imagining him as a piece of men's jewelry. But maybe she wouldn't imagine him as that because that was lovely, and he had a decidedly offensive edge to his voice.

"What the devil are you doing here?" he demanded. Offensively. Again.

"I heard something. Then I heard you, and I came to

investigate." She could be polite, though, despite it all, despite *him*.

In the dim light of what she now knew to be the dowager's parlor, she saw it—he rolled his eyes. "Yes, but why are you here at this address?"

"What did you drop?" she countered.

"Not that it matters, but I dropped a tumbler." He fell to his knees and stretched a hand beneath a drop cloth, waved it around a bit, then said, "Ah-ha." When he stood once more he held a crystal tumbler in his hand. He turned and grasped something on the cloth-covered table, and though she could not see what he did since his back was to her, she heard the familiar pour of liquid into the glass. When he turned back around, he held an amber-filled glass.

"Spirits so early in the day? You are a reprobate."

He winked. "Whatever you wish, love. I'm tired is what I am." He tilted the glass at her. "Cheers. Now go home."

"Absolutely not."

He sighed. "I suppose saying please won't work."

"Absolutely not. Why are you here? And inside? How did you get in?"

His hand not holding the tumbler fumbled at his waistcoat pocket before his fingers slipped inside. He pulled out something small and held it up between them.

"A key?"

He took another sip. "Excellent observational skills, Miss Fiona."

She'd grind her teeth to nothing talking with him. "A key to this house? Did Lady Balantine give you that?" Impossible to believe. She's a private sort of woman. Unless ... "Are you her lover?"

His grin died a swift death. "No! Why in hell would you think that?"

"You have a key."

"I made it, if you must know. Without Lady Balantine's prior knowledge or consent. Bribed a footman to make a wax mold. And I suppose I'd rather you know all those sordid details than have you think me the old woman's lover."

And *she* was supposed to be the criminal? "Your shame is misplaced, Lord Lysander. And your funds are misapplied. If you spend your money on things other than criminal activities, you'd perhaps not be in this situation."

"I do not misuse my funds." His body, which had been languid and long and lazy before, turned hard. "As you can see, I've benefited from having the key."

"But why do you need it?"

"To get inside." He finished his drink and snapped the glass down on a nearby table.

She groaned, covered her face with her palms. Impossible, infuriating man. "That much is clear. But what do you plan to do inside?"

"Same as you, I suppose. Have a look around. I would never have known the paintings were missing had I not had a key made."

"You're a devil."

He shrugged. "One does what one must." A glow, low and sultry sparked in his eyes. If a glow could laugh, it would. "Why are *you* here again?"

"I had you followed so I would know when you returned to London. I needed to speak with you, to make you see sense." She'd been denied a place in the practical whirl of life as long as she could remember, and she was ... she was cursed tired of it! She would not be shut out of having a say in her own future any longer.

He laughed, long and loud, and yes, that glow in his eyes fed on the sound, encompassed his entire body. If she hadn't been so enthralled by it, by him, she'd have been a bit insulted. As it was, she barely registered that she *should* be insulted.

When he recovered from his mirth, he pushed the fingers of both hands through his hair. "*This* woman? Wants to make *me* see sense?" Another chuckle. "Well, Miss Frampton, what is it you're determined to make me see sense about?"

"A partnership." She took several rapid steps forward, passing him by entirely to grab the crystal decanter on the table behind him. She took a long swig of it and tried to pretend it didn't burn. But the coughing and sputtering likely gave it away.

He merely crossed his arms over his chest and watched her with an amused eyebrow raised high on his forehead. When she stopped sputtering, he said, "I am not in need of a partnership. You see, I've just returned from Scotland, and while I found out nothing direct about the missing dowager, I did discover that there's a particular type of picture frame sometimes used to hide documents. I brought one back to London for a client, procured for pennies off an old duchess up north. I recognized it immediately. Lady Balantine has one, too. I fully intend to search the dowager's frame and, hopefully, discover something of import. Have you done as much while I've been away?"

No. She had not. "I cannot just ask our clientele about Lady Balantine."

The amusement faded, and he tilted his head. "Pardon me? I asked what you have done, not what you haven't."

"I've wanted to do it. I have access to any number of women who are friendly with the missing baroness. They come into our shop, but I cannot ask them outright what's happened to her lest I create an association between me and her in their minds. I can have nothing connecting me to her in the public eye. To protect my family." Frustration made her restless, and though she knew she'd regret it, she took another swig of the whisky. "Heavens that's horrid," she said as the fire in her throat calmed.

He sauntered toward the table—and her—and propped his hip against its edge, facing her. "Understandable. I suppose if I had not already interrogated all her closest friends ages ago, your poking around for information that way would be helpful. I have also queried her only son. A nasty man who answered my questions with grunts. Says he's not seen her or talked to her in years. No love lost between them, apparently."

Her spirits fell. All the way through the floor. "Are you sure they were telling the truth?"

"I am."

"Why would they tell *you* their secrets?"

He shrugged. "I am a marquess's brother. A handsome one."

"I cannot believe this," she said. "I'm the one who will hang at the end of a rope if this entire enterprise is revealed. But you are the true scoundrel. Having keys made, browbeating barons, seducing old ladies."

"No seduction necessary, love." He winked.

"I dislike you."

"The feeling is"—he leaned in low, the glow coalescing in his eyes once more, and tapped the tip of her nose—"not at all mutual." He turned, walked away, and she heard the *thunk* of the tumbler on the table before he turned back around, arms crossed over his chest, stretching the fine lawn of his shirt and the silk of his waistcoat across the breadth of his chest.

"What does that mean?" she demanded, plopping into a cloth-covered chair.

He sauntered across the room to a where a portrait hung on the wall. "It means I find you amusing."

His glow hidden by the dim shadows of the dark room, she could finally let his insult take her. "Amusing? And what does *that* mean?"

"It means, Miss Frampton, that I find you funny. A delightful little dragon that makes me feel a bit less tired." He cocked his head to the side and scratched the back of his neck. "The frame is like the other I saw in Scotland, but not identical. Hmm." He ran long, skilled fingers down each edge of the frame, then removed it from the wall entirely. Turning it over, he inspected every inch before replacing it on its hook.

He left the painting and fell into another chair-shaped lump facing her, bracing his elbows on his knees. "No hiding place for documents." He dropped his head between his hands. "Go home, Miss Fiona. A vain effort, I suppose."

"You tried. That's what matters."

His head shot up, and his dark eyes blazed as they pinned her. "You're comforting me? I thought you didn't like me."

She sat on her hands and shrugged. "You seemed to need it. But I'm also comforting myself. Your failure is mine as well. If we speak about this, I'm sure we can find a way my help is valuable to the search."

"We cannot."

"I can't simply stand by, clueless, while you run about investigating! This is my tragedy, too, Lord Lysander, and I insist I have a hand in fixing it. You cannot deny me—"

"*I* have interviewed everyone. *I* have searched every inch of this house. *I* have hired a damn runner. And you think—"

"*Every* inch?"

"Of course!" He exploded upward.

She stood, too, more slowly, though. She smiled, a true smile, one she felt to her toes. Because perhaps there was something she could do. Perhaps there was something he did not know. She'd assumed he'd known when he'd made his announcement—the art is missing!—at her home the other night. But perhaps not. Excitement buzzed in her veins, and the strides that took her from the parlor held more hope than the steps that had brought her, breathless, here.

His steps echoed fast behind her. "Where are you going?"

"To view the art collection."

"I've already looked at it. Dozens of times. There's nothing to see, the gallery is empty. The paintings are gone."

Of course he had been in that room before. He had a key. But she had something, too, hopefully. She continued walking, continued grinning.

He continued following. "You've passed the gallery door."

Ah. She did have something after all. "I'm not going to that gallery."

"But it's *the* gallery."

She turned then, squaring her shoulders and meeting his gaze. "Oh. My. It seems the baroness didn't share everything with you. It seems as if there *is* a way I can help you."

"What do you know, you minx?"

Oh, she could not wait to see the recognition light in his eyes that she wasn't useless. "There's a secret gallery. One Lady Balantine gave very few people entrance to."

"There is not." The click of his boots on the wood floor punctuated his words and his irritation.

She turned back around, continued her walk down the corridor. "Oh, yes, there is."

He hurried after her, following her straight into the dowager's bedroom.

She threw open the large wardrobe in the back corner of the room, and he came to stand beside her.

He waved a hand at it. "See? Empty. You are an imaginative one, aren't you."

"And you're an arse. Just wait, Lord Lysander, and watch." She stepped into the wardrobe, ran her finger down the right-hand seam at the back, and found the button. She depressed it, and the hidden door at the back of the wardrobe swung open.

"Hell." He stood so close his curse whispered over the top of her ear, sent a shiver down her spine.

She pushed open the door and sailed into the neighboring

townhome. "Not Hell, Lord Lysander. Lady Balantine's secret second home. Or, to be more precise, her secret art gallery."

He stepped beside her, turning in circles, though why she couldn't imagine. It was darker here than it had been on the other side of the wardrobe. "She owns the neighboring townhouse?"

"Mm-hmm."

"I didn't know. How'd *you* know?"

She stepped farther into the room, pushed back the curtains. "I suppose being the baroness's personal art forger has its benefits." Didn't find her so amusing now, did he? Eminently helpful, rather. Indispensable.

He clicked his tongue against the roof of his mouth. "How can you joke about such a thing?"

She clenched her fingers around the edges of the curtains. "What else is there to do?" She could not give up hope yet, so she dropped her arms to her side and faced him with a smile. "Shall I give you a tour?" She strode off without an answer.

"What if the paintings are here? You do realize, Miss Frampton, that they could be here. I had no idea this existed, so I have not looked."

"It seems the footmen cannot tell you everything." She smirked, but the expression hid a maelstrom of sincere emotions roiling in her gut. Were the paintings here? When he'd announced so confidently in their parlor that horrid evening that the paintings were gone, she'd assumed he had knowledge of this place. He did not, though.

Everything safe then. All her forged work still here, and in half an hour's time, she'd have it all gathered up and tossed into a fireplace, ignited and burned to ash.

Seven

Sunlight was a dusty thing gathering in pale pools in a room used to darkness. On the very edge of one beam stood Miss Fiona looking pleased and hopeful and with bright-pink cheeks likely lended to her by the whisky.

But she always seemed to be pink-cheeked, so perhaps not. And currently, Zander wanted to hug her, not just laugh at her, which until now had been his predominant reaction.

"Yes," he admitted, scratching the back of his neck, "the footmen didn't tell me all. I can admit when I'm wrong. Thank you, Miss Fiona, for the revelation. I'd very much like a tour."

And to so easily find the originals, after all these months ... relief almost dropped him to his knees.

She turned in slow circles, her gaze caressing the room as she clasped her hands before her, a curiously appealing move-ment that swept her skirts against her hips and tightened the bodice of her gown across her breasts.

Things he should not be noticing.

"The entire house," she said, taking a gliding step forward, "is an art museum, you see. No one lives here, sleeps here, or eats here. As far as I know, other than Lady Balantine, I'm the only one who's been here. Until now, of course. I do hope she won't be terribly put out with me for bringing you here, but needs must, I suppose." She stopped beside the fireplace and flattened a palm on the wall, her gaze caressing up and down the length of it, from floor to ceiling. "Each room has a theme, focusing on a particular type of art. This room is tapestries."

Zander came to stand beside her and touched his fingertips to the wall, felt the fine weave of silk. "I didn't notice." He turned in a circle now, looking closely. Drop cloths covered the furniture, but the walls had not been covered, and each one held a different tapestry. "How old are these?"

"I can't be sure. They could be authentic. But ... of course ..."

"They might not be." He leaned closer for a better view. "See this?" He pointed to a long faded spot. "The fading's not from light. The weave has been worn thin here, and in a pattern suggesting the tapestry's been folded. For decades. I say it's authentic. If it is forged, the forger has done as good a job as you. That crackling you painted on the Rubens ... perfection."

She ducked her head and blushed. "I should not be pleased at such a compliment, but it seems I cannot help myself. It's a devil's talent, I'm afraid."

He rocked back on his heels. "Still a talent, and a rather large one. Show me the gallery."

"You don't want a full tour?"

"Maybe some other day." His feet itched to find the Rubens. Surely they were here. The electricity of a discovery zipped through him, the same feeling he got when he procured a particularly valuable piece for a particularly grateful and wealthy client. Success. Funds. Helping the family. More than success—victory.

He slipped his hand into his pocket to find the broken

locket there and rubbed its edge. The action soothed him so he could follow her into the hallway without bouncing about like an ill-trained puppy.

Miss Fiona flashed him a look over her shoulder. "The hallways were left entirely blank, she said, to encourage contemplation."

"Odd woman, wasn't she? My mother would love her."

"She *was* odd." She shook her head. "She *is* odd. But I admire her. She always treated me well. Like she valued my help. She is odd, but she is *good*." An edge to her voice that dared him to disagree with her.

No point in that, though.

She found the stairs and made her way up.

He meant to climb silently beside her, but he found himself saying, "I feel like pins and needles are pricking me all over."

"Yes. Me as well." She grinned, and there in her flash of white teeth, he saw his own excitement mirrored. She understood what this could mean better than anyone. Deliverance.

"If you knew this place existed," he said, "and if you were so worried, why wait till now to visit it?"

"I did not have a key, now did I? And I confess, I never considered breaking and entering."

He chuckled as they reached the top of the stairs. "Fair."

She sailed forward without stopping and pushed open a door at the very end of the hall. He followed her inside with one long stride only to bump into her when she stopped abruptly with a gasp and a strangled cry. She wobbled, and he wrapped an arm around her waist to steady her.

A prickle of awareness—slim waist, curvy hip, tantalizing ribs just below things he was better off not thinking of—woke his every nerve, called his body into acute awareness. Of her. He yanked his arm away as soon as her feet were rooted strong to the floor. But he could not look away from her—the slightly parted lips, one long-fingered hand fluttering to her chest, her usually pink cheeks drained of color. A pretty woman indeed and an upset woman as well.

The gallery was bare, its blank walls patterned with squares of varying sizes whereby the wallpaper's brightness had been preserved by paintings hanging over it and dimmed by the sunlight and dust everywhere else.

Damn.

She stumbled away from his side, and when she reached the wall, stretched a trembling arm out toward it. "They're gone." Her voice as much a ghost as the missing paintings.

"Is that"—he raised an arm to point at a bit of wall with bright squares of a familiar size, found it trembling, too, and clenched his fist to tame it—"where the Rubens resided?" She nodded, one hand clapped over her mouth. "I think you need to sit down, Miss Frampton." He reached for her, wrapped his hand around her upper arm.

Her bobbing head began to shake instead. She needed to sit. But there were no chairs, and her body slowly dropped to the bare floor. He eased her down and joined her. She dropped her face into her palms, and her skirts spilled over her legs and his.

"A nightmare," she mumbled.

A nightmare indeed. And so soon after that brief ray of hope.

Miss Frampton's head popped up, and she looked at him with wild green eyes. "Perhaps she's loaded up the paintings and taken them with her wherever she's gone to."

He grunted. "Unlikely. If the dowager has such a neat little hiding place for her illicit art collection, why risk it during travel?" He eyed the blank spaces on the wall behind her. "Did you paint all of those missing from the wall?"

"Only some. And I cannot say whether or not the originals or the copies hung here. I thought—she told me—that she kept all my copies, but you've told me you have the copies at your house, and she has—had—the originals. I just cannot say anymore. Perhaps she offered the same service to others that she offered you." She shook her head, her eyes going crystalline.

Hell. No, no, no.

He patted the top of her head, and her chin sank toward her chest with each pat. "We'll find them. Don't worry." Should he really be comforting her? Her copies were safe at his brother's estate, and his originals were ... nowhere he knew of. Double hell. But his paintings were not the only ones she'd copied. She needed comforting, too.

They could soothe one another.

The thought led to action instead of more thought as it should have, and he cupped his hand around her neck, brushed his thumb up and down the warm, smooth skin there. He dipped his head low, their foreheads almost touching, and continued his rhythmic ministrations to the murmur of words he barely heard, needing to reassure her, to stop the tears.

Her body melted forward, her face coming so close to resting against his shoulder. Then she stiffened and pushed out of his embrace. With a scowl, she wiped the tears away.

"Do you think she's sold them? Your originals and my copies?" Her voice was soft but strong.

Good. She'd recovered.

He cleared his throat and jumped to his feet a touch too quickly. "God, I hope not. Come along." He offered her a hand.

She took it, and they left the room, closing the door silently behind them and returning to the dowager's home through the secret wardrobe door.

When they stood in the shadowy foyer, she said, "You said *we*."

He frowned at her. "Pardon?"

"You said 'We'll find them.' And that's a phrase that suggests you plan to include me in your search."

Hell. He had said that. Worse, he'd meant it. He rather owed her something after showing him the hidden gallery. And she stood to lose as much as he did if the dowager's careless handling of her art led them into trouble. Or if something sinister had happened to her and someone else had the art. *Double hell.*

All his reasons not to let Miss Frampton close remained, but his will to cling to them became sand between his spread fingers. It was her life, and she should be able to control it. He knew well how reliance made one vulnerable, knew the satisfaction and relief that came from taking one's own fate into one's own hands. He and his brothers had done so even before their father's death, taking work to prevent the flood of funds from the coffers, a useless task in the face of their father's deluge of spending.

"Yes," he groaned, "you can help, but frankly, I don't see how."

She bounced up and down on her toes. "You can come by the shop once a week, and we can share any new information we might have with one another."

"I can't do that. Your father will think I'm courting you."

She snorted. "No, he most certainly will not."

Zander wagged a finger in her face. "A single gentleman stops by the shop once a week to speak alone with his beautiful daughter? Hell, Miss Frampton, of course he will. I'm sure it's happened before. How the deuce aren't you married already is what I want to know."

He didn't really want to know that. It was neither here nor there, not of any usefulness to their investigation or to anything really. Except that, perhaps, a husband would have kept her out of trouble, kept her too busy in the bedroom to even think of forging anything. He pinched the bridge of his nose.

"Look, you can leave any information you discover in a location in the back of the alley. I'll check there a few times a week. That way, we never have to face one another let alone speak. And no one suspects matrimony is on anyone's mind."

"I don't think anyone would suspect that anyway," she insisted.

"You're daft."

"You're annoying. Besides, I thought you found me *amusing*. Let me amuse you, Lord Lysander." She fluttered her lashes, long and gold and hell—

His cock twitched. *Triple hell.* No good. The worst. She clearly had no idea the way her words sounded, like promise and seduction. And Zander, apparently, was willing to be seduced. No! He *could* be a gentleman. He whipped around and stomped toward the back door that led to the alley and the mews.

She chased after him. "You'll truly insist we participate in silly games because you fear a jeweler will take it into his head that his daughter is being courted by a marquess's brother? Do you hear that? *Jeweler? Marquess?* It is not a connection likely to be intuited."

He grunted and opened the door. The alley beyond it was clear, and when she joined him in it, he shut and locked up the townhouse door.

"We are not climbers," she insisted, more than irritation in her voice. He more precisely identified her tone as insulted.

"I'm not suggesting you are. I'm simply not willing to take chances. I'm in no position to support a wife let alone one as poorly off as I am."

"This is absurd. I think you're suggesting the note-passing nonsense to ... to fob me off. You have no intention of working with me to solve this mystery."

He stopped, turned on his toe, and towered over her.

She bumped into him then bounced back onto her heels even though they'd barely made a connection. Not that his nerve endings knew that. They had not only realized she'd brushed against him, they had decided they wanted it to happen again. But *more*.

"Listen," he said, ignoring his screaming nerves, "I'm not in any way out to fool you, Miss Frampton. I just want my damn paintings back, and I'm willing to do just about anything to retrieve them. But my brother recently married for love, the lucky bastard, and his wife had no dowry to speak of but for a cottage in Cumbria and a small annuity to go with it. It's a happy marriage but not a lucrative one. And during a time we needed lucrative." They'd needed Raph happy more than that, though. He'd deserved happiness after over a decade's dedication to cleaning up their father's mess. "All that being true and pressing and all that, I'm in no place to marry. It would be unfair to any woman who aligned herself to me. I don't even have a residence of my own. Do you understand? If I married, I would have to rely on my family for my wife's sake, and I'll not pinch them when they're already in pain."

She stepped back several steps, every thought in her head blazing clear in her eyes. He had the brief, mad desire to hear that litany out loud. It would likely entertain him for hours, days, a lifetime, even, but he wouldn't ask for her to vocalize those thoughts. What good would that do? So he shrugged it off.

Finally, she gave a tight nod. "Yes. I understand. There's a loose brick in the alley behind the shop, near the back door. I'll leave note of anything I discover there. And you?"

"Same, Miss Frampton. Thank you for being so unexpectedly reasonable."

She sniffed and paced past him. "Perhaps one day you'll do the same."

The impertinent, marvelous chit. He took several hard steps after her, then clutched his hands into fists, and glued his boots to the muddy ground. Arguing further would achieve nothing. When he had his temper firmly in hand, he walked to the end of the alley and swept his gaze both ways down the street. Gone. Good. He turned down the street in the opposite direction of Frampton's shop, each step hounded by what he'd told her in the alley.

His inability to marry. At all. When, by some horrendous quirk of fate, he'd always sort of, just a little bit, wanted to. He had fond memories of his parents' marriage—the looks they'd given one another, the jokes they'd shared, how they'd leaned on one another in times of woe. It had made him feel safe, loved, happy. Until, of course, he'd learned that the very ground they all stood on had rotted away, stability sold for a new painting or twelve.

Similarly, his hopes had been dashed this day. To find the dowager's secret gallery only to have the paintings gone. Seemed a decided step back. But it wasn't. It was merely that they'd not stepped forward at all. He'd always thought the paintings were gone, and they were. The tiny moment of hope had meant nothing but disappointment.

Damn disappointment—Zander's lot in life. Everything he did seemed to rot away to useless pulp. Hopefully this partnership with the Frampton chit would not end the same way.

Eight

Words were more difficult than images. So many of them could represent a single idea. Images, however ... You see a hill, you draw a curved line, more or less curved depending on the hill. A man has a long nose, you draw it that way. Easy. So was finding the right shape and color gemstone to create an effect.

But what words to use when you needed to tell a stubborn man that waiting wasn't working?

Fiona paced back and forth in front of the small writing desk in the workspace in the back of the shop. She'd put her tools away an hour ago in favor of attempting to find the right words like she could find the right curve of a brushstroke. Hm. Perhaps it was the same. When she painted, she pursued honesty, truth, exactness. She sat down at the table and picked up her pen. There were words for that. She scribbled quickly.

"Fiona!" Her father's voice from the front of the shop, a touch of irritation in it. "Lady Shellington wants to know more about your painting of the Thames."

She folded the letter as she stood. "Coming, Papa!"

If only Lady Shellington and those like her wanted to *buy*

those paintings. No, if only her Papa would sell them when they inquired. But he refused, saying a lady like his youngest daughter didn't sell her work. It would be undignified.

Ha. He knew the truth about Fiona's dignity now. She had little.

She made a quick stop in the alley first, sliding the brick loose from its home, sneaking the paper inside, then replacing the brick. The first note passed between her and Lord Lysander, and ten days after their defeat at Lady Balantine's art gallery. Too little happening too slowly. Hopefully this note would speed things along.

"Fiona!" her father roared.

She flung open the door and entered the shop once more. "Coming!"

But would Lord Lysander come? And when?

A fire glowed, low and dying, in the grate as Zander slipped into his bedchamber soon after the clock chimed twelve. It had been a busy day, but he'd made a pretty penny, and thankfully, he'd stopped by Frampton's before heading home. Wondering, unable to resist checking ... had she left him a note yet?

She had.

He lit a candle and pulled the slim piece of paper from his pocket, unfolded it near the flame. Finally, a clue. Miss Frampton had discovered something of importance. His own attempts to uncover the dowager's whereabouts of late have proved fruitless and frustrating.

He leaned close to the light, cursed, and pulled a pair of wire-frame glasses from his coat pocket, slipped them on. The swimming words focused, and he read.

· · ·

Dear Mr. B,

Nothing is happening. This cannot be the best way to conduct this investigation. I suggest we make a change.

Miss F

≈

Less than half a day was all it took to receive Lord Lysander's reply. When Fiona slipped into the shop to open up the next day, she entered through the alley door, checked behind the brick and found the note. She read it in the dim, early dawn light.

What the deuce do you think we should do instead? You know, you remind me a bit of my eldest brother, the marquess, though I cannot think of him that way. He is and always will be Raph. You are, and always will be, impatient, I presume. It's not waiting. It's biding our time. Hell, woman, please do find some-thing else to occupy your overactive brain.

P.S. Notice I have not written even a hint of our names. Please do follow suit.
    P.P.S. God save me from silly and amusing *women.*

Well. *Well.* He certainly had not had to write that last bit. She'd gathered in the past that he thought her amusing quali-ties were good things. Now she saw what he meant with that word—nuisance, ridiculous, silly. Same as always from everyone around her.

She was supposed to be finishing up the dreadfully dull still life she couldn't bring herself to work on, but she sat down and wrote a letter instead.

≈

Zander leaned against the alley wall in the late afternoon sun. He had a mind to stomp into the shop and demand she explain herself, but since that would defeat the entire purpose of sending the cursed letters, he did not. Instead, he read the note again.

Dear Mr. Muttonhead,

What the deuce do I think we should do? I'm so glad you've asked, as I have many excellent suggestions. First, we should locate all her former servants and interview them (unless you've done that already, and it seems you might have). Second, we should seek out gossip from the art world. Has anyone procured a Rubens recently, for instance? Third, we could certainly do something underhanded like put out rumors one of us intends to buy a Rubens. Then, we would wait and see who contacts us. I could put my considerable skill to work and forge another painting, put it about we have an original for sale and see if the dowager or someone else contacts us. As you see, sir, there are a multitude of options more productive than waiting.

As you can infer from the above observations, God has saved you from a ridiculous, silly, and amusing *woman because I am certainly not one of those, no matter what the rest of the world thinks.*

I wish I could meet this marquess of yours. He sounds utterly delightful. Much more so than his insulting brother.

Have a horrid afternoon,
Miss Brilliant and Bold

The hell of the letter was it made him want to laugh. The double hell of the letter was some of her ideas were not half bad. He located a third hell, too—he'd not meant to insult her and felt bad that he had. He pulled a pencil from his pocket and used the door to write, then he folded it, slipped it back behind the brick, knocked, and ran.

Fiona stared, mouth slightly agape, at the note in her hand. She could still hate him. She had that right, and he'd given her more than enough reason. But she could fully believe the man who'd penned the missive between her fingers was as charming as he claimed. She read it a fifth time and allowed herself a chuckle.

Miss Brilliant and Bold,

I think Raph would like you, too. Usually, people prefer me to him. He's a bit of a grump, and I'm absolutely the more charming of the two, but recent events have run me down, and I've not shown you my charming side as much as I would like. Perhaps that should be remedied. You have, shockingly, excellent ideas. But we cannot implement any of them in haste. Can you stay at the shop tonight after your sister and father leave?

I'll be waiting across the street for your answer,

Mr. Muttonhead

P.S. These names, as dissociated as they are with our true ones, are acceptable.

There was that bit about her good ideas shocking him, of course. But his suggestion that they meet in the shop after hours made up for it. She'd have to find an excuse to give Papa and Posey, of course. She could tell them she was working on a new painting or practicing a new brush technique, and that she'd have Daniel escort her home. Yes, that would do. She made her way toward the door to push it open and signal to him. She saw him through the shop windows first, standing as he had those first few weeks—a dark specter on the landscape, an omen that had brought to her life the chaos it had promised.

Shockingly excellent ideas.

Hmph. He could wait a little bit. She crumpled the bit of paper in her hand just as the bell above the front door tinkled. She turned, expecting to see Lord Lysander stride into the shop. He did not. The Duke of Crestmore did, however.

"Your Grace!" She grinned, striding toward him.

"Miss Frampton." He bowed low.

Formality ruled the shop, and they could not be as they felt toward one another here—brother and sister.

"What brings you in?" she asked.

He pulled a bit of paper from his pocket. "This. It's a new design. Do you think you can accomplish it?"

She took the paper and unfolded it. Pearls mostly. "It's exquisite. Your mother's design?"

Heat stole across his cheeks. "My own, actually."

She clapped hands over her mouth and danced a bit of a jig, propriety forgotten. "How utterly delightful." She studied the parure with closer attention to detail. "Exquisite and complex. Yet still simple. It's perfection." What stories would it participate in? What life would the lady who wore it lead?

"I hope so. Can you have it done by Christmas, do you think?"

She beamed up at him. "I shall try!"

He took her hands, squeezed them, though they both knew he should not, then shot out of the shop like his heels were on fire.

She shook her head, blinked at the place he used to be, then studied the drawings once more. "So very odd." She looked out the window. "No!"

Lord Lysander strode away.

She threw herself out the door and cupped her hands around her mouth. She yelled, "Oy!"

He stopped, one foot forward, hesitating over the ground. Slowly, he put it down, and slowly, he turned to look at her, scowl firmly in place.

Where the deuce was he going and in such a horrid mood?

And how to communicate to him that she agreed with his plan without crossing the street and speaking with him, an action that would thoroughly disgust him, considering his worry over being trapped into marriage through mere conversation. He'd likely take flight with her first footstep, screaming his head off, dodging between hacks, calling for a constable. Then he'd trip, be trampled beneath horse's hooves, and that lovely woman she'd met, his sister, would have to wear black.

Black would likely wash her out, pale as she was to begin with. But worse than that, she'd be so sad. So would the brother Lord Lysander had written about in his note, the married marquess. And then—

She shook her head. No. Focus. But just in case, best to remain on this side of the street. What to do? "Umm ..." She waved.

He scowled harder. From across the street, she could see the massive and massively disapproving indentation between his brows.

She rolled her eyes, then jerked her head toward Frampton's behind her. Hopefully that was clear. She finished off with a smile wide enough to make her face ache and returned indoors, dreaming of what might happen that evening when her family went home and she stayed. When Lord Lysander snuck inside and, together, they plotted how to save themselves.

Nine

When Zander knocked on the alley door, the sun had already dropped below the London skyline, and Miss Frampton's family had long since closed the shop for the day. Only Miss Frampton the younger remained inside, and inadvisable as this little evening exploit was, he could not help but look forward to it. What absurdities would the woman's mind cook up? He'd already considered a few of the possibilities she'd written in her note. The one about putting out rumors they had a Rubens to sell was particularly good. Perhaps the dowager herself would show up on her own doorstep to fill her personal galleries with priceless works of art.

The door creaked open, and Miss Frampton's heart-shaped face peered out at him. She bit her bottom lip, and dragged her eyes up and down his frame, as if she suspected he was not himself.

The suspicion, the mistreated bottom lip, the white teeth peeking out at him beneath her fiery green eyes—stole his breath. Just a bit. Just one little breath he could not push through ribs and teeth to mingle with the air.

"Come in," she said finally, stepping aside, and he found his breath again, everything as it was before. She smiled up at him, a wavering thing. "I must admit to being slightly anxious about all this."

"Forgery has serious consequences." He spoke too harshly, but he felt a bit sour. He should not be thinking of her bottom lip. He was unavailable by choice, by circumstance, and she was too. Why'd she not mentioned her suitor when he'd brought up the danger of others misinterpreting their relationship?

"Not that, Lord Lysander." She waved a hand between them. "This. Even a jeweler's daughter knows not to be alone at night with a man." She led him into a workroom at the back of the shop. The walls were lined with narrow drawers with tiny knobs for handles, and a large, beaten table took up much of the space. In the corner, near an empty fireplace, a small armchair sat like a squat brown bear, a matching ottoman pushed right up against it. It was clearly a workspace, but it seemed cozy as well. Their home had been cozy, too. They were clearly a family that took comfort seriously.

Miss Frampton wore a green muslin gown with a gray shawl pulled close over her shoulders, and she bustled about the room. With no bonnet and no gloves, she seemed most at home. "Have a seat. I'll find us something to drink." She knelt near a cabinet, opened it, and half disappeared inside it as she dug for something.

He sat, doffing his own hat, stripping his hands of his own gloves, and digging a fingernail into a dent in the tabletop. If she could be comfortable for tonight's discussion, so could he. "If you're so worried about impropriety, Miss Frampton, you should have asked your suitor to stay."

She popped upright, a wine bottle in one hand and two murky glasses in another. "My suitor?" She shook her head, standing and placing her bounty on the table between them. "I have no suitor."

"Then who was that fancy fellow who waltzed into the shop earlier, took your hands in his, and left you with a love note?"

She blinked, her gaze going far off. When she came back to the room with him it was with a laugh. "Archer? Is that why you ran away?"

"I didn't run. I simply did not wish to wait for your answer while you made love in front of all of London."

Her face contorted in disgust. "Archer? Make love to *me?*" She shivered. "He's a duke. A friend, to be sure, but most certainly nothing like you imagine. And I would never ... I have never ..." She made a retching noise. "No thank you. He's a friend. Nothing more."

Zander lifted an eyebrow. "A friend?" Her visceral reaction to his assumptions suggested she spoke the truth, yet doubt remained, a stubborn burr between his ribs. The eager way in which the man had greeted her, the ease she'd had with him. "He may be now, but—"

"Absolutely not. He's like a brother, and I would like to move on to a more productive conversation now. You are stubborn, aren't you? Get an idea in your head and don't let go. Well, please do let go of that one." She sat next to him and splashed wine into both cups then scooted one across the table to him. She took a sip of her own, going thoughtful and distant again. "Though I have wondered a time or two if he and Posey might have feelings for one another." She shook her head. "Apologies. I tend to spin stories, and they are not productive. Now"—she pulled a wrinkled bit of paper from her pocket, and he recognized his handwriting on one side, hers on the other—"which of these ideas of mine do you think best?" She smoothed the paper on the table.

He sipped the wine, felt the burn down his gullet, then

leaned back in his chair, letting the front legs pop off the floor, and folded his hands over his belly. He believed her about the duke. The bit about her sister having a *tendre* for the man did it. Made him feel lighter. Of course it did. He no longer had to worry he'd be discovered alone with another man's intended. Deuced awkward, that. But also ... hell, he tried to be honest with himself because he often kept honesty from everyone else, and he couldn't pretend—not to himself—that the threat of a suitor's fist in his face had been the only thing plaguing him. He'd stormed off, after all.

They'd looked so pretty in the frame of the shop window, so perfect with the duke's golden curls bent toward Miss Frampton's darker yellow locks, her chin tipped up, both of them grinning like fools.

He'd turned green. No reason for it. But he couldn't deny it. And the lightness he felt now? Relief that she didn't belong to another man.

Hell.

He rapped his knuckles on the table, annoyed with himself and about to feign annoyance with her because of it. "Trying to sell a forgery," he said, "is an obviously brainless idea."

Her mouth dropped open and her eyes widened. Hurt flashed there, and her pink lips curled into disgust.

He couldn't. His pride demanded he wound, but that organ nestled in his chest, protected by bone and muscle, wanted to protect her, to give her the honesty he usually reserved for himself alone. He hurried to add, "But also a good one. Apologies for the gruff way in which I phrased it. It's not brainless. You're not brainless." The chit seemed sensitive on the topic of her intelligence. "The plan is good. Merely rough."

The flush of hurt bloomed into one of hesitant pleasure.

He took another sip of wine. Sip? No, more like a gulp. It had been a long day. A long week. A long year. He'd slept little, worked hard, and couldn't seem to keep his temper when he used to be the most charming of his brothers. Now he growled instead of grinned and insulted pretty women instead of flirting with them, turned green with jealousy when he should feel nothing.

The wine burned resolution into his veins, though. He would be nicer to her from now on. He downed the rest of his wine and gave her his most charismatic expression, making sure that one lock of hair fell right across his eye.

She cocked her head to the side. "What are you doing?"

"Smiling at you."

"I see that, but why."

"Because I have been unpardonably rude during our short acquaintance, and you do not deserve it."

She laughed and swiped his wineglass away. "No more for you." She poked the paper. "Now let us focus. Imagine ... *me* insisting we focus. Mama and Posey would love to see it."

"Most women find me charming." He wanted *her* to find him charming.

"Have you growled and cursed at most women since meeting them? Have you revealed their sordid secrets to their families?"

He winced. "We should restart our acquaintance."

"But why?" The sincerity of her question settled about the room, and a lock of yellow hair rested in the curve between shoulder and neck Zander always found irresistible, his favorite part of the female body. On Miss Frampton it was doubly arousing.

He dropped his head and raked his fingers through his hair. "I feel bad for all that—the insults and the ill-timed revelations. I'd like to make amends. You're friends with a duke. Do you think you can be friends with an art curator?"

She narrowed her eyes. "You didn't want to work with me a week ago."

"And I've come around, haven't I?" More like his willpower to keep the woman distant had crumbled entirely. "I'm still hesitant about the entire thing, but it's your life and your fate as much as it is mine. Of course you must take part. On an"—he growled a bit as he finished up—"active level. More than notes." And he'd just have to do anything and everything to keep her safe. And to keep her father from getting ideas about their relationship.

Her nod came slow as dripping honey.

Honey—the color of her hair, though now in the deepening shadows it seemed even darker than that.

"I suppose we can be friends," she finally said. She smiled, a barely-there expression that very nearly knocked him unconscious.

What had they been talking about? Where in hell was he? Did he even have a name? He took a deep breath then cleared his throat.

"We should focus." He pushed the bottle of wine away despite his urge to grab it up and take a giant slug of the liquid.

"That's what I've been trying to do, Lord Lysander."

"Of course, you can't paint another forgery. That idea is right off the table."

"I think you're correct. I had determined some time ago not to copy any longer. That bit of my note was one of my less-practical fancies."

"You can't forge something new, but there's no reason we can't let everyone think we have a painting we don't have. Only a few people knew the true extent of my father's art collection. Collectors will easily believe I've got something they want."

"Yes. Very fine indeed. But it has to be something Lady Balantine wants. Or something her captor wants."

"Captor?" He scratched an invisible line into the weathered tabletop. "You think she's been abducted?"

"What else? You don't think that?"

"I've considered it." Feared it even. "But we've no proof. She's eccentric. I grew up in a house of eccentrics, and I know what they're like. She could have merely decided to up and move elsewhere."

"With no notice to anyone?" She leaned away from him. "Without alerting her friends or providing a new address?"

He shrugged.

"I disagree."

He reached for the bottle, poured himself another glass. Odder things had happened in the art world than the abduction of a woman who owned priceless paintings. "Truthfully, I don't know what to think. It's more likely she realized she didn't want to return the original Rubens and so ran off with them."

Miss Frampton shook her head. "I do not think she would do that. Though you call yourself her friend, you clearly do not know her very well."

"And you did?"

"I *do*. Please do not speak of her in the past tense." She tapped the side of her wineglass with a long, slender finger, and he could not help but remember how talented those fingers were. He'd seen her work. It had possibly fooled his father for a time. But not forever. The stipulations of the will said all. He'd known.

"Well then." He needed more wine after all. "Tell me why I'm wrong."

"She's thoughtful. She gives to several charities. She supports an orphanage or two. She has one son, of course, but you already know he's awful. He dislikes her. She has no family other than him and his wife, but he refuses any sort of close connection. So she delights in helping other families."

The description was plausible. It would explain why she provided Miss Frampton steady—even if questionable—work. It would explain her willingness to buy the paintings from Zander and return them one day at a lower price, but ... "Even with all that, she can still be greedy when it comes to art. The fact she has a personal gallery no one but you has ever seen proves that. And, if no one has seen this gallery, as you suggest, then who is there to know what art she has, to abduct her for it or to steal it from her?"

Miss Frampton's teeth tore at her lip again.

"Many art collectors are drawn to rare objects, Miss Frampton. They are drawn to things valuable not because of their monetary worth but because they are one of a kind." He slipped his hand into his greatcoat pocket and clasped the broken locket. He pulled the locket out and tapped it on the table in a steady rhythm.

"I cannot deny what you say, Lord Lysander. Only ... I hope it is not true. I refuse to think it of her."

"That would mean our Lady Balantine is in trouble, or she was in trouble and is now no longer troubled by the woes of life, if you take my meaning."

"I do, and I do not like it." She sniffed and took a drink of wine. "Let us assume she is still alive and hatch a plan to bring her back to London."

What an optimist she was with her pink cheeks and bright eyes and determination to do whatever it took to support her family. Even break the law. He understood that impulse if not the optimism. The world was broken. He knew that better than she, obviously. But she had not seen how those with money could have whatever they wished, those without be damned. A system he abhorred, though he certainly took advantage of it, procuring whatever it was the rich wanted by any means necessary, accepting their payments. To help his family. Just as she had tried to help hers.

No, he could not shatter her likely hard-protected optimism. "Bring her or her captor"—he could not very well say murderer after she'd asked him not to—"back to London. Because if she has been captured, it's the fiend who abducted her who has the paintings now." He knocked the locket against the wood. *Tap, tap, tap.*

Miss Frampton finished her wine and slapped her hand over his, stilling the steady beat. "That is quite a distraction."

He curled his fingers around the locket and froze. Partly because she'd been so brazen as to touch him and partly because neither of them wore gloves. Their skin rested warm together, and that warmth spread past knuckles and tendons, spread up his arm and through the entire network of his body —to nerves, blood, muscle, and bone. He snatched his hand away.

"What is it?" she asked, her gaze flicking down to his clenched hand.

"Nothing of consequence. A broken locket." He pocketed it. "I like to keep broken things about me. Things no one wants because, at some point, the thing was wanted. It may be forgotten now, but it held value for someone once." Hell, he'd had too much wine. To be spouting such nonsense.

But she brightened and leaned closer to him. "Do you know what my favorite painting is?"

"How should I?" He flinched. He'd devolved once more into a growling beast. "Something famous, no doubt."

She shook her head. "My sister painted it when we were little. It's of my mother and father." She bounced out of her chair and across the small room. "Come here. Look." She nodded at a framed painting to the side of the fireplace and above the armchair.

He rose slowly and joined her, peered into the frame. Blue sky and green grass, a man and woman holding hands. Sort of?

The limbs were different sizes and there was no sense of proportion or perspective.

He hissed. "I assume your sister does not have your talent, then."

"Not an ounce of artistic talent. She's an excellent head for business, though, and if given a good design, she can fashion a gorgeous and durable bit of jewelry. This is one of her last paintings. She gave it up soon after."

"I can't blame her. Looks like my brother Raph's work. I swear he has ten thumbs on one hand and none of them know how to hold a brush."

She laughed, and it sounded like gold threads wrapping round him, like sunlight shattering the shadows of the night. Hell. Neither of those things *had sound*. Definitely too much wine.

"You love your brother," she said. No question. A direct statement.

"I do. I love all my brothers, though they're often right pains in the arse."

"How many do you have?"

"Four. Maggie—Mrs. Blake—is my only sister. But she's more delight than pain."

Her whistle bounced off the close walls. "Four pains in the arse is a lot to have. I wish I had more, but ..." Her voice trailed off as she stared up at the child's painting. The woman in it stood. "The doctor said my mother should have no more. Not after ..." She shivered. Her shawl had slipped from one shoulder, and she pulled it back into place.

"Cold?" he asked, rushing to the empty grate. "I can light a fire."

She shook her head. "Thank you, but I'm fine. Let us return to planning. I should get home shortly."

They sat, and though he ached a bit to ask about her mother, he did not. He did not need to know more about her.

91

What he knew already was far too appealing, how it made him want to know even more, a greater danger. He'd not indulge the impulse further. He'd make use of her cleverness, and when they'd accomplished their mission, he'd never see her again.

Ten

They left the shop by the alley entrance, and though a chill snaked through the spring night air, Fiona felt warm to her very toes. Confident, too, that together, they would find the dowager and the paintings. He would put it about that he had a rare Rubens in his possession and wanted a buyer. Knowing the state of his family's finances, not a soul would question his wish to sell it. Then they would wait to see if the dowager bit. Or if someone else bit. Then, if it was not the dowager, they'd ask questions.

A breeze whipped her skirts as she set her steps toward home, and a hand wrapped tightly around her upper arm pulled her to an unexpected stop,

She yelped and swung around to glare at Lord Lysander in the darkness. He merely locked her arm snug into his and pulled her close.

"Don't stray too far from me," he grumbled. "After dark, all streets of London are dangerous."

"I'm well aware." But she did not pull away. It felt rather nice to have someone unreasonably protective over her. She looked up at him. She'd evaded the question in his eyes from earlier in the evening. About her mother. The memories were painful, and he'd not pressed. That made her want to settle them into his palm like tiny gems.

"You were curious before." Her voice sounded fragile in the night, like a wavering star about to fall to earth, and she cleared her throat before speaking again. "About my mother."

"No need to discuss it if you do not wish to."

"It's no matter. It is as much a fact now as the color of the sky."

"She's not always been in a bath chair, then?"

"No. She fell. Down the stairs. Hit her head, too. For quite some time, she was unconscious. Weeks. When she woke up, she was not quite herself. She regained her mental faculties, but never the use of her legs. She has always helped my father with the books, and during her illness, father failed to do the job she'd done so well for years. He was worried about her. To distraction. And by the time she was well enough to return to her work, much damage had been done to our finances. In addition, we had to pay doctors and buy a good chair."

"You said you had no intention of forging paintings any longer," he said. "Does that mean your family is doing better, your motives for criminal activity not quite so pressing?"

She heard the smile in his words, and she put her own smile in her response. "We are better. But the shop is still not as profitable or stable as we should like. Yet, no matter the pressure, I will not do it again. I've decided to ..." No reason to tell him.

He elbowed her, a gentle nudge. "You've decided to what, Miss Frampton?"

Heavens, the way he said her name, as if it were poetry, as if it were starlight, as if it were the thing most likely in the entire world to bring him pleasure ... she could not survive it, so she thrust words into the world to cover the echo of her name on his lips.

"I want to design jewelry."

He stopped walking, yanked her to a stop, too. "No."

"Yes. I'm no good at painting. And I do not like it."

His bark of laughter ripped the night sky open. "No good? You're a genius. Don't try to lie to me."

"I can't paint my own scenes. I can only copy. That's what I have a genius for—forgery, not creation. I cannot *create* with paint, and it vexes me." Tears pricked against her eyes. She hated crying. She wouldn't, so she squeezed her eyes closed. "But jewels and gold ... I see stories there. If Papa would give my designs a chance, they would do well. I'm sure of it."

"Fiona." A soft whisper at her temple. "I've no doubt your designs will bewitch all of London. And abroad."

"I've not given you leave to use my name," she snapped, though his belief in her made her want to croon instead.

"'Miss Frampton' is too stiff a moniker for a moonlit night." His voice fell low and dark and full of promises best kept in the shadows after midnight, promises best whispered, best kissed into skin. The heat of his body lessened from full conflagration to fireside warmth, and he tugged her back along the path.

"A great loss," he said in lighter tones, "if you give up painting, but it's your decision. A great loss, as well, if your other designs never see light. I am determined not to dislike your father, but he's not proving helpful in that endeavor."

Their steps took on the same pace and length, and she did not look up at him as they walked, but she felt his nod nonetheless, the curt movement shifting muscles in his body, the tremors of which passed into her own.

"I understand, too," he said, an unexpected declaration, "why you forged those pieces." He swallowed hard. "You were just trying to help."

She threaded her fingers through his. Scandalous act, but she did it anyway. They wore gloves, and a double barrier of cotton separated their skin, but the palms of their gloves must both be worn thin—or the heat of his body incinerating—because she swore his skin nestled close to hers as she squeezed his hand.

"We'll find the paintings," she said. "I know it. And your family will have their inheritance, and I will have my safety." Her steps faltered, slowed.

He unthreaded their fingers and patted the top of her hand. "Let us be done with unhappy conversation. Tell me who your favorite artist is." False lightness attempted to lift his query into the air, but it sank.

"You think me weak," she said. "You think I cannot handle discussion of undesirable eventualities." Everyone thought her weak and silly and—

"I do not. I did not ask you the question to spare you pain. I merely … It's the exact opposite, Miss Frampton. You do not run from difficulty. You face it head-on. Even I can see that in our brief acquaintanceship. I happen to think that those who fight the worst of life for those they love deserve little breaks. Moments they can just be and enjoy life instead of worrying about the next crack in the earth that might swallow them whole."

She looked up at him. The moon loved his face, turned his skin silver-gold and swept his hair into darkness. He seemed an ethereal thing of shadows and fairy tales. Hades perhaps—a man of the darkness who loved the light. What a lucky woman his future Persephone would be. Not her. She was of the dark like him, willing to do whatever she must to survive, existing in a gray area between right and wrong, redefining those words to suit her worries and solutions.

He was beautiful, and his dark eyes looking down at her seemed to offer a mirror for her to see herself in before they blackened entirely and swallowed her whole. Nervous energy lighting her veins on fire, she shifted from foot to foot, began to step back, to step away from him and the velvet trap of his gaze.

But his warm arm snaked around her waist, kept her close and stole her breath. She licked her lips, and a fire flared to life in his midnight eyes as they dropped in a flash to her mouth. Made her think of kissing, it did. Odd when she'd not much thought of kissing in her life. Too busy thinking of other things. She'd looked once upon the delivery boy's lips with curiosity. And several times, when exhaustion did not claim her in the privacy of her bedchamber, she'd thought about men's bodies, all the little hidden parts of them, in fact, wondered if they looked in life how they looked on canvas, in marble.

Seek out answers to such wonderings, though? No. Who had the time? His arm around her waist promised answers if only she'd melt into it.

He leaned lower over her, his arm a steel support against her lower back. No man had touched her there, and the newness of the embrace ignited sparks along that reach of skin and bone he'd claimed. The sparks climbed higher, igniting every inch of her and turning her lungs to ash, making her heart beat the rhythm of a racing horse. Her lungs came back to heady life, though, resurrected with an inhalation of nighttime wafting off Lord Lysander's skin. He smelled of night, yes, but of sweat and wine as well. He smelled ... good, the type of good that gave rise to another word—more.

But more of what?

His arm tightened, pulling her closer as he dipped his head, and soon her belly pressed up against his. Hard, so very hard where she was soft. So surprising. But that shock dissipated in the eventuality of his lips, drawing ever closer to her, the charming rogue decimated from his gaze, the determined scoundrel alone left there. That scoundrel focused more than she'd seen him all night, and on her.

But why? A jeweler's daughter and forger, the bane of his existence, yes?

His nose almost touched her own, and he inhaled, pulling in a deep breath on which he shuttered his eyes. He meant to close the scant remaining distance between them. And kiss her. And her stomach tumbled over itself, her hands knew not what to do, that space at her back where his arms held her to him screamed for things she did not understand, and inexplicably, her breasts tingled, tightened, and she panicked.

She snapped her head to the side between one breath and the next, and the kiss that should have been stopped, his lips oh-so-lightly brushing her cheek, his breath fluttering warmth there. And now she did not have that kiss, she cried, her heart a sobbing mess because she wanted it, and she hated herself for giving into fear.

She slammed her eyes closed, so she felt, not saw, the hand that cupped her cheek, that nudged her face back to center, felt the feather-light brush of his lips skimming the skin of her other cheek and finally, finally, resting at the home of her lips. The kiss was as light and soft as the body that held her was hard. Nothing to be feared at all. In fact, something to be ... savored. She parted her lips on a breath, and he surged closer, sucked her bottom lip, his fingers digging past clothing and all propriety to mark her very skin.

No wonder she gasped.

A surprise when he startled, broke their connection.

His hold on her loosened, disappeared entirely as he clasped his arms behind his back and took one seemingly enormous step away from her. She sought out his gaze for an answer. Why had he stopped? And when she found his eyes, she found them closed, his eyelids an adamantine gate shut between them. And that severance rocked shame up her spine. She dropped her gaze to the ground between them so she did not have to see the disappointment, the mockery in those dark eyes of his.

She cleared her throat and whispered into the wind, "William Turner is my favorite artist."

London settled languid as a lazy cat around them, stilled for a moment, uttering not a single sound. No harness jingles or horse neighs, no boots on gravel or gates creaking open. No angry wives calling husbands home or children chasing one another down puddle-dotted streets. And in that silence, he offered her his arm. She took it. As if they'd never kissed. Better to pretend so because she'd quite obviously embarrassed herself with her cowardice and then her inexperience.

"William Turner," he said, returning them to the slow amble toward her home. Their footsteps crunched with a faster pace now. Now that he likely wished to be rid of her. "A talented man, indeed. My favorite, too."

Awkwardness forgotten, she swung her head around to peer up at his face. "Truly? Many think him too modern. Too different."

"Many don't like to feel uncomfortable, and his work will do that to you."

He understood.

"You and I, though." He squeezed her arm to his side, a brief return to the iron closeness of before. But soon, too soon, he freed her and held her lightly once more, an escort for the short remaining distance to safety only.

Should she talk about what had not happened between them? Assure him, first, that she had not minded the kiss. It might have been gentlemanly guilt that had stopped his lips from exploring her own. Then she would let him know that, yes, she had not known what she was doing, but she could learn, could improve, but—oh—what a folly that was, yes? Did she want him to kiss her again? To teach her how to do it better? No!

Maybe.

It did not matter. For he did not seem intent on such a conversation, or an education, and perhaps she should follow his lead. But the need to speak her mind crept like insects all over her insides.

He rattled her arm. "You're bouncy."

"Apologies. I am, but—"

"We're here." He brought them to a stop and looked up at the line of terrace houses that cast his face in shadows.

"Yes. Lord Lysander, I want to say—"

He dropped her arm and stepped away from her, sweeping into a low bow. "Good evening, Miss Frampton. I shall alert you as soon as I hear from a potential buyer for our nonexistent Rubens."

She reached an arm out toward him, to stay him. "Yes, but, Lord Lysander—"

The sharp turn of his body sliced her sentence in two, and the unsaid half of it fluttered useless to the ground. His long strides took him out of reach quick as could be, and she turned for home, found it warm and loud and welcoming.

But not for her. If she joined her family, her father's face would turn into granite and her mother's eyes would fill with worry.

"I'm home," she called, then made her way upstairs alone, what she'd meant to say to Lord Lysander still brimming inside her. Before she could shut her bedchamber door, Posey was at her side, and they entered together, speaking at the same time.

"What do you think the duke's new design is for?" Posey asked as Fiona said, "Have you ever been kissed?"

They stared at one another for a breathless moment. Fiona had not even realized Posey had seen the duke in the shop earlier.

Then Posey took Fiona's hands and dragged her toward

the bed. "Where does that question come from?" she asked. "Have you been kissed? When? By whom?"

"I've not." A lie of course, but it had been a truth up until, oh, ten or so minutes ago. "I was merely curious. Mother's talk to us"—years ago now, when they'd barely begun to be women—"left out the details. But we can certainly discuss the duke's design instead."

"No. No. Let's discuss this. Hm." She wrapped one arm around her belly and tapped her cheek with her other hand. "What to tell you. Mother spoke of more delicate topics, the act between a married man and woman. She didn't discuss kissing. Hm. *Yes*, I suppose, is a good enough place to start. Yes, I have been kissed. And I've kissed someone in return."

"Who?"

"I'd rather not answer that."

"Rather a good way to increase my curiosity."

"Nevertheless, on that point, I'll ask you to mind your own business."

"Very well, but ... did you enjoy it? Mother said what married men and women do is enjoyable, but I cannot assume kissing is the same."

Posey's face slipped into a smile. "It is quite enjoyable."

"Is it the sort of thing that is enjoyable with every man, or does the individual doing the kissing matter?"

"Excellent question." Posey tapped her cheek again. "Here is where, I suppose, I admit I've kissed more than one man."

"Really?" She should not be surprised. Posey was seven years her senior. Most women were married with babes by that time. Of course she'd had a kiss or two.

Perhaps Fiona should be more concerned with the fact she had not. Seemed unnatural. Not quite right. No. She didn't believe that. She'd never wanted to kiss before now. And that seemed right, natural. She'd never followed others standards, and she would not begin with kissing.

Posey nodded. "Both men provided pleasant enough experiences, but … yes, I believe it does matter. One was just that. Pleasant enough. The other …" She pressed her palm into her belly and released a shaky exhale. "It was like my entire body had turned pins and needles, but it did not hurt, merely offered the most exquisite pleasure."

Fiona narrowed her eyes. "It sounds like he should have asked for your hand."

Posey's face fell. "He did." Quiet words. "But I quite turned him down." Forced cheer if Fiona had ever heard it, and in this family, she most certainly had. "Do you think me very wanton for kissing two men?"

"No." Men kissed many women over the course of their lives, after all, and it was just plain ridiculous that women could not enjoy the same plethora. "There is a man I would like to kiss." Close enough to the truth, there. She would like to kiss him. Again.

Posey bounced up, curling her legs beneath her and placing her palms on her knees. "Who? You must tell me."

"When you tell me who you kissed."

Posey grunted. "Well then, we are at a stalemate. Fine. But I can guess easily enough. Daniel."

Papa's fake apprentice? Daniel was handsome and cheerful and kind. She'd considered kissing him before, but would it feel like almost kissing Lord Lysander had? Like fire and steel and the sky crashing down around them? She did not think so.

"Not Daniel," she said.

"Keep your secrets, then."

"Shall we discuss the duke's design now?" She had the answers she sought. Kisses were better with different men, and kissing did not necessarily mean marriage. Not if she kept it secrets.

She would have to keep the kiss secret, for she would kiss him again, disrobing of fear and taking that caress she'd run from tonight. He could not take a wife, and she did not desire a husband, another innocent to entangle in her sins. But she could kiss a man in secret and enjoy it, and she meant to do just that. It would be excellent practice for living the life she wished instead of the life her parents wished for her.

Eleven

L ying required subtlety. And perfect timing. And the silk merchant gazing in adoration at the sketch Zander had pilfered from an old lady in Wales offered a perfect opportunity to set the lie he and Fiona had crafted into motion. Subtly. And at the perfect time.

Perhaps *pilfered* was too strong a word. He'd paid her, but much too little. She'd not known the worth of the sketch in her possession, and he'd taken advantage. Felt like pilfering. But Mr. Katsky was pleased he'd gotten it at such a cheap price, and he'd show his pleasure by increasing Zander's payment. A nice little bonus for swindling the old woman.

And Mr. Katsky, as his residence well proved, had more than enough to give a bonus. His London townhouse had more gilding than a palace, and every surface contained some bit of art or another, all of it expensive.

Zander tried not to accidentally brush against the paintings and stood still as the statue placed carelessly on the corner of the table he and Mr. Katsky leaned over. There'd be less of a bonus if he broke something.

The bigger bonus was the expression on Mr. Katsky's face

as he gazed at the sketch unrolled on the table before them. Not a Rubens but in the same style. Likely one of his students who would have been expected to copy his styles and techniques to perfection before producing work in a style of their own. He should remember to tell Fiona that, that she wasn't a forger so much as a student doing what a student must to become a master. Would that ease her guilt a little?

Hell. He wouldn't think of her, wouldn't put back little bits and pieces he wanted to share with her, wouldn't crave to ease her way in the world. Wouldn't relive that most innocent of kisses, that most erotic of gasps when he'd pulled her lip between his teeth. But he couldn't seem to help it. He'd been doing it all week. So much so that he suspected he'd become infatuated. He had, at some point during their short acquaintance, developed a schoolboy crush on the jeweler's daughter. Started thinking of her as Fiona, too. This wouldn't have happened if they'd kissed. *Really* kissed. Not that soft prelude, but the full promise of the action, the fireworks leaping beneath his skin, the ravaging of her mouth, extension of the kiss to other places just as soft, just as warm.

If they'd kissed like that, this fixation would have found its release in learning the taste of her tongue. But now the unknown questions of her body plagued him as well as the little hints she'd given him. The memory of her gasp could make him hard, curse it all. It hung over him, chained him to the unknown, drove him to imagine and dream and wonder what it was like when he should know by now. And the knowing would release him, and—

"Lord Lysander," Mr. Katsky said, "you have once more proved your value. Such an exquisite piece, and such a steal." Yes, it had rather felt like stealing. Still sat heavy in his gut. Mr. Katsky's face fell, and his shoulders sagged. "It is a shame, though. That it's only a student's work."

"I don't know. If the student proves as skilled as the master, there's no shame at all. The brush strokes—"

"Brush strokes? Who cares about those? It's the name that matters, Lord Lysander." He grunted. "You know that. Better than most of us, I suppose."

An opportunity. Zander seized it. "True. Do you know, I've a real Rubens for sale."

Mr. Katsky's head popped up so quickly Zander feared it might snap right off his neck. "A real one?"

Zander rolled up the sketch and replaced it in its protective tubing. "Yes. My father's. Mine now. Soon to belong to someone else entirely. If I can just find the right buyer." He gave a white-toothed grin that would make Fiona roll her eyes. "Naturally."

Miss Frampton. And why should he care what made her roll her eyes? He shouldn't. But he did. Like a green boy after his first time laying his body alongside a woman's. Yet they'd laid nothing beside one another but hands. And, for a brief, breathless moment, their bellies when he'd pulled her close.

"Who is interested?" Mr. Katsky asked.

Zander listed names he would know, names that would incite his jealousy and ... he named the dowager.

"Her?" Mr. Katsky's brow furrowed. "I've not seen her for months. Thought she'd hied off to the Continent for entertainment."

Zander shrugged. "She's interested." Perhaps silly to throw her name in the ring, but if she was merely gallivanting, paintings in tow, hearing her name in a ring she'd not tossed it into might bring her home. "Are *you* interested?"

He scratched his chin and lifted his glasses to the top of his head. "Perhaps, perhaps ... Depends. I'll let you know in two days' time. I'm attending an auction. Secret of course, a bit of an ... event."

"I've heard of no auction." And he heard of everything in the art world.

"As I said—it's a secret. An event solely for *collectors,* not curators and procurers like yourself."

"Ah." He'd get no more information on it, then.

Mr. Katsky wiggled his brows. "A masquerade."

Scratch that. Zander lifted his own glasses to the top of his head and leaned a hip against the table, waiting. Not long, either.

"Lord Currington is hard up, and he wants to sell his collection, but he doesn't want it to seem like a desperate move, so he's invited only those of us with the deepest pockets to attend, all in disguise. Dominos too, even. Guests required. To help with the charade, I suppose." He snorted. "As if we don't see through it. He claims to be bored and in need of a good time. The man just needs blunt. But"—he hooked his thumbs in the suspenders showing in the gap between the bottom of his waistcoat and the top of his trousers—"a good time shall be had nonetheless." He laughed and winked. "The mistress is looking forward to a night out on my arm."

"Hm. Of course." Scoundrel. Men who cheated on their wives were the worst sort. As far as Zander was concerned, one of the few things his father had ever gotten right was adoring his mother. Love was precious, and if discovered on this wretched earth, should be protected. Of course, many did not marry for love. Marriage was a contract in which two people bettered the circumstances of their pocketbook or of their social sphere.

Zander knew it. He might have to bow to it. Didn't mean he wanted to.

"I only tell you because Currington has a Rubens I'm interested in, as well as a few others. The wife won't mind if I procure one, perhaps two more, this month. But if I drain our accounts more than that, everyone in London will hear her wrath."

"I don't wish such a sound lecture on you, Mr. Katsky." Frankly, he didn't wish this man on his wife, but he could do nothing about that.

"You'll understand one day, Lord Lysander. Just stay out of the leg shackles as long as you can."

"I shall certainly try."

"I'll pay your fee today." Mr. Katsky popped the top of the tube and released the sketch into his hands.

Zander waved the words away as he took his leave. He never discussed payment. He was a marquess's son who worked in trade. Worked in a shady trade at that. The least he could do to save his pride, the social standing that gave him value in his client's eyes, was to act like the money didn't matter. When it alone mattered.

The butler handed him his hat, and he stepped out into the busy London street, thinking.

A masquerade doubling as an art auction. All the most interested collectors in London, likely some from further afield, grouped in a single location for one likely scandalous night where fortunes would be made (because Currington needed to make a fortune) and lost. Poor Mrs. Katsky. At least her husband had a modicum of self-control regarding his art acquisitions if not regarding his amorous exploits. Unlike Zander's father—though his eye never roved to another woman, it had roved over every piece of art in Christendom—who bought ravenously without considering the consequence.

He found his feet leading him to Frampton and Son's. He'd made an interesting discovery today, and Fiona would want to know. Everyone of interest would be at the auction. Perhaps even, if alive and free, the Dowager Balantine. Zander would be there, too.

Fiona would want to be. He stumbled over his feet.

Damn. She'd want to attend with him, and he couldn't let her. For so many reasons. She was a sexual innocent if not a moral one. She'd not even been able to face his kiss. He'd recognized the blinding pink in her cheeks for what it was—fear of the unknown. The woman had never been kissed until he'd kissed her. He'd felt that truth in every movement of her body, in every sound she'd made. He couldn't bring her to a masquerade where men brought their mistresses, likely took advantage of their disguise to do what they pleased in full view of the other guests.

Added to that, if they were caught together in such a situation, he'd have to marry her. He would marry her, no questions asked, neither of Raph's fists required, though they'd no doubt be hovering to do him harm. And he could not burden the family with the cost of a wife, a forger for a wife at that, with the shadow of a noose hanging over her.

And finally, she couldn't join him because if he had her near again, he would absolutely finish that kiss, take it to its natural conclusion. A kiss, long and sultry and *thorough*, was the only way to purge himself of this infatuation, and he would take it. To free himself and her of a growing obsession that would do neither of them any good.

But he could leave her a note. He would not deny her information in a matter so delicate for them both. So he slunk into the alley beside Frampton's and hastily penned a note with the slip of paper and stubby pencil he kept in his pocket, his fingers brushing against a piece of wire he'd taken from the floor of the workroom the night they'd planned their attack there. He left the note behind the brick and knocked, then ran, his hands slipping into his pockets once more, brushing against that wire again. Stiff silver and gold threads twined together, discarded as useless, forgotten beneath the beaten worktable. Until he found it and saw its worth.

Twelve

The sketch unfolding beneath Fiona's hand winked at her. She winked back. A good sign. A wink meant she was capturing something true, something she never saw in her paintings. But the necklace taking shape beneath her charcoal pencil seemed lively. It liked a good time. The perfect strand to warm a ... debutante's neck? No. Too ostentatious. It needed a red gown, certainly, not pallid white. This necklace and its winking rubies were meant for garden trysts and kisses under starlight and—

Oh. She should not think about kisses. Trouble was, she could think of very little since Lord Lysander had kissed her, since she'd been a coward and turned her cheek to his seeking lips and he'd turned her right back to him then stepped away when he'd learned how ill she performed.

She could do better with more experience, though. She had no doubt. But with only one kiss to warm her memory, she knew so little. How did one breathe and kiss at the same time? Was one to kiss at a straight angle or tilt the head a bit? Should other parts of the body be touching? And were bites— like the one he'd given her—perfectly allowable? She thought so, thought it marvelous, thought she'd die if it never happened again. She'd likely never kiss again, would die without answers to all her questions.

She had dreamed of the kiss last night, a waking vision before sleep had taken her. She'd not turned away at first but met him confidently, as if she had a right to his kisses, and while her mind had remained in control, it had been a delicious vision that sent starlight skittering across her skin and grew an ache between her legs.

But then she'd fallen asleep. And the dreams had continued, but they had changed from a young woman's fancy to a spinster's embarrassment. Her dreaming mind had conjured disasters. They'd kissed. He'd gagged. She'd woken mortified then fallen asleep again. And they'd kissed, and he'd laughed, that word *amusing* hanging over them both. She'd woken again, groaned into her pillow, and when she next awoke, cheerful morning light proved unpleasant company for her still-present mortification.

She tried adding another row of rubies to the necklace on the paper, but the vision had vanished. Frustration slammed through her, and she slammed her feet to the floor.

She had determined to kiss Lord Lysander again, but what if ... what if ... what if she was horrid at kissing, having never had the opportunity to practice.

Practice! Precisely what she should do. She just needed an opportunity to practice before kissing Lord Lysander. Of course that meant mortifying herself with some other man, but that did not seem to matter so much.

She put her sketchbook away and entered the front shop. "Posey, have you seen Daniel?"

Posey looked up from a display case she was rearranging. "He just returned. I believe he's in the mews." She stood slowly, her grin growing with each inch she gained above the case. "Why do you wish to speak with him?"

Fiona rolled her eyes and left, Posey's laughter ringing in her ears.

In the mews behind the shop, Daniel brushed the horse in long smooth strokes, and he looked up when she entered.

"Good afternoon, Daniel," she said, stopping just inside the mews. This ... was a horrid idea.

But ...

Not as horrid as kissing Lord Lysander and having him cast up his accounts on her slippers.

She must do it.

"Good afternoon, Miss Frampton." Daniel put the brush down and dusted his hands off on his riding breeches. "Can I help you with something?"

"Well ... yes. Um, are you busy? At the moment?"

"Not as much as I'd like to be. Done with morning deliveries. Only one more this afternoon."

She stepped closer. Casual steps. A saunter really. "Good. Excellent. Not us not having nearly enough jewelry to deliver, of course. That's decidedly not excellent, but I am glad I'm not inconveniencing you with my request."

"And what request is that, Miss Frampton?"

She stopped her saunter and closed her eyes. She had to say it. She had to. She must.

"Willyoukissme?" She smooshed all the words together and said them so fast, they barely made sense.

"Pardon?"

No surprise he'd not understood. She took a steadying breath. "I was wondering—and you may say no, mind you—if you would kiss me?"

His mouth opened, then his teeth closed, but his lips didn't, creating a very clear picture of ... *no*. That expression meant no. "You see, Miss Frampton, you're very pretty, but there's this girl. I've barely said a word to her but—"

"Daniel, is this lady real?"

His eyes widened.

"You do not have to create a lady love in order to get out of kissing me. I am not offended, and I said you could refuse."

His entire body drooped with relief.

"I asked because I've only been kissed once, and I'm not certain I'm doing it quite right. And ... there's a fellow I'd like to kiss. With more skill this time. But ... I'm afraid I'll embarrass myself with my ignorance. Again."

"But ladies aren't supposed to know how to kiss, Miss Frampton. Your innocence is part of the pleasure for us fellows."

"Pishposh." Zander had not seemed overjoyed by her ignorance. He'd turned from her. "Viewing a painting by an incompetent artist isn't pleasurable because the fellow has no idea what he's doing. But you're correct in that women aren't supposed to have prior knowledge of it. A disappointment, that."

His eyebrows slanted together, forming a quite serious V above his nose. "If it's important to you, I'll kiss you. A small one, mind. Because you're my friend. But you're also my employer's daughter, so don't tell your father!"

She brightened, straightened. "You will? How wonderful." She scurried forward. "And father will never hear a thing. Now, how do I do it?"

He held his hand up, palms toward one another, arms bent at the elbow as if he meant to grasp her upper arms. But he floundered, seemed unable to let those hands land anywhere on her.

"Hands are not necessary," she reassured him.

"Actually, they are. Most of the time. If you're doing it right."

"Really? Fascinating. And where do you put them?"

Daniel groaned. "That's something a bit beyond kissing, Miss F. It's kissing adjacent, and I'll not help you with that."

She shrugged. "Fair. I only asked you for help with the one thing." Besides, surely she did not need to do anything *kissing adjacent* with Lord Lysander. The kiss would be enough.

He eyed her. "Just ... close your eyes."

She did. Leaned forward, too, and puckered her lips. It was not what it had been like at all with Lord Lysander that lonely London night, but that had happened quite naturally, quite magically, and could not be recreated here. With Daniel. The *who* seemed to be an important component of kissing. She began to see what Posey had spoken of—kissing differed from man to man.

Daniel chuckled. "Not the other stuff, Miss F."

She straightened and let her lips go loose, fighting back mortification. "Please do not laugh."

"Apologies. That's better. Now ... just ... hold still."

The sounds of shuffling, the feeling of human warmth so near but not touching.

Then there was touching, the light, barely there touch of his lips to hers. He puckered, ever so slightly, and she parted her lips on a breath to see what happened.

But nothing happened except that he leaned away from her.

She opened her eyes. He stood before her, hands on hips, peering quizzically into her face.

"There then," he said. "Done. How was it?" He grinned, a peacock sort of look as he stroked his hair away from his face.

"Underwhelming." The kiss had contained none of the heart-stopping anticipation, none of the curling desire for fruition that had consumed her, terrified her, the night Lord Lysander had held her in his arms.

His hand dropped and his gaze startled to hers. "Well don't ask me again, right?"

"I do appreciate it, Daniel. Thank you. But one last question."

His eyes flickered left and right. The man might bolt, no other words, just boots taking him far away from her. "What kind of question?"

"Was I horrid at it?"

He slumped, scrubbed his face with his palms, and spoke through the barrier of his hands. "You did everything just fine in the end, Miss Frampton." He groaned. "You're just not the right gal for me."

"Do not be worried I'll get attached, Daniel. You're not the right fellow for me."

"*Bah.*" He waved her away and returned to the horse.

She'd not embarrassed herself, then. At least not with the kissing. Daniel may avoid her for a while, and she'd suffer that awkwardness gladly because she'd obtained the gold nugget of knowledge she'd been after. She'd kissed a man, and he'd not gagged. Brilliant. She could now kiss the man she actually wished to kiss with a modicum less worry.

She stepped into the alley, and someone stepped out of it at the other end. At a quick pace too. She rushed after the figure, no reason but that curiosity drew her, and she saw him —tall, dark hair beneath a beaver hat, his trim figure familiar.

Lord Lysander. She thought of calling after him then thought better. Instead, she flew to their loose brick and pulled from it a freshly penned note.

When she'd finished reading, she read it over once more, slower this time to make sure she understood.

He was going to an auction, a masquerade hosted by Lord Currington, and she was not to come along. He'd not even told her when it was happening, the cad! Anger boiled her bones, and she stomped back into the shop and flung herself into the chair she'd vacated earlier. She needed distraction from wanting to throttle Lord Lysander. He'd promised to include her, and yes, he'd sent her a note, but ... she wanted to go with him. *Of course* she wanted to go with him. He'd known she would, too. It was why he'd been so cursed stingy with his information, telling her but not telling her, keeping his promise to include her in the investigation while keeping her at arm's length.

She opened her notebook, seeking that distraction, but the rubies in her sketch still winked up at her, this time mockingly. She'd just kissed Daniel so that she would be better equipped to kiss the man who had promised to include her, had seemed to think better of her intellect than most, then had betrayed her with his high-handedness. He'd likely call it protectiveness.

No.

She flipped to a blank page and started a new sketch. Inspiration had finally struck. This sketch featured paste diamonds instead of rubies, a black velvet ribbon instead of a clasp, and eyeholes so she could see the look on Lord Lysander's face when she did exactly what he wished her not to do and claimed a right to a say in her own life.

Thirteen

Zander hated masquerades. The dominos were always itchy, and the ribbon tied at the back of his head pushed his hair out in ridiculous directions. He wasn't usually vain. Except when he wished to be, and it suited his foul mood to let his vanity be piqued. Additionally, he could see the mask in his peripheral vision, and that sent growls of annoyance through him, though the disturbance to his actual vision was slight. How would anyone properly view the art in order to purchase it?

Currington was a fool of the first order. He should simply admit to his dire straits and offer his collection to Sotheby's instead of pretending. Instead, he'd gone to the trouble—and expense, it must be noted—of a masquerade ball. The ballroom was huge with balconies circling it above from which garlands of some white flower draped. Three chandeliers hung from the ceiling, flickering with a city's worth of wax and flame, and a string quartet played beneath the center one. Extravagance to hide rising poverty. Ridiculous. Currington and this event were as fake as Fiona's forgeries. But unlike her copies, everyone knew this night was an illusion.

Whole thing reminded him too much of his damn father —the extravagance, the refusal to face facts, the clear disdain for duty. Zander had plenty of faults, but he knew how to care for those who belonged to him, and he knew extravagance like that surrounding him now came with a price dearer than pounds and pence.

How many times had he, Raph, Theo, Drew, and Atlas rushed to save their family from this precise fate—an auctioning off of all the family's belongings, a ruination in the eyes of society, a failure to the generations of Bromleys who had come before them? Too many times. But they'd always done it. Just in time. They'd saved him, and themselves, the shame of having their lives picked over, auctioned off. And by doing what other men of their station, men like Currington would scoff at them for—work. Theo's satires, Zander's clients, Atlas's body in the wars, and Drew's tutoring. They'd all worked when the alternative was this—a spectacle of their failure and a parade of curiosity seekers.

Zander tugged at his waistcoat and too-tight cravat. He much preferred a less formal manner of dress. He wasn't made for the country like Raph and Atlas, but he did prefer the comfort of rolled-up shirt sleeves, something he usually couldn't have unless he was in the privacy of his own home. Or, to be more precise, Maggie's home or Theo's flat or Raph's estate.

He possessed no home of his own, no place to take a woman of the heart and make her comfortable. Even if he wanted such a woman, she'd have to dash about with him from one residence to the other. No, he could not do that. He wouldn't even be thinking about it except for the blasted infatuation with Miss Fiona Frampton.

Rage flashed in his breast, and his hands found the shape of fists. Another reason for his foul mood ... she'd been kissing another man. Only the tightest self-control had kept Zander from pounding the lad into the dirt, and only the cold parting of the two kissing bodies had convinced Zander to leave the damn note and run.

He should be done with the cursed infatuation after witnessing that.

He wasn't.

He wanted her in his arms to teach her how men kissed properly. They didn't stand an arm's length away and hinge at the waist to peck a woman's lips. They took her body and soul and gave themselves the same.

Bloody hellish infatuation to make a man consider giving a woman his soul as well as his body, make him think of all the ways his bachelor life could not accommodate a wife. And think on those facts with ... *hell*! How did he think on them?

With worry. With exhaustion. And a little bit with disgust.

The trouble, likely, was that he'd been around Fiona in such comfortable spaces—fire-warmed parlors, crowded work-rooms, shadowed personal galleries striped with dusty sunbeams. When a woman who made you laugh did so in places like that ... it turned your guts inside out. Made a man think of home or the lack of one and exactly what that word—home—meant.

Another irritant to rub his insides raw.

"You are looking like you want to kick something or some-one." Theo, of all people, spoke from right beside him.

Zander kept his gaze trained on the crowd, searching for the one face he hoped would appear—the dowager. "I do rather. Kicking something would be a great step up in the world for me. What are you doing here?"

"I'm on the hunt for a patron."

A decidedly feminine clearing of the throat followed Theo's proclamation.

Zander finally looked over at his brother to see he had a woman draped on one arm.

"Hello," Zander said, irritation dissipating. "And who are you?"

"Zander, meet Lady Cordelia Trent. One of our dear papa's leeches. The one with the house."

"Not for long," Lady Cordelia said, "and not tonight. Tonight, I'm your mistress."

Theo bit off a curse. "You're here to find another protector."

Lady Cordelia gave a saucy smile and winked. "Is that what we're calling it?"

Zander whistled and took another look at the lady.

She was tall and statuesque, nearly perfectly proportioned in every way, and her thick Titian hair was piled high on her head in elaborate ringlets. A golden domino covered the top half of her face, leaving open for everyone's observation only a pair of plump, deep-red lips. A breathtakingly beautiful woman, yet ... Zander still possessed his breath. Seemed only tiny art forgers could steal it these days.

"Are you positive she's an artist?" Zander asked. "Looks like she's the art."

Lady Cordelia's eyes danced behind her domino. "Thank you, Lord Lysander."

"Don't humor her," Theo said.

"Look, Theo ..." Zander leaned in close. "You're not really trying to find her a ... protector in that sense, are you?"

"Of course not. She merely delights in infuriating me." A statement made of sharp teeth to crush bone.

"If you didn't make the activity so diverting, I wouldn't do it so often." Lady Cordelia's red brow lifted above her mask.

Theo's jaw clenched enough to make dust of his teeth.

"How did an earl's daughter come to be ... essentially ... my father's ward, Lady Cordelia?" Zander asked.

She shrugged, her jaw as hard as Theo's. "I'm sure you have assumptions." She looked out over the crowd with a sigh.

"He saved me. Your family is not the only one capable of falling on hard times."

"Fair," Zander said. "Father had a soft heart. And an eye for beauty."

"Zander," Theo barked, "are you here on behalf of a client?"

Lady Cordelia jumped, hands clutching her belly.

Zander chuckled. His brother lacked conversational finesse. And patience. "No. I'm here on behalf of myself." And the fabulous little forger he was trying to forget. "Do you have any idea how this event is supposed to work?"

Theo shrugged and looked to Lady Cordelia.

She shrugged too. "I know no useful information, but I certainly plan on discovering some." She dragged her gaze down Theo's body. "Do you have any ... *information* I could discover, Lord Theodore?"

"You're driving me mad," Theo mumbled. "Don't say such things in public."

"In private, though ..." she purred.

"Not then either! There is no *in private*."

She chuckled. "I'm teasing you, my lord. I merely meant that I am happy to help you discover my next position."

"I don't need your help with that," Theo snapped. "I told you not to come."

And then their already brittle conversation devolved into a round of bickering so futile even Zander put his attention elsewhere. Who did he know here tonight? And could he divine their identities behind their masks? And would the Rubens lover be here? Would the dowager make an appearance?

He scanned the room with a hungry gaze, looking for answers to all of his questions, until it fell on something—someone—standing at the top of the stairs leading from the balcony to the dance floor, that stopped his heart from beating.

She wore a gilded mask covered in paste diamonds that flashed green in the reflection of her eyes. Her heavy hair, coiled on top of her head like a crown, glowed like candlelight. She wore a blue gown, its color deep and shifting like the ocean, now a foamy blue and then dark blue of the fathomless depths. He'd rather see her in green, but the blue made him needy, made his legs move toward her, made him think of stripping the gown off her. Slowly. He'd push the hem up her over knees, smoothing his palms from ankle to calf over hopefully silk stockings. Then he'd release those from their garters and peel them down to stroke her softer skin up, up, over knee, all the way up to her center, and then he'd press a kiss right to the warm inside of her thigh, and—

A hand on his shoulder made him curse.

"What's caught your attention?" Theo asked.

"She's not supposed to be here," Zander growled. "How does she even know where *here* is?"

Theo followed his gaze to the top of the grand staircase where Fiona Frampton stood. "Who's she?"

"The jeweler's daughter," Zander hissed.

"Aaahhh. Her. Well, she's fine to look at. Ow!" He swung to look at Lady Cordelia. "Did you just flick my ear?"

"You should not notice other women when I'm about." She raised her chin.

"You're a nuisance. And I'll look at any woman I like. You're my father's project, not my—"

"Mistress?" she crooned.

"Bloody hell." Theo thumped Zander on the back. "Have fun with your, *ahem*, nefarious miss." He nodded at Miss Fiona. "I need a drink. And to find a patron for this termagant."

Said termagant followed Theo into the throng, and Zander pushed in the other direction. Toward the staircase. Toward Fiona, who bit her bottom lip and gazed out at the crowd below, one hand tangled in her blue skirts, the other lifted to the very low bodice of her gown. Absent-mindedly, she stroked the line where the bodice met her skin with one finger, and the movement became a lodestone for Zander, a guiding star, a seduction.

Triple hell. He must end this infatuation fast. And he must get her home even more quickly. He ran up the stairs, and she finally saw him, the green eyes behind her domino going wide with recognition. Pleasure curled through him. She knew him even disguised, as he knew her. As it should bloody well be. He growled, knowing he should want to suppress the thought or deny it. Knowing he'd do neither. Then he slipped his arm through hers and tugged her toward the exit.

She tugged right back, snapping her arm from his hold. "No. I'm staying." A hiss on her pretty pink lips.

He leaned close enough to smell her sweet scent. "You cannot. If we are caught—"

"We will not be caught. We are disguised, and no one here knows me. Even if they do frequent the shop, Posey is the one everyone interacts with. And finally, I am not of this world. They will never expect a jeweler's daughter to attend, uninvited, a secret masquerade. With what funds would I pay for one of the paintings up for sale?"

"Fiona—"

"I'm staying. I understand the dangers, the risks, but I will not let you get caught in a matrimonial web you do not desire. I am a nobody, Lord Lysander. You will not be forced to"— she lowered her voice and leaned even closer, lifting her face to whisper in his ear—"marry me."

His body shivered. He wanted to haul her to him and part her lips with his own.

He locked his jaw, though, and his hands into fists and offered her his elbow. "Very well." He could not argue her points, except the bit about forced matrimony. If he ruined her reputation somehow tonight, if their identities were discovered, he would pay for it. He would marry her. "Stay close."

She took his proffered arm, and as they left the final step together, the string quartet struck up a waltz. He swept her into it, moving his hands in a heartbeat to her lower back and hand, pulling her close. He shouldn't. But he did. And he didn't give a damn.

"We're not here to dance," she said after a breathless moment.

"I need time to think." He needed time to hold her.

"We do not need to think. We need to look."

He wanted to look at her. He knew the reason he should not do so, should not want to do so, but he did not care. Not right now with the curve of her spine elegant against his palm and the warmth of her talented, long fingers wrapped in his own. Through two layers of gloves, he felt how perfectly her hand fit into his. He tightened his hold, pulled her so close their torsos nearly touched. If she breathed harder, the soft curve of her belly and the gentle rise of her breasts would press into his chest. He was going to do it, pull her close and kiss her. Here. In front of everyone. But he couldn't.

With reluctance knit into the very fabric of his every bone, he put distance between their bodies, and said, "That mask. Did you make it?"

"I did." Her voice was deep and breathless. "What do you think? Is it too large? I wanted to hide as much of my face as possible."

The diamond-studded domino curved elegantly beneath each dark-yellow brow and molded to the hills of her high cheekbones. Her nose—cute, pert—stood out, as did her lips —pink, kissable. But with the silk gown and mask, with her hair more elaborate and smooth, she looked an entirely different woman from the usually disheveled miss dressed in wools and velvets and impish grins. She was right. No one but he would recognize her.

Maybe this was allowable, then. Maybe he could have this night to give in to infatuation, boil it up hot so that it evaporated entirely. A good thing, in the end. Anyone who looked on them might recognize him, but they'd see him with a mysterious woman on his arm, a woman fit for his own professional mystique—beautiful, valuable. They would not know that her value went deeper than beauty, though, deeper than the diamonds on her mask. As with most things, Zander saw the true value. She was no rusted button or broken locket, no discarded piece of glass, but it was her imperfections that drew him, those things others would dismiss her for.

Yes, allow the infatuation control tonight, ride the emotion and connection like a horse running from all the demons of hell, then dismount when exhaustion brought them both limping into the dawn.

He lifted his head to reassure himself his conclusions were sound, that no one looked at them—at her—with recognition in their eyes. *Hell*. At least three sets of eyes did peer at them. But not with recognition. No. These men's gazes gobbled up Fiona's frame with ravenous hunger. With intention.

Zander tightened his hold on her once more. Infatuations were not so possessive. But that's what roared through him—the word *mine* on a wave of anger at anyone who might touch her tonight. He could not guess where such possessiveness would lead him.

"Are you well, my lord?" Fiona asked, squeezing his hand.

He found a grin beneath the boiling need and tossed it at her. Charming as could be, easy, as if nothing inside him had shifted tragically toward who knew what. "I'm quite well, considering the circumstances. How did you discover the time and place?"

Her turn to grin, but not a charming ruse, a real smile that lit her eyes and put a bounce in her step.

"Whatever it is, you think you're quite clever, don't you?" His grin turned true, too.

"I do."

"So do I."

She beamed brighter than the candles.

And he stumbled over his next words, finding it difficult to utter the simple statement. "Tell me ... I mean how did you ..." He huffed, tried again. "Tell me how you did it, then. Find out the location of the auction."

"I've a shady contact. A boy named Thomas. I give him various items he desires, and he does various tasks for me."

"Such as ...?" Did he even want to know? Yes because it was bound to be amusing, bound to make him want to hug her tighter.

"Such as follow marquess's brothers about London and report back when they've returned from their travels."

For a red second, he didn't understand. What marquess? What brother? May he rot in hell! Then it clicked, and the hot jealousy rolled away like a violent wave receding back into the ocean.

"You had the boy follow me about?" he asked with a chuckle.

"Yes. My apologies, but you were not being entirely helpful at the time. I would, in fact, do it again if necessary."

"Minx. Well, how did this Thomas discover details I did not wish you to have?"

"High-handed, that's what you are. You've no right to keep details from me. You're not my father or brother or husband. And even then ... I do not think I would marry a man who would keep secrets from me."

His gut clenched, but he found himself nodding. "Clever woman. You know your worth."

She ducked her head, hid her face. Shame, that. He'd hoped the compliment would turn her into a star once more so he could look on it again.

"Tom asked about," she mumbled toward their feet. "Discovered Currington was hosting the event at his own home."

He groaned. "I should never have given you Currington's name."

Her head popped up, and she peered at him. "Why did you?"

"I wanted to give you *something*. I felt bad, if you can believe it, keeping you in the dark when you only wanted to be a participant in it all. When you have a right to be involved."

Her lips parted on an almost imperceptible inhale. Sharp and tiny, he would not have noticed it had they not been so close. Then she shook it off, whatever it was that had caused that gasp.

"Well, guilt does not quite make up for the trouble you caused poor Tom. I've promised him a new pair of shoes for the ones he wore out running all about London."

"Noted, Miss Frampton. And I'll pay for his shoes. Two pairs if he needs them." Young ruffians often did.

Her steps hitched, and he tightened his arms to give her support.

"You called me Fiona," she said. "On the stairs." She flicked a glance over her shoulder toward the staircase. "And the other night, when you were walking me home."

"Ah. Apologies. Emotion quite carried me away, and I forgot formality."

"No. Do not apologize. I think, perhaps, we should dispense with formalities."

Did his cock tighten because the sound of his name on her lips was an eventuality now? Yes, it did.

"Very well," he said, his voice low and needy even to his own ears, "Fiona." He'd said it in a fit of anger earlier. He said it now with intention, slowly rolling it over his tongue, enjoying the sound and feel of it.

Her eyes closed with a shiver, and he knew, knew without a damn doubt, that she felt what he did. That the shiver was her own tell of lust and desire, and when she spoke, it was to wrap his name up with a saucy curve of her lips.

"Lysander."

"Will you call me Zander? I confess I dislike my given name. My father named us all, and he was a rather fanciful man. Theodore and Andrew made it out fine, but not the rest of us. Lysander, Raphael, Atlas, Magnificent. Tell me, Fiona, what are we to do with those?"

She chuckled. "I rather like it. Lysander. But ... Zander ... I suppose I can do as you wish." She opened her eyes, and they were brighter than the diamonds dancing in her mask.

Hell. To hell with convention. To hell with caution. To hell with everyone but her. No one would care anyway, not here, not with their mistresses in tow and champagne bubbling through their blood. He crashed her body against his, held her tight as he swept her around a curve of the dance floor, and lowered his head into the crook of her neck to whisper a promise, a vow.

"The first dark corner we find, Fiona, I'm going to back you into it and steal a kiss and make you forget that boy in the mews behind your shop." That last part, born of hot possession not cold, calm sense. But he meant it with every broken bit and bent bob that made up who he was.

The cheeks below her mask burned red with something more than exertion. "You saw that?"

"You told me you had no suitor."

"I don't."

"Good. I'm going to kiss you so the idea of suitors quite flies from your head." Dangerous words, to himself as well as to her, but he could not seem to stop them.

Her hands clung to his shoulders, her breath quickened, and she turned her head until her breath fluttered near his ear. "Swear it."

He'd been right. She wanted him as he did her, and the spiraling rhythm of the waltz wound its way into his very soul, making him dizzy, turning the candles above into blazing stars. He grabbed her hand and tugged her off the dance floor.

Just an infatuation. Just an infatuation. How the hell could it be anything else? He barely knew the woman. He did not know her favorite color or how she liked her tea. He did not know what dishes she liked for dinner or if she enjoyed mornings. Did she prefer solitude to company? He knew none of this.

All he knew was that she was talented with a brush, that she was a determined minx who would not give in to fear. He knew she made friends with dukes as well as with street urchins named Thomas and that she looked as breathtaking in wool and muslin as she did in silk and diamonds. He knew she loved her family as much as he loved his, and that she would sell her soul—would give her very safety—for them. Had already done so. He knew she was better than him by miles, ocean lengths.

And he knew it was an *infatuation*. But he'd given the night, this only night, to that temporary emotion, to let it live and burn bright until it piled in ashes round his feet come morning. So he kept his head bent to her neck and pressed his hand on her back lower, scandalously low, flirting with the round curve of her delicious arse, and he whispered. Whispered every hot thought that flitted through his head, giving them passage on his lips with ease. No lock, no key there. And as he flew her round the dance floor, her body moving like wind across water next to his, the world dropped away. And he did not care. The men and women—gone. He did not care. The masquerade somewhere lost in time. He did not care. The missing dowager, the paintings, all of it dissipated like so much rain into the soil. He did not care.

Each spin around the ballroom brought them closer till two bodies moved as one and until he could no longer touch her and not touch her *more*.

He spied a curtained alcove, pulled her toward it, and found it empty. He deposited her inside and fixed her with a hard gaze. "Do not leave here. Keep the curtain closed. Do not take off your mask, and—"

"Do not breathe, Zander?" The whirl of the dance still flushed across her cheeks, and her breast rose and fell too quickly. Her hand fluttered up to absently and innocently tease the line of the low bodice.

Hell. He laughed. Groaned, too, arousal and mirth a heady concoction. He needed to cool off, and she needed to rest. Infatuation was supposed to live and die tonight, not bloom into something entirely different. If he insisted on treading this path, and he did, he must tiptoe.

So he killed his mirth and gave her one more glare for good measure. "Breathe, Fiona, but do not leave this alcove. I'll return shortly with something to drink." He pulled the curtain closed and followed in Theo's direction. Laughing loud enough to break through the sweetly vibrating strings.

God, she amused him, and he liked nothing better than to laugh. It was the only thing some days that made the dark world brighter. Laughter was like his broken bits of glass and shattered lockets—thrown away by others but hoarded by him because he knew, had always known, where true value lay.

And now he knew it lay in her.

Fourteen

⌒⌒⌒

B eyond the curtain, danced a world she'd not known existed. Oh, she'd known, she supposed, in an intellectual sort of way, but she would never have been able to guess, when she'd teased Posey about sneaking into ton balls, that they would be like this—all golden candlelight and champagne dizziness, all garland-hanging fairy tale and shadow-shivering danger.

Danger only because of the man who had ordered her to stay put.

Ordered her—and with a glare to show he meant business. She rolled her eyes.

Made her want to leave, that did. She knew her own stubborn nature well. Stubborn. Not foolish. She knew the risks, and she would not further them with pointless stubbornness. So she turned in the small space, found her breath, and tried to find out the nature of her surroundings in the dim light. A sconce on one wall provided a feeble, flickering light, and a narrow couch that could likely seat no more than two snuggled close together rested against the wall opposite the curtain. She sat and kicked her feet, craning her neck to see through the small cracks on either side of the curtain and out into the whirling ballroom beyond.

He'd held her close, touched her like he intended to start a scandal, and made mad promises into the shell of her ear she would not let him forget.

He'd kiss her tonight, and every nerve in her buzzing body told her it would be more than Daniel's quick buss, more even than the dance that had buzzed her blood and pooled liquid low and warm between her legs.

Why did he want to kiss her, though? That was what she could not understand. Was it merely some misplaced jealousy over Daniel? She should not care about the answer. Knowing it would serve no purpose. Kissing and alcoves, come to think of it, also served no purpose, not at an auction like this where the object of their pursuit might be hiding. If they found the dowager tonight, if they discovered someone else with information on the missing paintings, they would find themselves closer. Closer to the end of their association. Perhaps at the very end of their association. It all might end tonight.

A consummation devoutly to be wished. The dowager, the paintings, the maddening mystery—all put right. Her family's livelihood and reputation as well as her own fool neck —saved.

She did not devoutly wish it. Not as much as she should. Not, at least, for a few more magic hours. What had she so recently been thinking about *not* being a fool?

Wrong there. She was proving quite foolish indeed, particularly over one man.

Her fingers wrapped tight around the front edge of the couch, fingernails digging into upholstery and padding.

Ah. There—the reason for dancing and kissing. She would not find such excitement with Daniel, and no man until Lord Lysander had roused her curiosity so. Did not bode well for it ever being roused again. On the one hand, she should be grateful if her entire life was uneventful as long as she was not hanged for her crimes. But she'd become greedy since meeting him, wanting more each time he grinned at her, willing to do what she must to take it like the little thief she was.

Perhaps thief was too strong a word and not quite the right one. She'd never stolen anything, though she would not deny forgery often allowed others to steal ... She shook her head, thereby shaking her unfocused fancies away.

What had she been considering? Dancing? Kissing? Ah, yes. *Lysander.* Zander.

If this were to be their last night together, she would certainly make the most of it. She was innocent but not blind. She knew the men beyond the curtain wooed women who were not their wives. She saw the way they'd been holding those women. It was the same way Zander had held her— close, intimate, promising. When men and women wore masks, they dared more than usual, dreamed out loud instead of silently.

So would she.

The curtain brushed back, and the light of the ballroom fell prey to the shadow of a large, male body before the curtain returned to its place, almost kissing the doorframe.

Kissing. She hoped so.

Zander held a glass of champagne out to her. "Drink slowly."

She took the cool glass and rubbed it to her forehead then against her lips, assuaging the need of her hot skin.

He groaned.

"Sit," she said, patting the couch behind her with her free hand.

"I don't think I should." He sipped the champagne and angled his body away from her.

She summoned bravery. Not hard to do. It usually skimmed right beneath her skin. "Zander."

Another groan.

"You made a promise, and I would like you to make good on it now. Seems a perfect opportunity, as we're hidden and all. The auction has not yet begun, and—"

"I've changed my mind."

"Not very sporting of you." She sipped her own drink, using the burn to focus her brain, which wanted to flit away as if it drifted on a champagne bubble.

He rubbed his temples. "I've been conflicted all evening. We have a purpose for being here tonight, Fiona, and it is not this, but *damn*"—a hissed curse, almost silent—"do I want *this*." He downed his drink and slammed the sweating, empty glass on a long, thin table that ran the length of one side of the alcove.

The knock of the glass against wood popped Fiona to her feet, and she gasped as he moved quickly, so quickly, to stand directly before her. The fingers of one hand trailed up her arm, over the satin of her glove, and onto the bare skin above it, then down again, then up as his gaze did the same, raking over her, devouring every inch.

"You're an innocent. Your kiss the other night said as much."

"I've practiced since then."

His touch disappeared and fists appeared at his sides. "With the boy? In the mews?"

"Yes. I wanted to … prepare. For kissing you."

"Hell," he hissed. "Words like that carry my control away like a strong wind."

"I'll tell you if you scare me. Or if I don't understand. Or if I no longer wish … whatever it is you do."

"We will not go so far as to scare you. We should go no farther than this."

She stepped closer, and he hissed like she'd stabbed him in the gut. He closed his eyes and shoved a hand through his hair, knocking his domino askew. She reached up to fix it, but her fingers paused as they brushed the ribbons at the back of his head. Not just because her bounce up onto tiptoe had brought their bodies into heated contact—breasts to chest and points more southern meeting, too—but also because his hands wrapped around her, biting pleasure points into her waist, her lower ribs. And also because, though she hardly needed a third reason for all thought to flitter right out of her head, she'd had a better idea. The only way to fix the mask would be to remove it.

When they kissed, she did not want them pretending to be other people. She did not want them hiding. So finally, she tangled her fingers into the silky strands of his hair, found the ribbon, and pulled to remove and pocket the thin silk domino. She settled back down on her heels and met his gaze, daring him to object. He did not, though he smirked, an expression she hoped to heaven she had the opportunity to kiss off his lips.

Before he could say a word, she removed her own mask, sighing at the relief from the weight that had rested on her nose. His gaze darted right toward that appendage, and he rubbed his thumb over the spot that was angry from the heavily bejeweled mask.

"There's an indentation. It's red." He scowled. "You'll have to put it back on, but ... perhaps you can wear mine instead."

She chuckled. It felt natural to chuckle with him, as if they'd been doing so for years. "And you'll wear mine? I would like to see that."

His gaze traveled downward to her mask, dangling from her hand, and he shrugged. "It would look excellent on me." He winked then flicked the ribbon of her mask. "This is bloody brilliant."

"No, it's not. It's necessity. And likely gaudy." She'd made it for the evening alone, a look to obscure her identity and to help her fit in with the glittering crowd. She was not the shiny sort, and well she knew it.

His head dropped to one side. "Are you looking at the same thing I'm looking at?"

"Yes." She gestured to the mask, holding it up for him to see.

He lifted his hands toward it. "May I?"

She dropped it into his palms.

He ran his fingertips over the front. "I could not tell from far away, when I first saw you, but the surface is not entirely encrusted."

"No. And they are not real diamonds." They were paste. Fake. Like her paintings. Like her.

"Paste?" He lifted an eyebrow with a whistle. "They look real. Impressive."

She blushed. Difficult not to feel pleasure at the compliment from a man who dealt daily in valuable things. "I used wire and spangles to reflect the light. As well as the foil behind the paste jewels."

"It works. The wire and spangles also, I suppose, keep it from weighing too much."

"Yes." She trailed her finger around the edge of the mask in his hands. "And these wires"—she rubbed her thumb over a bundle of them—"are twisted to look like flowers ... floral jewelry is quite fashionable at the moment."

"From far away, it appears to be one thing, but you see more about it and understand it better the closer you get. Take a closer look, and you see just how complex and intricate that design is."

"It's not brilliant. I'm not capable of brilliance on my own. I've told you that. But it is rather good. And I'm fine with that for now. But this." She stroked the edge of the mask. "It's a tad too heavy and clunky. Imperfect."

He hummed, a thoughtful, throaty sound, as he rotated the mask to look at the back side of it. Then he handed it back and reached a hand into his pocket. "Do you know ... my entire life, my father chased the *perfect*. The perfect sculptures, the perfect paintings. Perfection, beauty, truth through art. Do you know what I've always chased?"

"A wage?" she asked with a grin.

He laughed, and then he pulled his hand out of his pocket. "I can't deny it. But also this." He held up a thin strand of wire. No. Two wires—one gold, one silver, twined together.

"What is that," she asked.

"It is from your shop. I stole it. I hope you do not mind."

She shook her head, shrugged. She cared much less about the loss of discarded material than she did about the loss of this moment between them. She would not discard it. Not even fifty years from now. It felt too real, too precious, and when she had grown old and gray, she'd take the memory of it out of her pocket and hold it up to the candlelight for inspection as he held up that wire, and with just as much reverence, too.

"It looks like it was meant to be thrown away," she whispered.

"Do you know why I stole it?"

"Obviously not."

"I stole it— No, never mind that description. I did not *steal* it. I rescued it because the thing I have been searching for as long as my father has been searching for perfection is the *imperfect*."

She blinked, trying to understand, finding herself a failure. "I do not mean to offend when I say this, Lysander, but what nonsense. No one likes the imperfect."

"I do. I love imperfections." He pocketed the wire once more. "I have an entire collection—bits and bobs no one else wants. A broken locket, a chunk of glass, more buttons than

I've attempted to count. I'll show them to you if you like. Little imperfect things others toss away. But at one time that dull button used to shine and give someone pride. Perhaps the broken colored glass was an old church window filtering sunlight on bowed heads. Maybe this wire was at one point meant for a duchess's wrist or ear." He tweaked hers. "Even though no one remembers their worth ... I do. Perhaps *because* no one else remembers ... I do." He held his hands out to her, palm up. "See. I specialize in imperfections."

He seemed to be telling her something greater than the meaning of his words. Rattled her it did. "If you like imperfect things," she said, keeping her tone light, playful, "I've much to offer, my lord. I daresay once we investigate my offerings, you'll find you do not like imperfection as much as you claim to."

His knuckles brushed down the line of her neck. "What imperfections are you offering me, Fiona?"

"Oh, let us start small. What think you of these freckles across my cheeks?" She risked a glance up at him, her heart screaming at her to stop, for surely this way lay its doom.

His hand switched trajectories, a gloved thumb smoothing across her cheekbones and down the bridge of her nose. "Most women want to get rid of their freckles, I suppose." His voice was low, deep, thoughtful.

"Yes." Her voice was a husky whisper, though the topic of conversation hardly allowed for such a response. "I've ... I've even tried a lemon concoction a time or two. To get rid of my own."

"Don't do that again." Another demand, another order, and this one, too, she'd likely heed. He tilted toward her until the very tip of his nose tapped the very tip of hers, then he straightened. "Those freckles are adorable. I'd mourn if you wiped them away."

She found some sense to construct a sensible reaction. She

snorted. "And my ears ..." Fumbling for something now. "I've known my entire life they are too big, and Jake the errand boy when I was fourteen made sure I understood that, too ... Do you find those adorable?" What a cursed foolish question, as if she were fishing for compliments instead of forcing him to admit he lied. He, like everyone else, loved perfection. He dealt in it daily, buying the perfect works of art to raise men in society's eyes.

"Go on, then," she said, irritation creeping into her voice, "admit you like big ears." *No one* liked big ears.

He tilted his head, his gaze meandering to the side of her head and slope of her neck. He threaded his fingers through the hair at her temple and brushed it back, revealed an ear, and made the sort of sound in his throat usually only heard by hungry men staring down a large dinner. "I want to nip at the lobes."

Her breath caught in her throat.

"Do you have any other compliments to give yourself?" he asked.

"They're not compliments. They are flaws."

"Not to me. To me, each flaw makes you who you are, and you, Miss Fiona Frampton, I like very much. You are intelligent, and you are creative, and you are kind and loving and a determined little minx, and you are"—he inhaled and exhaled and rested his forehead against her own—"so bloody beautiful it hurts."

And she fell in love with him just a little bit.

Not because he called her beautiful or recited a litany of compliments that weren't really true. She was not those things he said. She was a big-eared, freckled, unfocused criminal. But she had the feeling that if she said that to him, he would punish her, somehow, for abusing herself, as if he'd taken it upon himself to protect her. Even from herself.

No, she did not fall in love with him—just a very little bit, mind you—because he saw her differently than she saw herself. She might be falling just a slightly little bit in love with him though because he looked at a piece of discarded wire and saw something beautiful and useful. And how many others saw the world that way? He spent his time purchasing overly expensive art for other people, but in his own life, he valued those things his clients would sneer at. And if her heart had been hollowed out in this moment to make room for him, it was because of *that*.

"Fiona, what are you thinking?" His forehead still pressed against hers.

"That I'm none of those things you say I am. I am not ladylike enough to please my parents. I want to follow my father in his work, not waste my time on proper accomplishments for ladies miles above me. I cannot pretend the way they want me to, and I cannot create with paint, so I do not want to, but I have no time to work on my jewelry designs because I must always paint horrid still lifes. and I will never be as they wish me and—"

He stopped her speech with a kiss. A brief one, short and hard, that punishment she knew would come, and then he rested his forehead against hers again. "I do not want to hear you describe yourself unless it's in glowing terms. Are we agreed?"

"Not at all. I reserve the right to describe myself however I please and however the mood strikes me. But ... would you very much mind kissing me again? On that point, I think we might find some common ground."

His hands curved round the back on her neck, hard and gentle at the same time, drawing her forward, unforgiving and possessive as his fingers speared into her coiffure, as his thumbs tipped her chin up. Such force she gasped, and he took advantage of her open mouth to plunder it.

She drowned in a maelstrom of sensation headier, more

dizzying than the dance had been. Unable to separate the feel of his lips from the pinpricks of pleasure his fingers drew at her neck and from the scandalizing press of his body against her own—hard edges, lean muscle, and pulsing desire all evident despite the layers of clothing that separated them—she let herself fall into it, gave way and gave up. And let her body do as it pleased.

What did it please?

Touching him. Spearing her fingers through the hair at the base of his skull, tugging on it just a bit. He moaned, and the sound made her moan, too. And she'd never moaned before but for a tart or biscuit or cake or pie. But now she knew more delicious treats—his kiss. Which ... now that they settled into the rhythm of frantically beating hearts, she began to understand. He tasted of champagne, of course, but something minty underneath as well. Or was that her own taste mingled with him from where she'd chewed on a mint leaf before coming?

Didn't matter. She could hardly finish the thought because soft lips and probing tongue pried her own lips apart with hard insistence. That tongue swept into her, and her legs went weak, and she clung to his shoulders—wide and strong and hard beneath her hands.

He left her lips, dragging his teeth over her bottom lip with a quick nip before rolling over the point of her chin and down the length of her exposed neck. When he arrived at the place where shoulder met neck, he stopped, kissed—a soft flutter of a thing—before nipping her there, too, a sharp bite of pleasure that caught a gasp in her throat.

She almost did not notice his hands leaving the cradle of her neck, the warm blanket of her hair, but when recognition rocked through her, his fingers already caressed the low line of her bodice with one hand and gathered her skirts in a fist with the other. The hem of her gown rose as he bunched the material at her hip.

What did he intend to do there? And at her bodice? She could guess. She'd seen enough embraces in the tavern near her home, on the streets in alleyways near the shop. People liked to pretend these things were hidden well, that unwed woman had no knowledge of them. Fiona's mother had certainly armed her with the basic facts of what went where and the repercussions of it. As had her own observations, gained from eavesdropping on conversations not meant for unmarried ladies' ears. Oh, she *knew*. But the bulk of her three and twenty years had been spent learning to paint. Between painting and running the shop, she knew about men and women and what they did together in the dark, but she'd had no opportunity, nor indeed the desire, to do more than know. On an intellectual level. Until now.

She'd seen men's hands on other women's bodies where Zander's hands now rested on her. This went past kissing. It trod a road that led to a different land altogether, one she would not seek experience in before walking it with the man who now held her. Because she wanted only this man to lead her, to show her.

She clutched at his neck again and drew his head back up to her lips while his fingers dipped beneath the silk of her bodice, beneath the stays and the flimsy shift there. And he found, with barely any light and no compass but his own instinct, the tight, aching bud of her nipple, making her gasp.

He took the sound in a teeth-clashing kiss that unbalanced their bodies. They stumbled backward onto the tiny couch, and he caught her, twisted them so she landed atop him, their bodies half sitting, half sprawled in a tangle of legs and clinging arms and seeking lips, still seeking. Because not even a fall would stop them from finding one another.

Found him had she? Yes, she rather thought she had, whatever that meant, and letting him go? An impossible thought.

"Fiona." He whispered her name like a sigh of adoration near her ear, and her head fell back, opening up more territory for him to explore.

Exploration—something her fingers itched to do. She dragged them down, over his shoulders, and flattened them on his chest. He shivered, turned their kiss into a breathless, needy storm. She'd done that. Touching him felt like power, felt like access to perfection she'd never claimed before in her life. She curled her hands into fists on his chest, letting her fingernails scrape against his waistcoat, making his shoulder roll back and his hips arch up. He snaked one hand between their bodies to knead her breast, returning to his ministrations before their fall, and she ... she wanted ... well, he had tasted her body, and now she wished to taste his.

But a cravat was in the way.

She curled her fingers beneath its top edge and pulled it down as much as the tight wrap would allow, as much as she could without choking him, and nudging his jaw to the side with her nose first, she dipped to place a kiss right below it, dragging her lips down to the edge of the cravat. Too little skin, but feeling bold, she wished to taste it all, so she flicked her tongue out and did. Salt, the sweat of him, and something like soap. Mercy, he smelled divine, tasted better and—

She cried out, a sound he silenced with a hard kiss. "Quiet, now," he whispered, "think of those dancing beyond that thin curtain."

But how when he'd pulled her bodice low and kissed her there, laved his tongue across her nipple, and then sucked. He returned to those ministrations once she'd tamed her volume, and he pressed the heel of his palm tight into the place where her legs met, the place she ached the most, and she almost screamed again.

"Stop?" he asked, breathless.

"No," she demanded, determined.

His hand moved, reached for her skirts, and tossed them up around her waist, revealing her leg, clad in white silk stockings with a small black garter she'd decorated with a small paste diamond for no clear reason. Her own amusement, perhaps. She hoped he noticed now, though, hoped he approved. His fingernails scraped up the silk to the sensitive flesh of her inner thigh, then his fingers explored higher.

She gasped and raked her hands through his hair when he stroked her at the apex of her legs. His lips and teeth gently ministered to her breast while his fingers stroked that never-touched place between her legs. Touched now, and something lit inside her that she'd never felt before, as if her body were a candle that had been waiting for a flame to give it purpose. His every stroke made breathing more difficult, and when his fingers pressed to the smallest part of her—the place that throbbed the most—she cried out once more, burrowing the sound in the curve of his neck as he slipped a finger inside of her. *Inside of her.*

She'd think more on that later.

Right now ... thought could stuff it. She wanted to *feel*.

"Have you ever touched yourself here?" he inquired, voice low and sultry and somehow as inside her as his finger.

"No," she admitted, though now that he mentioned it ... why hadn't she? Would it feel as good if she did it?

"You will now. And think of me."

"Yes." A truth.

His thumb began a rhythmic circling, and she moaned, pressing her body up into his hand. What was this, and why had Mother said nothing of it? Of the building and the aching and the pleasure and the need for more, something just beyond her reaching. His movements seemed to help her, to drive her closer to that something she did not understand. His ministrations at her mouth, her breasts, her core, tightening her up like a clock about to chime.

A bell rang beyond the curtain. Curse the bell. She growled and deepened the kiss and then his thumb pressed and flicked, and his other hand tugged gently at her nipple, and she ... she ... she became a night sky of shimmery diamonds, a glinting necklace laid against a bed of black velvet, falling, reflecting rainbows of light. Breath caught in her throat, her chest, and the ringing bell from behind the curtain disappeared behind the beating drum of her heart and the words he whispered in her ear, not that she understood those. She heard, felt, only the tone of them—soft and sweet and lovely, making the falling diamond feel of her nestle into something warmer, heavier, satisfied.

The bell rang again. His body stiffened beneath hers, and she realized the string quartet no longer played. When had that happened? He pushed to sitting, putting her to the side and rearranging her clothing, his gaze fixed on the bodice as he raised it, straightened it, her shoulder as he righted her sleeve, her hair as he smoothed it away from her temples. Each little bit of her he organized felt like a closing off, as if he was meticulously patching the gaps that had opened up between them so they could reach through to one another no more.

"I believe that's the signal for the auction to begin," he said when she was presentable.

"Oh. Yes. Right." The reason they were there. Not for kisses but for intrigue and discovery.

He righted his cravat and coat, and the thick muscles in his thighs flexed as if to stand.

She laid a hand over the one closest to her, almost melting into nothing at the feel of the hard muscle. "Wait."

He stood slowly, letting her hand slip to her side, and peered down at her. "Yes?"

"I'll climb over that wall you've erected."

He blinked, shook his head as if he did not understand.

She stood and, with tentative hands at first, lifted her fingers toward his hair, smoothed it back away from his temples. Then she met his gaze with more confidence than she touched him. "I am not a woman who will claim a man's forever because of a kiss—"

"That"—he pointed hard toward the couch—"was more than a kiss."

"I will not tell a soul, Lord Lysander Bromley. But I will not be shut out either. I will climb whatever walls you build. Do you understand?" She poked him in the ribs. "And explode that one you've currently shoved up between us. I'll not have it. So do not even try."

He swallowed hard, his jaw tightening. "I have no clue what this is. It's the damn truth, Fiona. I'm laid flat, and I ... but you know my reasons."

"I expect nothing from you. I've never expected to marry, and—"

"Why the hell not?"

She shrugged, smoothing the wrinkled damage he'd done to her skirts, unable to meet his gaze. "I'm not entirely certain. There have been no suitors. Perhaps that fact ... stuck with me, molded my expectations early on. And I do not expect you to be my suitor, but ..."

"Yes?" he prompted, running one finger down her cheek.

She wanted to banish those gloves keeping his skin from hers just as she'd banished the walls between them. "But ..." But she did not have the words. There were few options for women—wife or whore or spinster. There should be a few more. She'd like something outside of those, something that allowed for touch without ruination. "I do not expect you to be my suitor," she repeated, waving away the growl that rumbled from his throat, "but I would still, while we are connected, like to kiss you."

"Fiona." Her name almost a curse on his lips.

"If I never marry because my life ends short at the end of a rope or because I'm taking care of my mother for the rest of my life or working secretly for my father or because I'm just plain and unremarkable ... for any of those reasons, if I never marry, there is no one to know I once met a man who saved me from my innocence, who taught me the beauty of imperfection." Yes. That was it.

She searched for her mask as she thought through the new truth blooming in her breast. When she found it, he took it from her and tied it on, and she freed his domino from her pocket and did the same for him.

All the while, she considered the new truth, spring green and certain. She was supposed to remain perfect for her husband, perfect innocence, pristine and untouched. All women were. But she'd never been perfect, so why try now? And why not sink into that imperfection in the arms of a man who understood its value?

Her voice stronger than before, she said, "I will never marry because I cannot be the type of woman a man will want. I will always have forgery attached to my past, and marriage would align and endanger any man with that crime. But I still want to know, to feel, to touch and be touched, and—"

His hands wrapped around her upper arms like lightning, and his lips lowered to hers just as quickly, and in a flash, he kissed her again. A kiss blinding enough to cast the meager candlelight in shadow. When he lifted from the kiss, his eyes lit with the dark flames of hell, and a new desperation clung to him. Then he took her hand and led her out of their hiding place. The crowd in the ballroom streamed toward a pair of open double doors at the opposite end of the dance floor, and Fiona and Zander followed. His hand held her like a manacle, his arm a chain that bound them together. Here. Tonight.

But did the chain mean agreement?

She pressed close to his side and popped up on toe to reach his ear and whisper, "Teach me, Zander, for no one else ever will, and I've always loved to learn."

He hissed a curse, but he did not say no. Indeed, his hold on her hand increased, crushing, possessive.

She liked it. She'd not drop the conversation. She wanted to have him as long as their association lasted, and that might not be very long, so she held on just as tightly as he did and promised herself that after the auction, they'd continue what they'd started with a kiss.

Fifteen

The room the guests filed into was scarcely smaller than the ballroom they'd left, but this one was filled ceiling to floor with paintings of all sizes. On small tables throughout the center of the room, clear cases sat squat and shining, jewels glittering beneath their glass, and statues clustered in corners. A small army of masked footmen handed out more glasses of champagne. Fiona took one from a passing footman but put it back down on another footman's tray when Lysander did not do the same.

"Shall we abstain?" she asked, leaning in and reaching up so her whisper could reach his ear.

"Yes. We must keep our wits about us. We should not have had some earlier, but I meant to cool us off."

She chuckled, squeezing his arm closer to her side. "Cool? I'm a fire. A furnace. The very sun. If I were Icarus, I'd be in terrible danger."

"Focus, Fiona. That is why we must abstain. I need your mind at its quickest, its sharpest. And I fear I've already muddled it enough for the evening." He looked down at her like he'd like to muddle her some more, like he would do so if they were not crowded round by others.

The others. She began to peer past masks, looking for familiar faces. No matter the revelations of the last half hour, there were bigger problems to attend to tonight. Focus was indeed necessary.

"How does this work?" she asked.

"It appears as if Currington is going to run it like a larger auction house would. Usually, they open the house a few days before the actual auction to those who wish to purchase something. At that time, buyers decide what they want and how much they're willing to pay for it. It seems tonight is to be the walk-through."

"Have you ever attended one? A walk-through?"

"Yes. To procure pieces for clients. Usually, it's crucial to hold your tongue when viewing the art. Stay no longer than ten seconds before each piece and never speak of a piece unless it's to criticize."

"Why?"

"The footmen are listening. They'll report back to Currington, tell him who wants what and how desperately, and he'll know exactly where to apply pressure, exactly how far he can extend his victims' pockets when they extend an offer."

Fiona *tsked*. "Appalling."

He threaded their fingers together and squeezed her hand. "Oh, my little fraud? Is it appalling? Tell me how."

She sniffed. "Perhaps it's not so appalling." She would not add hypocrisy to her sins. "What should we do?"

"The Rubens are over there." He nodded his head to the side without looking.

She stepped in that direction.

He held her firm in place. "We cannot get too close. My current client will recognize me. He has an eye on those pieces and is sure to be hovering in that direction."

"Do you think he's—"

"No. He's not who we're looking for. He's so much money that procuring items through any other means will not have occurred to him."

"Right, then. We're looking for someone who's in need of funds."

"Perhaps. Or someone who is such an art connoisseur the act of owning the art is all that matters, and they will procure it however they can. Anyone here tonight could have stolen the dowager's paintings."

"Including the dowager," Fiona mumbled.

"Including her. Keep your ears open, especially when we pass by the Rubens. Any mumbled aside could be a clue. Keep the titles of my originals firm in your mind, and listen for them in the whispers in the air. Listen, also for any mention of secret collections like the dowager's and whispers of paintings for sale that should not be." Lysander escorted her around the room, stopping here and there, spending a bit more time looking at pieces not crowded round by others, standing with their backs to large groups, but close enough to hear their conversation.

"Hell," he hissed, peering at a tiny gold-flecked icon.

She leaned closer to the painting. "What is it?"

"It is a fake." Each word clipped. "And at least three people are eyeing it, willing to pay with their children's lives for it, too, I've no doubt. Hell. Stay here." He bolted off before she could answer him.

She inspected the icon more closely. It appeared to be of the Virgin Mary and the infant Jesus, faded round the edges. Typical for such an old piece. She looked for the telltale signs of forgery, of aging a piece to make it look older, but she could not find them. How could Lysander tell? She flashed him a glance where he stood shoulder to shoulder with another man. Neither of them looked at the other, but their lips moved lightly in conversation, then Lysander spoke to another man and another, before joining her once more.

"There," he said, "they know now. Currington will not be pleased. But none of those buyers could afford the price he'd push it up to, and the only thing that would run them off is the truth of its authenticity. They'd beggar their children before they gave up the hunt." More than a sneer there—outright disgust.

"How did you know it's a forgery?" she asked.

He pointed to a corner. "Do you see this color? Not used in true icons. Only developed in the last ten years, actually."

"Why"—she blinked up at him—"that's brilliant."

He grinned. "Me or the concept of only using period-correct colors to forge?"

She shrugged. Let him think what he would when the only correct answer was him. He was brilliant. Not only his knowledge and sharp eye, but also his empathy. If those men would not look out for their families, he would—and even at the risk of angering another.

He dragged her away from the icon and toward the jewelry at the center of the room, and the first piece they passed was a ruby necklace.

A familiar ruby necklace. Fiona gasped. She had not meant to, but the sound of surprise broke free before she even knew of its existence. What else was she supposed to do?

Lysander stopped, looked at the necklace, then at Fiona. "Recognize it?"

She nodded.

"Has it been brought into your shop to be fixed? By its owner?"

She shook her head. My, the heat had risen in the room. Insufferable, it was, and pooled almost entirely in her cheeks.

"Do you recognize it for some other reason? Because you've seen it on the owner's neck in public?

She shook her head once more.

Lysander stared hard at the necklace, then shifted quick as a breeze, and wrapped tight fingers around her wrist. He pulled her toward a pair of doors at the side of the room that opened into a hallway. Soon, the dim light of the hall surrounded them, and he surrounded her, her back pushed against the wall, his body pressed close, his knee splitting her legs and nudging them apart.

His head dipped and his breath whispered in her ear, "You made a copy." A lover's embrace meant for, it seemed, hissing accusations.

Correct accusations.

She swallowed hard. "Yes." She pressed her palms flat against his chest. "You know this about me. I've stopped. But ... that one is real, so you need not let your anger consume you."

He growled. "Hell, I'm not angry."

She cocked her head to the side. Even her heart seemed to stop its hammering to listen. "You certainly seem enraged." Or in lust. One of the two. Both perhaps.

"I wanted to speak, and this was most expedient. A moment of privacy gained through the appearance of uncontrollable ardor."

Ah. Now she understood. "Pretending a ... a sudden bout of lust?"

He rested his head against her shoulder, bringing the entire length of his body closer to hers. "Forgive me." Waves of his warm breath stole across the skin above her low, low bodice, and her body tightened. Her breasts ached.

"Are others looking?" She dared not look left or right.

"No. All others in this hall are ... as we are."

She did look right then, the only way she could look with his head resting on her left shoulder, and yes—there, a bit down the hallway—another couple embracing, a woman was pinned to the wall as Fiona was by a man as dark-haired as Lysander. Hopefully the woman enjoyed the pinning as much as Fiona was.

"How clever of you," she said, breathless. And meant it.

"How did you come to have the Currington bridal gems?" His voice was a harsh, heavy rasp as his hands lifted to her bare upper arms, stroked up and down in that sliver of a space between her sleeves and the tops of her long gloves.

"The what? Oh, the rubies." Was that what he wished to speak of when the couple just down the way was not speaking at all? Oh, wait, the other woman did mutter something —*please*—and then she uttered a few more words—*God yes.* Well. *Their* conversation seemed preferable. She looked to Zander, who still rested his forehead on her shoulder, his eyes clenched closed, his jaw working as if he were a cow chewing cud. He likely would not be amenable to such blasphemous conversation.

"I, ah, the dowager has a particular fascination with bridal parures. You did not know?"

"No," he hissed.

"Had we more time when I took you to her secret gallery, I would have shown you the room she keeps them in."

"How did she procure them?"

"I did not ask. She provided the set, and I ... um ..."

"Yes, yes, I am aware of what you did."

"She promised that the originals were going back to their owner, and that she would have the fakes destroyed when she died. It is good to see she kept her word there at least."

He snorted, but then he stroked the side of her neck, waking her up, muddling her mind, though she needed to be sharp. His knee seemed too close to her body. It pressed her skirts up between her legs, and—mercy—she wanted him to press more, ached for some greater pressure she could not describe.

Each word difficult because breathing was a difficulty, she thought. "We should return to the auction room or ..." A risk. She'd take a risk. "I begin to doubt this ruse of lustful abandon is necessary for a private conversation. There are doors outnumbering us on either side of this hall, more than enough to slip into and—"

"Discover others further along than we are and less fully dressed."

"Ah. I see. Either way, I do believe you've pinned me here not to speak with me, but to ... touch me." Her hands clawed into the lapels of his coat, and she pulled him tight against her until his hard chest crashed into her soft breasts. Aching again, too. My what a world the body could learn in a small hour. Breathless, anticipating, careless of the conversation, she just wanted him closer, all of him, arched against her and into her.

He flattened his palms on the wall on either side of her head and dipped in low for a hard kiss, wild and wanting and too, too short. He pushed himself away from the wall, from her, and offered her his arm.

She almost melted. Only the wall held her up, but she launched herself toward him, grabbed for his arm to steady her legs, and somehow they found the door to the auction room.

And found it blocked.

The woman in the deep-purple gown took up the entire space, her feathered turban waving about like an excited child bidding for attention. She blinked up at them with oddly familiar eyes, her mouth partly open, her skin flushed. Had she been watching them? Fair. They were in public pressed against a wall, after all.

Why were her eyes so familiar? That gray-blue ... They widened. She gasped and covered her mouth with a black-gloved hand. And then she ran, twirling and twisting between the prospective buyers in the auction room and disappearing behind a glass case.

"The dowager?" Fiona's voice scratched a hoarse whisper up her throat.

"Precisely." Zander's voice held the predatory growl of a jungle cat, and he pulled her into the room, after their prey.

Fiona ripped from his grip. They'd never weave through the crowd together successfully. Better to part ways. Where was the purple silk? Where was the feathered turban? She was so cursed short! Everyone towered above her, and she had to go up on toe, then jump, just to see.

"Where," she growled, pushing between two men, "is that woman?"

The dowager was short, too, though, and even with her towering headgear, the tall black-and-white columns of gentlemen would hide her well. But Fiona had her own column, and he chased ahead of her toward the ballroom, after —yes, there—a flash of purple skirts.

Fiona followed. People were looking now, though, and while no one here knew her well, what if her mask slipped? She hitched up her skirts and ran, eyes on her be damned.

Ahead of her, Lysander slipped out of the auction room and into the ballroom, and she lost sight of him for several breathless seconds while she scrambled to keep up. When she tumbled into the drawing room, out of breath, gaze darting every which way, she found him. Alone in the middle of the dance floor, arms limp at his sides.

She hurried to him. "Where did she go?"

He shook his head, the lines of his face grim and heavy. "I don't know." He pointed toward a series of doors that opened up into the gardens. "Could have gone that way." He pointed toward the stairs. "Or that way." He swept a hand toward those shadowy alcoves that had hidden them earlier. "Or in any one of those. The problem is if I choose wrong we lose her. Damn. We've probably already lost her. The slippery thing."

She tugged his arm then darted off toward the alcoves. "I'll search here, and you search upstairs. If she's slipped into the gardens, she's likely already darted off toward a carriage and is gone."

"No." The single word echoed, resolute in the air like a heavy fog.

"What can you mean 'no'?"

"I'll not leave you down here alone, a room away from a horde of lascivious men too deep in their cups."

She could not argue that point. "Let us search the alcoves first. Quick. Then go into the gardens." They were too close to answers to stall. She rushed to the curtained-off corner and threw the draper back. Empty. And the next and the next— the same.

He searched the other side, calling out, "Empty!" as he went. They met near the doors that opened out into the gardens, and Fiona eyed the stairs that would take them to the upper-level balconies of the ballroom. Were they making the right choice?

His hand cupped over her shoulder. "I do not think she would have gone that way. She's agile for her age, but those stairs and that gown and turban? It would have taken her longer to ascend them, and I'd have caught her. Much easier to hide or escape out the back."

She inhaled, the air filling her lungs deep but shaky. "Yes. Let's go."

They pushed into the cool evening, the night an inky black that swallowed them whole. He grabbed her hand and tugged her toward the front of the house.

"This way. Toward the carriages."

They ran, and she had to crush her skirts in one hand so she did not trip over them. The coaches waited before Currington's home in a long line, like giant frogs on lily pads, squat and sluggish except for the restless horseflesh reined to them.

"Which one?" Fiona gasped.

Lysander craned his neck left and right, up and down, bending his body, a low hum emanating from his throat.

A horse's whinny, as if disturbed.

They jerked toward the noise.

The slash of reins whipping through air and the slap of their leather upon horse backs. Then the rumble of wheels across gravel.

"Her!" they said together, giving chase. Their legs pumped into motion at the same time, running toward the front of the carriage line.

But not fast enough. Lysander stopped first as the carriage pulled away, faster on the empty night streets than they could follow.

Fiona folded in half, her hands slamming into her knees as she gasped for breath.

Lysander's hand rested on her back. "I'll take you home when you're ready."

She straightened, shaking her head. "No. Back to the gardens. Perhaps that was not the dowager. She could be hiding still."

"Unlikely."

"We must try!" She stomped toward the garden gate. She'd let herself forget their purpose this night, losing herself in his touch and his gaze and unabashed regard. Near him, her crimes did not feel so heavy, the unknown pitch of her future did not seem so dark. She'd allowed herself to loosen and to forget, and she'd lost the answers as soon as they'd appeared. "Perhaps there's someone else inside who will have information."

"You know the dowager is our best chance, Fiona." He

followed her, though she only knew so by the heavy crunch of his feet on the gravel of the garden path behind her.

She would not look around, would not let moonlight on his face distract her. She set her steps down a dark garden path, shaking the bushes.

"What are you doing?" he asked, a chuckle on the edges of his voice.

"Trying to scare her out."

"The dowager is not a bird or rat to be shook from a bush." He did laugh then.

She whirled on him, took two pressing steps toward him until she could shove her finger at his hard chest. "Do not laugh at me."

"Do not amuse me so."

"Will you laugh when I swing from the end of a noose?"

"You won't." A dagger had slipped between his words. A promise to anyone who thought to harm her?

"You've lost your originals, Lysander, but the copies I've made are lost, too. You own the originals. Your family's coffers and comfort may be at stake, but my life is forfeit if ... if ..." She pressed her heels into her eyes. "I'll *not* hang." Then more softly. "It's my own fault."

"You won't hang." His arms slipped around her. "But running about making noise is not the way to save yourself, little dragon. Breathe less fire. Hoard more treasures."

She laughed, a startling thing that cracked open the shadows around them. "I have no idea what you're talking about."

He led her deeper into the shadows beneath a tree with small white blooms. He sat and patted the hard marble beside him, imitating her earlier gesture in the alcove. Like him then, she did not sit now. She paced back and forth before him in short bursts of three steps, turn, three steps, turn, dislodging blooms from low-hanging branches. She clasped her hands behind her back, the weight of her mask pressing, pressing, *cutting* into her face. She tugged at the ribbons at the back of her head and cried out, an angry rumble of frustration, when they did not give.

A hand at her waist, a quick, hard tug, then she was falling, but not far, and not onto the ground or hard marble, but into the warm lap and strong arms of the one who had tugged her.

"Zander," she breathed.

He swatted her hands away from her head and with slow, careful fingers against her skull, loosed the mask, dropped it to the ground at his feet. His feet. Not hers. Because hers could not reach perched as she was atop him, a little bird with a lovely nest.

"Thank you," she said. "That's better."

He rested his chin atop her head. "Listen, you dragon. The dowager is back in town. If she ever left. We know that now, and we must focus there instead of running about lighting the entire town aflame. Since we met, you've been spouting flames at danger, thinking to burn it to ash, but douse the flames and save your family, yourself, in one violent fit of defiance. Sometimes rescue plans take more nuance, though."

"Did yours? Does yours? For your family?"

"I thought it did. I believed myself to be quite, quite sneaky. Smarter than them all. But my father knew the whole damn time. Played me for a fool."

"Perhaps he did not want to embarrass you or ... or create a rift between you by pointing out your thievery."

He snorted, tightened his arms around her. "I doubt that. None of us, me nor my siblings, were what he wanted out of his progeny. Too rough and tumble, not nearly enough refined or, of course, interested in the arts. I'm sure he relished forming a will that would pressure us to make art, relished leaving us inheritances that he knew were worthless, and—"

"What do you mean pressure you to make art?"

A harsh bark of laughter. "A stipulation of the will. Even if the paintings we were willed were the originals, we cannot have them until we each produce a work of art deemed valuable by my mother. My brother Raph and my sister Maggie have both won their inheritances, but—ha—there is nothing worth selling to inherit. In the end, I have ruined my family as much as my father did."

She snapped her head upward, bumping his chin.

"Ow." He plucked at her earlobe. "Don't throw your flames at me, dragon."

"I will if you deserve them." She smirked, liking the way he called her dragon. Not, perhaps a conventional endearment, not one other women would welcome, but he'd recently spoken of relishing, and she relished that—the power of the word and the fondness with which he said it. "Have you tried to win your inheritance, fake though it may be? Have you sculpted or drawn or—"

"No. I've no talent. For any of it. I have an eye for what is good, what is true, what is exceptional, but unlike you, I cannot make these things myself."

She turned and wrapped her arms around his neck, buried her face in his shoulder and cravat to best hide her sudden fit of giggles.

"What's the meaning of this? Should I be insulted she laughs at such a time?"

"No," she shrieked on a laugh flung sky high. "No. It's only ... it's only we are the same, don't you see. Each of us unable to create—"

"Hold on. You *can* create—"

"Not how I want to. They will not allow me to." She laughed some more into his shoulder, clinging tight to him as he clung to her. When she had recovered enough to speak, she said, "We are a pair. Perhaps I should create some art for you to show your mother, then you can get your"—the laughs returned again, crowding out her words, but she squeezed them through anyhow—"forged inheritance."

"'Tis not funny." But he laughed, too, a deep rumble that rocked her, turned her mirth to something else entirely, like earth-warm fireflies glinting into diamond stars in the night sky. A transformation.

He pressed a kiss to the top of her head. "You'll be safe. We'll find all that is missing." A promise. She intended to believe him.

Sixteen

Lysander woke unwillingly at who knew what late hour, reluctant to let the dream woman he'd held all night go. But sunlight across paper-thin eyelids eventually banished his hold on her. When he opened his eyes and pushed to sitting, scratching his head where it slightly ached from the pressure of the knot holding his domino together last night, he realized he did not want to let her go. Hated it. Which likely meant the infatuation he'd been attempting to rid himself of last night ... was not an infatuation. What it was, he would not explore. No reason to. She'd been too eager in his arms last night, too ready to continue their inadvisable actions, scandals if they were ever found out.

He flopped back down on the bed. Last night. A debacle from beginning to end. At least they knew the dowager yet lived. He'd make a visit to her townhome today. Unlikely she'd returned there when she knew they were after her, but worth a try. He knit his hands together behind his head and studied the ceiling. He should call on Fiona, too. See how she fared after such a shocking night. Likely well enough. She probably had a plan already spun and expected him to step in with no hesitation. She'd be animated—explaining, arms waving, hair falling, eyes wild, lips mobile—and he'd want to kiss her.

He grew hard, and the coverlet draped over his lower half tented. "Damn."

A knock on the door.

"Double damn. One moment please," he called out.

"You've a note, Zander." Maggie's voice. "That's all. It's been waiting on you all morning. It's past noon, you know." He'd not known. "I'll slip it beneath the door."

Silence, then the thumps of fingers fumbling about wood and the slight shush of paper, and then, "Will we see you at all today?"

"Oh, I'm sure. Getting up now." And he did get up as the sound of her footsteps receded behind his chamber door. He knelt and picked up the note, his name written on it in curling, ostentatious script. He unfolded it and read, and a boisterous waltz broke out inside him. Impossible. Was it to be that easy?

He flew into movement, cleaning his teeth and any bits of himself that smelled stale or worse. He threw on the cleanest clothes he had and shoved his feet in boots, and after a much too slow hackney ride, he burst through the front door of Frampton and Son's, waving the letter. "I need to speak to Fiona."

Her sister, the only one in the shop, looked up from where she leaned across the counter, book open before her. She scowled. "Lord Lysander. What are you doing here?"

The first time he'd stepped foot in the shop through the front door, and it seemed he was about to be kicked out. "I need to speak with your sister." He looked toward the door that must lead to the workshop at the back. "Fiona!"

Miss Frampton circled the counter to stand before him. "Do you have permission to address my sister so informally?"

"He does." Fiona stood in the doorway, her head tilted to the side, a bevy of questions in her eyes. "What is it, Zander?"

He shook the letter at her. "An invitation. To the dowager's house. For tea. This afternoon."

She looked at the nearby clock. "Oh. We're late. I'll grab my pelisse."

"You can't go anywhere with him, Fiona," Posey protested.

Fiona slipped her arms into a gray wool coat and swept across the room toward Zander as she buttoned it up. "I already have, Posey. He's no harm." She stopped before him and looked up, a fragile smile on her lips, so small it almost did not exist. "You came to gather me instead of going over to her home yourself?"

"I've learned my lesson, Fee. You're quite valuable. You might see something I miss or know something I don't, and I'll not do without you." He offered her his arm, pretending those last words—*I'll not do without you*—didn't have a significant double meaning.

She stared at him, mouth slightly agape and eyes like stars.

"Where are you going?" the elder Miss Frampton demanded.

"You heard the man," Fiona said, her voice a breezy cloud. "To tea."

"I'll come too." Posey bustled away. "You need a chaperone."

"No. Someone must mind the shop, and Papa's asleep." The breeziness had fled, and Fiona had her dragon claws out now.

The sister must have known it, too. She turned slowly, eyes narrowed, and Zander saw dragons ran in the family. "One hour, Fee. No more. Or I'm coming after you."

Fiona took Zander's proffered arm, and as they left the shop, she greeted the afternoon air with a bounce in her step.

"Thank you."

"For what?" he asked, turning them toward a hack.

"For including me."

Such a small thing, and he cringed to know he'd denied it to her over and over again. "Do others make it a habit not to include you?"

"Where it matters most, yes. I'm the youngest. I was never supposed to know about or feel our worries as a family, our rising poverty, our struggle to face off against old Foggy. They wanted to keep me safe from it all. But I only wanted to help."

"Perhaps they should not have left you to your own devices."

"Oh yes, the forgery thing is entirely their fault." Bright words, playful, but her body drooped as he handed her into a hack and sat beside her, thigh brushing thigh.

"I don't think that," she said, her voice small. "I blame no one but myself."

He swallowed down the lust, suppressed the rising physical reaction and chucked her chin up. "Think of how close we are to answers, dragon. We've an invitation to answers! You'll know where your paintings are in half an hour. Less. Then we'll set about getting them."

"We, we, we. *Our*. Do you mean it truly?"

"Yes." He kept making promises to her. Didn't seem able to stop. He hoped to God he could keep them. Though no number of promises or fulfilments of them changed his situation—a floating no one, whose every pence went into the family coffers to repair the roof on the estate or fix up the dower house for rental or to pay mother's new companion. Or for his own boots and cravats. He'd never known where the money for all of it came before a decade and a half ago. It had all appeared quite effortlessly, daily magic taken for granted. And now he knew where it came from. His own sweat. His brothers' sweat.

This infatuation turned ... something else ... could not give her what she needed, what she did not know she wanted—stability, the same stability she'd tried to buy from the dowager with her talents.

The hack rolled to a stop, and he helped Fiona out. The dowager's townhome rose before them.

"Stay close," he whispered. "We cannot know what to expect inside."

She whipped to face him, and her gaze felt like pins on his skin. "You suspect some nefarious plan."

"I don't know. Just ... remain close."

She nodded, and he knocked on the door. A butler—one he'd met many times before—opened before he could put knuckles to wood a second time.

"Lady Balantine has been expecting you, Lord Lysander. Do come in." The butler bowed low and stepped aside and led them both to the parlor where Fiona had discovered him the day he'd used his purloined key.

The dowager sat with her back to them near the fireplace, but she bounced to her feet and rushed to them, arms stretched wide and welcoming when the butler announced their arrival.

"My darlings," she crooned, wrapping both arms around them for a bone crushing hug. Where did a woman of sixty or more years obtain such strength? She stepped away, folded her hands before her, and beamed at them. "I knew it was you together last night. It was, wasn't it? Oh, do say I guessed right. No"—she lifted up a hand to stay speech Zander had no intention of providing—"you need say nothing at all. The mere fact you showed up together says it for you." She sighed, a long, delighted sort of sound. "You've found one another and fallen in love. I have wondered, often, I must confess, if I should introduce the two of you. Both so pretty and young, so talented and clever. A perfect match really. I *am* pleased, though I wish I could have brought you together myself."

Zander looked at Fiona, who looked at him. Her red-cheeked expression clearly said, *Do you have any clue what she's going on about?* He shrugged. *No clue*, he tried to communicate without speech

"We're, um, not together. That is, we've not fallen in love," Fiona said.

The dowager laughed. "That's not what that steamy and scandalous exhibition in the hallway at Currington's suggested. No, my dear, you won't be able to fool me, though you fool the rest of London." She winked.

Zander turned back to Lady Balantine, smoothing out the frustration and impatience coursing through him. "My lady, will you please slow down? No. We must speak clear sense for a short while." He lightly settled an arm around her shoulder and led her back to her chair. "Let us be methodical about this. I'll ask questions, and you answer them. Yes?"

The dowager sat with a chuckle. "Yes, if you insist. Though everything seems perfectly clear to me."

Fiona, who had been stuck in the doorway, shook herself loose and ran across the room, her arms waving wildly. "Clear? You've been missing! I feared you dead, and here you are, happy and whole—thank God—and going on about me and Lysander being in love, as if love mattered in the face of complete and utter ruination. You've no idea the tales I've been spinning of my own demise. My imagination knows no bounds, and—"

"Darling Fiona," the dowager drawled, "do sit. You do not wish to start foaming at the mouth. How unladylike. And in front of your suitor?" She shivered. "And I've not been missing! I've known where I have been my whole life."

Fiona did sit, dropping with a thud into a nearby chair.

"Now," Lady Balantine said, "why in heaven did you think me dead?"

Zander inhaled deeply. He needed to wrench control of the scene from these two. "May I ask my questions and give this drama a semblance of order?"

The dowager blinked. "As you wish, darling. Shall I ring for tea now that everyone's arrived?" She clapped her hands. "Oh, I had no expectation you would bring Miss Fiona, Lysander, but I'm so pleased you did. It confirms everything."

"You were dead!" Fiona exploded.

"We only feared she would be," Zander corrected.

Fiona dropped her face to her hands with a groan.

"I'm not dead," the dowager said with a grin. "That makes it better, yes? Aren't you pleased, my loves?" Her confidence wavered a bit, as if she was only beginning to realize that her plans were not going accordingly.

What were her plans?

"Why did you invite me here?" Zander asked.

Lady Balantine's grin returned in full brightness and confidence. "I wished to speak with you last night. I was certain it was you I saw in the hallway with the woman." She smirked at Fiona. "I could not be sure it was Fiona. Why would she be at such an event, after all. But it had the look of her, and that mask ... such an absolute brilliant riot. Only one mind could create it, one set of hands craft it. Brava, Fiona. I adored it. Can I have it?"

"Ye-es?" Fiona said.

The dowager rolled on. "Excellent. Most excellent."

"Why did you run from me?" Zander demanded.

"Oh, that. I didn't know if you'd recognized me, and if not, I didn't want to risk being recognized. I was not supposed to be there, after all." Her lips pursed into a pout. "I'm not allowed to buy anything else. Herbert dislikes it so. Says art is a waste of good blunt and will have nothing to do with it. And I dare not upset him in this because we've just reconciled, of course, and—"

"Herbert?" Zander pinched the bridge of his nose. "And who is that?"

The pout disappeared. "My son! We've never been close before, but he showed up last year to get to know me better. He has a new baby and realized he wanted me near, part of the family. Never understood why he shunned me to begin with, but that's all in the past now. No hard feelings. I've just returned, actually, from his country seat. I've been helping his wife with the babes. They have a difficult time, it seems, poor dears, keeping a nanny about. At their wits' ends, they were. Until me."

Fiona held up a hand, palm flat, stopping the monologue. "You've been in the country?"

"Yes. Derbyshire."

"For how long?" Fiona asked.

"Hmm." Lady Balantine tapped her lip and considered the ceiling, as if she kept an almanac there. "Oh, almost a year, I think. Yes. I remember it now. It was rainy, and the leaves on the street were green. A summer shower when Herbert came home and swept me away. You should *see* little Annie. The new baby, though she's a bit older than a year now. Cheeks like apples and hair so yellow it's almost white. And the elder one, Johnny, he's a perfect copy of his father." She chuckled, glanced at Fiona. "Almost as if you'd painted him from the original, darling. Oh!" She popped a hand over her mouth, her gaze flicking to Zander. She plied her hand away from her mouth just enough to mouth to Fiona, "Does he know? About the F-O-R-G—"

"Yes," Fiona barked. Then she groaned. "He knows."

She caught Zander's eye. "I don't remember her being quite this difficult to talk to."

He shrugged. "You likely never had something you needed from her so desperately before."

"How are you being so patient?"

"She's here, isn't she? I suppose we have time."

"Wait," the dowager interjected. "What do you need desperately, Fiona, my love? Tell me, and you know I shall provide."

Zander stepped forward. "She needs information. As do I. Where are your paintings?"

The dowager froze. The only point of movement in her entire body were her eyebrows slicing toward one another. "My paintings? Why, safe and sound right where they always are, of course." She turned a bewildered gaze first to Zander and then to Fiona. "Why do you ask?"

Zander and Fiona shared a gaze.

"Have you seen them since you arrived home?" Zander asked.

Lady Balantine's gaze clouded over. "N-no. But"—a weak chuckle—"they are always there. Right where I left them. Of course ... I've never left them for quite so long before."

"Perhaps," Fiona said, "you can show us ... just so we may confirm they are still about? You know I become nervous."

Lead the woman right to the bad news. Show her instead of tell her. Either a brilliant strategy or a horrid one. They'd find out soon enough.

The dowager patted Fiona's hand. "Of course, of course." She turned a sharp eye toward Zander. "I think it's time to show you *everything*, Lord Lysander. Are you ready for a remarkable discovery?" She bounced to her feet. "Follow me, darlings."

They did, huddled together and at a slight distance from their hostess.

"Do you have smelling salts, by any chance?" Zander asked, his voice low.

"No. Do you think she'll need them?" Fiona whispered.

"I did when I first discovered the missing pieces."

She bit her bottom lip. He knew what that lip tasted like, and his body begged him to taste it again. His mind agreed. Only … something, some still-resilient bit of him held fast and steady against his entirely inadvisable not-an-infatuation.

"Can she really not know anything about it?" Fiona shook her head.

Zander grasped her hand, squeezed it, pulled her closer, as if they were alone and not a single thing stood between them, as if he had a right to. "It will all be well."

The dowager cast a look over her shoulder. "Ah, young love."

Zander dropped Fiona's hand, and Lady Balantine chuckled. "Need not hide it from me, darlings." She tapped the corner of her eye. "I see everything, and I highly approve."

"She's not seen everything yet," Fiona hissed.

The dowager led them upstairs to the small room Zander had believed to be her only gallery space, and she opened the door with a sweeping gesture. Then froze.

Zander ran up behind her, wrapping an arm around her shoulder and, when she melted into him on unsteady legs, moving the arm to her waist to better keep her upright.

Fiona rushed forward, too. "My lady, you must sit."

"Where have they gone?" Her gaze fixed to the empty walls. "All of them. A lifetime's collection"—a sob broke through, and her face paled—"where?" More shriek than query. Then her entire body stiffened, becoming stone, and she jolted out of Zander's arms. "No." A low moan. She jerked around him and ran down the hallway. "No, no, no. Surely not. Surely not."

They followed, running after her as they had last night.

"She keeps in excellent health for a woman of her age." Zander panted for breath between words.

Fiona hitched up her skirts and ran faster. "We'll be sure to follow in her example if we keep having to run after her."

He ran faster, too, but the dowager still beat them, and they found her stepping through the wardrobe and into the second townhouse before they could stop her or help her or ask her to slow down.

"My lady," Zander called, "Please do slow down. Sit. You'll hurt yourself."

She did not listen, and they ran up the stairs after her, breathing hard. When they reached the top of the stairs, they saw the door to the painting room open, and they heard a low keening echo in the open space.

"Oh." Fiona clutched her heart but slowed her feet, tiptoeing toward the dowager as if they did not wish to disturb her mourning.

Zander had heard such sounds of grief before from his mother's lips after his father's death. No matter his father's sins, the man had loved his wife. And she him. He tried to remember that on the days he wanted to scrub his father's name from the earth. But then those days he tended to remember that his father had not quite loved his children more than his art, and that stung too deep.

The dowager sat in a crumpled heap in the middle of the gallery, much as Fiona had the last time they'd been here, and Fiona joined the older woman, wrapped her in a hug, rocked her back and forth. Zander knelt near them, offering what strength and solace he could, but he could not quite find true empathy for her, not when she seemed to love her art and mourn its loss as if it were a husband, a child. His jaw was hard, his teeth grinding, and he took several voices to relax the angry muscles.

Finally, sobs subsided, and Lady Balantine rose on shaky legs, supported by both Fiona and Zander.

"Let's take you back to the other house," Fiona said, clutching the woman's arm.

Lady Balantine nodded with watery eyes and dislodged curls, and they got her almost into the hallway when she turned to Fiona with wide eyes. "Your paintings. Your ..."

"Forgeries." Fiona's mouth was a grim line. "Yes. They are gone."

The dowager snapped her gaze to Zander. "And your Rubens ..."

"Gone as well, my lady."

"Oh." Her already pale visage lost what was left of the blood in her cheeks, and with one final moan, her eyes rolled back in her head and she fainted.

Zander caught her with a grunt. "Devil take it! When did I start making women faint?" He swept her into his arms and picked his way carefully down the stairs and into the other house, where they found her bedchamber and laid her on the bed.

"Well"—Fiona collapsed with a sigh into a shadow-drenched chair in the corner of the room. "Technically I did not faint. I only pretended to. Have other women fainted around you recently?"

God, what an amusing woman. He should not laugh but he wanted to. He would not laugh, but he dropped to the floor beside her chair, breathing in her soft scent as he let his head fall back to rest on the cushion beside her leg.

Today was not amusing. Today the plot thickened and the shadows gathered. Today they'd found answers but also more questions. He closed his eyes.

And her fingers crept like tendrils into his hair, tugging gently, smoothing it away from his forehead, taming, stroking against his skull in a caress of comfort he'd not known since childhood.

Could dragons soothe as well as snort?

Seemed so.

Today had knocked him flat and not simply because they'd gotten everywhere and nowhere at once. More shockingly, today he'd realized he'd found a woman who could make him see the world's brightness in the dead dark of midnight, and if he was not careful, he might never want to let her brightness go.

Seventeen

⌒⌒⌒

M en's hair should not be so soft. Unfair, it was.
Horribly so. She never, in fact, wanted to slip her
fingers out of Zander's hair, though she should
not have dared to slip them in there to begin with. Not with
the dowager fainted on the bed, not with her clear lack of
knowledge of the paintings' whereabouts. So much for her
idea that she might be touring Europe with the paintings by
her side. An unlikely scenario to begin with.

As unlikely as Fiona's fingers stuck for eternity to a handsome man's scalp.

But that might very well happen, too, because she simply
could not concede the area she'd won with such casual boldness. He'd brought it on himself, really, seeking her out this
morning to have her by his side, telling her he could not do
without her observations, her knowledge, making her feel
useful instead of disposable. He'd assured, really, with all that,
her fingers would be eternally fussing in his hair.

"Zander," she ventured.

"Hmm." The sound rather like a purr as she stroked a lock
of his hair behind his ear.

"What do we do now?"

He opened his eyes, those dark orbs staring straight into her, though muscle and bone to the ephemeral bit of Fiona that she'd never thought another person would see so well. "I wish I knew. I'm rather ... at a loss."

"Yes. I was afraid you'd say that."

He lifted his head, and the side of her thigh hated the rush of cold air, missed the light pressure of his head nestled against it. He turned to view her more fully, and his hands found her waist, squeezed pinpricks of heat into her with each of his fingers, even through shift and stays and gown. "There's still the rumor we've put about. That I've a Rubens for sale. We'll see what comes of it. Don't cry, Fee."

She hadn't been going to, but he'd said her name with such tender care, and, well, now she just might.

A moan from the bed brought them both to their feet and to the dowager's side.

Fiona knelt by her bedside and placed a hand to her cheek. "Lady Balantine. Lady Balantine, please wake."

"My paintings," the lady moaned. "My art."

"Come to, my lady," Fiona pleaded. "Please."

Zander placed a hand on her shoulder. "Patience. She'll come to."

And then she did, popping upright, her waist as the hinge between two boards.

Fiona lurched back with a gasp, falling against Zander's legs then scrambling off them as the dowager broke into a chaos of sobs. Fiona jumped onto the bed and wrapped the older woman in her arms for the second bout of tears in less than half an hour. She whispered consoling words into Lady Balantine's ears, and Zander shoved his hands in his pockets.

"I've been looking for them," he said weakly. "I'll keep looking. We have contrived another plot, but we must wait for it to produce results." He sounded so resolute, so sad, too, and she wanted to tackle him to the ground and demand to know the reasons for the waver in his voice."

The door to the room burst open, and a tall, thin man with a floppy mop of brown hair flew through. "What in the devil's name is this? Mother, who are these people?"

"Ah." Zander pulled Fiona from the bed. "The son, I presume."

"I am her son, but that does not answer my question."

Lady Balantine sniffled. "Herbert, these are my friends and business associates, Lord Lysander and Miss Frampton."

Herbert stiffened and curled his face into a sneer. "What are you two doing in my mother's bedroom? While she wails inconsolably?"

"I was doing my best to *console* her." Oh how lovely her fist would feel in his face. Where had he been when his mother was so distressed? Where had he been when her paintings were stolen? Where had he been for years while his mother filled her lonely life with paintings and statuary that could not talk back to her? "You listen, Lord—"

"Not now," Zander hissed near her ear.

"I think you should leave. Now." The baron pointed toward the door.

But Fiona stood her ground, fisted her hands. "No. I'm not leaving unless her ladyship wishes us to."

Lady Balantine reached for her. "It's all well, darling. Come back later when I've recovered from the shock. We'll have much to speak of."

Zander's hand curved round her wrist and did not loosen easily or quickly when Fiona tugged, but she tugged again, and he let her return to the dowager's bedside.

"Are you sure?" Fiona asked. "I can stay and—"

"No. Go, dear. I need to be alone for a while."

"Did you hear my mother?" The baron shoved a finger at the door. "Leave."

"We are," Zander growled. He gathered Fiona to his side and ushered her through the door, which slammed shut behind them.

Out on the street, Zander quickly helped her into a hack. For several moments, the only sounds were from outside the conveyance—the rumble of wheels, the whinnies of horses and rattle of reins. Inside the hack, they both seemed to breathe too slowly, too softly, to make a single rustle of the air around them.

But all the things she wanted to say boiled up in her, and Fiona's body began to move. First, her toes tapped, then her fingers on the hard wooden bench. Then, her teeth bounced about on her bottom lip, and she clenched and unclenched the muscles of her legs.

"You have something to say?" Zander said. "I recognize it bubbling up in you. You can't sit still."

"We must talk."

A breath more of silence, conversational hesitation that allowed Fiona to gather her bouncing thoughts and put them into some sort of order.

"Yes," Zander said. "We must plan. Though I'm not sure exactly what more we can do. I'm beginning to feel—"

"No. Not that." She did not wish to hear the word that would end his sentence, likely one to ring a bell of doom, to sink her soul low, but he was right. They were at an impasse in the matter of the paintings, and there was really only one topic of conversation to be had. "I mean we must talk about last night's kiss."

"I don't see why. Things that happen in masks aren't real."

"Oh?" She arched a brow. "As I recall, we had removed the masks."

"Ah. Yes, well—"

She threw herself across the hack to sit beside him. "Zander. I have little patience or elegance. I pursue what I want with, as you well know, little consideration for my own well-being."

"You say that as if you're proud of it," he said, folding his body into the corner farthest from her.

"I am, rather. Not all days does it do me in. Sometimes it rather makes life better."

"And this supposedly beneficial, definitely chaotic quality of yours is pertinent right now because—"

"I want you. Oh, don't sputter. And don't try to jump out of the hack. It's moving much too quickly. You'll hurt yourself. I don't want you, as in your name or your hand in marriage. I am aware of your reasons for remaining a bachelor."

He lurched forward, holding his empty hands out to her. "I have nothing, Fiona. Everything I have I give to others except for the means to clothe myself well, a necessity of my occupation. My clients want to see the little lordling when they look at me to know they are getting insider information as they climb their way toward social suitability. But other than clothes and food, Fiona, everything goes back to Briarcliff and Raph, my brother and his home, my home. The only home I have. I cannot provide one for a wife myself." He fell back into the corner, into the shadows, his arms falling lifeless at his side.

A muddle. Because when she said she didn't want him that way, she didn't fully mean it. It had felt like the right thing to say, because it felt like what he wanted her to say, needed her to say. A small part of her brain and a hidden part of her heart had begun to paint a portrait, though, of a man and a woman that looked a bit like them, of children and perhaps a dog. Or cat. Both. Why not? It was a dream, after all. All of them living in a little terrace home near the shop, within reach of Mayfair so he could visit clients and curate art collections, so they could visit that lovely lady, his sister, and take strolls through Hyde Park on days she was not designing a new piece to make Foggy's eyes pop out of his head.

She could see it so well. But neither of them had any means of bringing the picture to fruition. That did not mean, however, that she could not have him in other ways. In what little time remained between them.

"Not marriage," she said softly, watching London pass by in a blur outside the window. "An affair. Brief." But necessary. She turned her head and met his gaze.

He slumped in the shadows, but his dark eyes blazed like stars in the semidarkness.

She folded her hands in her lap and kept that gaze without letting it consume her. "I do not want to wed unless I feel a passion for my husband, and at this moment, I cannot imagine feeling such a passion for any man but you."

The stars in his gaze flashed out as if he'd closed his eyes. "It will pass. With time."

She rather thought it wouldn't. It would be with her when she drew her final breath. "I expect nothing from you but pleasure, lessons I'll likely have little chance to practice in my life. But for now. With you. Keep in mind I am no lady. I am a jeweler's daughter. And a forger. You cannot ruin me." The brief grin she flashed slipped from her lips slowly as she planned her next words. "I would like to know all that you can teach me, and you will find me an eager student, an eager participant."

The hack rolled to a stop, and Fiona took in a heavy breath, filling her lungs with his silence. He did not stop her from opening the door and descending, and before she closed it, she found him in his dark corner, the vague outline of his body, the pale shadow of his face.

"If you are willing, I will be in the shop tonight past midnight. Waiting."

His eyes flew open, and she could see those stars once more.

She'd wait tonight for him to come to her, but she would not wait now for a reply. She slammed the hack door and fled to the safety of the shop.

Posey looked up from the counter as Fiona entered. She wove her way quickly around it and took Fiona's face in her hands. "Fee, you do not look well. You're red as a rose." She growled at the door, "Did Lord Lysander hurt you?"

"No. And he's not outside. It has merely been a trying hour or so."

"Why did you rush away with him?"

"Lady Balantine has returned to town. But she has no idea where the paintings are. It had always been a thin hope that she would have some idea, would have moved them to another location or some such, but"—Fiona pressed her eyes closed, finally letting the significance of the final few hours penetrate her fully—"that is not the case."

"Then the"—Posey glanced around the shop to make sure they were alone—"paintings are truly gone?"

"Likely sold."

Posey licked her lips and smoothed her skirts as she often did when thinking. "Should you ... leave?"

"Leave? I'm supposed to design a bracelet for Lady Ankling."

"No. I mean ... should you leave the country? Flee to the Continent? Farther, if necessary. I would miss you terribly, but better that than—"

"Please do not say it. I'm only in danger if someone notices they are not real."

"You're terribly good, yes?"

Fiona nodded, though even the most skilled forger had weakness. Being caught was always a danger.

"I wish you'd never—"

"Me as well."

Fiona stumbled toward the workroom, and Posey returned to her place behind the counter as the shop door creaked open. The chair Fiona pulled from beneath the workbench made a screeching noise, but Fiona barely heard as she slouched into it. With numb fingers, she pulled her notebook to her and opened it to a blank page, took up her charcoal, and began a mindless design. When done, she turned the page and sketched another. And another. And another, and she did not stop until Posey entered the room and reminded her of the time. They closed the shop and returned home arm in arm.

Fiona ate dinner in silence, and she prepared for bed in silence, donning a clean shift and wrapper and brushing her hair out in mindless strokes. She braided her hair and laid in bed until she heard the clock strike the midnight hour. Then she donned her boots and her pelisse to hide her dishabille and her cloak to hide her identity and made her way back onto the street before their house.

"Hell!" A hiss like an angry snake. "You are not so daft as this suggests, Fiona." A hand wrapped around her elbow and pulled her into the shadows.

She was not afraid, and she did not jerk away because she knew who held her arm, wanted him there. Well, not precisely there—holding her elbow angrily in the street—but this was moving in the right direction. And her numbness from the entire day began to shake away.

"I'm glad you know it," she snapped, yanking her arm away and setting her steps toward the shop.

He followed with long, angry strides, his boots slapping the street. "But this, *this*, makes me question everything. You've snuck out to walk the London streets past midnight. Alone. That is precisely what I consider daft behavior."

"I am aware of the risks. I was willing to take them.

Besides, I'm not alone." She hated to sound smug. But also … she didn't.

"You did not know I would be here."

"But you are." Oh, he was, and that meant tonight they would continue what they'd begun at the auction. Her stomach flipped over, and her stride lengthened. She nearly ran.

He didn't though. His long legs strode beside her at a normal pace. "I almost wasn't. But in the end I couldn't let you traipse to the shop alone in the middle of the night."

She stopped and grasped his arm to stop him, too, then she looked up into his face. "Is that the only reason you came? Because if so, I suppose I should return home."

"Double hell." He jerked her forward. Toward the shop.

A thrill rippled through her, and she almost skipped the rest of the way. She unlocked the door quickly and pocketed the key before the world went upside down. His hard shoulder beneath her belly, his backside in the very center of her line of sight. The brute had tossed her over his shoulder!

"Put me down," she demanded. Useless. She'd had to whisper it, hadn't she? So no lurkers on the street would hear her. But he likely didn't hear her either.

He kicked the door closed and carried her all the way back to the shop. When the world tumbled around her once more, she landed on a hard surface with a thud that shook the breath from her.

The worktable. She sat on it.

His angry face, hovering above her.

He slammed his hands down onto the table on either side of her and leaned in close. No candle or fire gave light to the room, and she felt him more than saw him, the warmth of his breath on her cheek, the heat of his body everywhere else. "I'm enraged. At you for risking yourself as you've just done. And at me. Because I can't say no."

His lips. On hers like a magnet. He needed no light to find her.

She moved like the slash of charcoal against paper when the ideas poured forth with ease—quick and without thought—wrapping her arms around his neck and pulling herself up to deepen the kiss. He'd parted her lips with his tongue last night. She did the same to him now, and he did not hesitate to let her, then to push her legs apart and step between them.

"I need closer," he growled.

She ran her hands down his back. Was that allowed? It felt right, and it was the best way to give him what he wanted. She wrapped her hands low around his back, just before that muscular rise of his backside, and used the long strength of his body anchored to the floor to pull herself across the table until high on her inner thighs met his hips. He arched toward her, increasing the pressure of their bodies against one another. His hands flew from the table to the line of buttons closing her pelisse, and he made short work of them, flicking the fastenings open and peeling the pelisse down her shoulder, discarding it.

"You," he growled as he did so, "vex me."

"I thought I amused you," she breathed.

"In spades." He kissed her neck, bit it so she yelped, then licked it.

"Is that ... is that usual? The biting. I've been wondering—"

He kissed the spot and the warmth of his breath spiraled across her skin.

"Oh, never mind if it's usual. I don't particularly care because—" She could not breathe. He yanked one shoulder of her wrapper down. "Because ..." she tried again.

He yanked the other side of her wrapper down, untied the thing entirely, and with eyes dark with desire, pushed it open, looked on her body, covered now only by the shift. "You are well prepared for this encounter."

What had she been trying to say?

He stilled above her, and she used the pause to gather her breath and her wits. Oh yes. She liked it, the biting. That's what she'd been about to say. She opened her mouth to tell him, but he descended once more, ravaging her lips like a starving man. His hand clutched at the bodice of her shift, almost quivering. He pulled from the kiss and laid his head on her forehead.

"Fiona," he said, his voice deep and dark as onyx, as the hell he so often evoked, "I am not going to ruin you tonight. I refuse, but I cannot deny you." A brief huff of hard-edged laughter. "Nor me, the delights of pleasuring your body."

If her body had not already been hot as coals, it would have burst into that heat then, but all she could do was continue to simmer in her need, her blood sizzling along her veins, stars flaming across her skin, an explosion waiting to happen.

"I am not a good man, not truthful or talented or kind. I take advantage of people and situations, and I'm about to take advantage of you. Do you understand?" His grip tightened on the bodice of her shift, and he pulled her closer.

Her head tipped back on her neck. Her eyes found the sensual outline of his lips and could not look away. "I do."

He dragged his lips up the column of her throat with an inhale that seemed to make him twice as broad of shoulder as before, and when he came to her lips, making her body shiver, making her hands cling to him anywhere they could, he said, "Tonight, I'm going to make you scream, little dragon. I'm going to make you roar."

Then he wrenched her bodice down and cool air spiked across her breast. He kissed her where only he had ever touched, where no other man would ever touch her. Only him, and never again if not him.

She clutched at his waist and let her head fall forward, onto his shoulder warm and soft and too fully clothed. She raked her hands up his back, and though the pleasure he spiraled at the nipple of her breast was exquisite, she lifted his face to her for a kiss she took control of. Just as she took control of his cravat, tugging on one end, his fingers flying to help her, then unwinding, unwinding, unwinding until his neck—strong and corded—opened up to her hungry gaze. She kissed that neck, kissed the line of his jaw.

"Do ... do you like that?" she stammered.

"Hell yes. There's this little spot behind my ear that—" He hissed. "There. Yes, you vixen."

"I want to learn all your secret spots."

"You'll hoard them?" He leaned away, his gaze glued to her breast, his hands coming up to cup them, squeeze them.

"Yes," she moaned. "All mine."

"All yours."

Good thing he agreed.

His hands slid down her ribs and cinched her waist for one brief breath, and then he slid his hands, fingernails dragging slightly against her skin, down the tops of her thighs as he lowered to his knees before her.

She tilted her head and looked down into his gleaming onyx eyes. "What are you—"

"Do you remember the auction? When I touched you"—he blew softly against the juncture of her legs—"here."

She shivered. "Yes." Of course she remembered. Diamonds and black velvet. "I felt ... I felt ... every muscle tight and hard like a diamond *is*, but every nerve in my body, my blood even, sparking with fire, as a diamond looks. In the heat of flame or light." Or his touch.

"There are other ways to make you feel like that."

The mere idea that he might be about to apply one of those ways sped up her heart, made her ache to touch him more, to get the business started. "How fortuitous. I assume you're about to show me one of those ways?"

That grin widened, a thief's smile, one that promised mischief. Then he gripped the hem of her shift and pulled it up, pooled it around her hips, pressed her legs farther apart, and settled kisses on the sensitive inner skin of her thigh. Kissing slowly, methodically, inch by inch, higher and higher until his mouth teased where his fingers had at the auction.

And then, well, other than the inky curls on the top of his head, she saw very little. But felt everything. At first, each lick and tease and suck and kiss seemed odd, each sensation the actions curled through her, indescribable, but the more he worked between her legs, the more boneless her body became.

She flattened her palms on the large worktable behind her to hold her weight, but they too had lost their strength. She collapsed backward onto the same table she sat at every day, the table where she spread wire and jewels and tools and paper and ink designs and tried to create something of her own that would not ruin her. Hard and cold, provided a solid surface, changing only with the years, only when the work done upon etched its mark.

Would they mark this table, too? She certainly would never look at it without a blush again because here he spread her open and created her anew—skin of diamonds and hair of twisted gold, eyes of emerald and ruby lips, a woman crafted to receive pleasure, whose every nerve screamed his name and whose fingers had found the silk of his hair, tugged it, urging onward, toward more.

And oh, he gave more.

He nipped the sensitive flesh of her inner thigh, and her fingernails dug into the wood, the only outlet for her ferocious need and wanting, for the desire he flamed higher with each lick and suck and puff of warm breath. He kept his hands busy, too, caressing up the outside of her thighs, fingernails scraping the worn linen of her shift down her skin then back up, a roughness of sensation to counter the delicate whirls of pleasure at her center.

Delicate? No. They screamed and cursed and demanded, and her hands found his shoulders, dug into linen to flesh and muscle as he did at her thighs, and had he called himself imperfect? A bad man with no talent? Ignorant, is what he was, of his own worth. Of his ... of his ...

Her back arched off the table, and she cried out his name as pleasure took every diamond of her body and ruby of her mind and broke them, scattered them, left her open and raw and tingling. Breathless and boneless, all her thoughts went the way of the jewels. That is, gone entirely.

His mouth left her body, and his hands dug tight into her legs, and for a moment, his rapid breathing gave the room a heartbeat. Then his body covered hers, large and warm, and he gathered her off the table and carried her across the room. He settled her in the armchair by the grate and left her. He did not go far, only to find a tinderbox and light a fire, then he picked her up once more and settled in the chair with her on his lap.

Sleep or hold him to her tight so he could not walk away? A true conundrum as drowsiness took her.

"Don't leave," she said. "Not yet."

"Not yet." But the two words sounded more like a single one.

Soon.

Eighteen

Fiona woke warm and cozy and cuddling against something rather hard. Should be uncomfortable. Felt like heaven, but where ...? Ah, yes. Now she remembered.

Zander had laid her bare on the worktable and poured her body to brimming with pure pleasure. And it wasn't enough. As her body came to full wakefulness, all bits of her touching all bits of him, she wanted more, knew she would not let him go until she had it. Had him. She nuzzled his chest and scratched her fingers down his chest, stretching against him. If she were a cat, she would have purred. She felt like purring. Finally, she opened her eyes and lifted her face to his, found him looking at her, his dark eyes hard and glittering.

"You didn't leave," she said.

He brushed a lock of hair behind her ear, and where his fingertips brushed her skin, she burned. "Not yet."

Not yet meant something else, especially with the surety of time—soon. She licked her lips and found her courage and spoke. "Zander, thank you."

"For ruining you?" No humor there.

She took a deep breath to decimate her hesitation. "For making me feel so wonderful, for trusting me that I know what I want for my body and my life." He nodded, his jaw tight. "Zander?" No movement, as if he'd turned to stone. "Would you give me more if I asked for it? Would it ... hurt you to give me more?" She rubbed her forehead and closed her eyes. "That's not precisely what I mean. What I mean, I suppose is, will you feel much guilt if you show me more? Because I want more. From you." Only from him.

"And where would I do that," he said finally, his voice hard. "On the table again?"

She winced, feeling the promise of bruises from earlier. "If that is what we must do."

"There are other ways. You could straddle me in this chair."

"Oh." Her hand fluttered to her lips as she tried to imagine the pose. "Yes, that seems ... nice."

"Nice?" He inched closer, those dark eyes feral now. "What if I took you against the wall? Would that be *nice*?"

"I'm not positive since I've not tried, but—"

"Or if I laid you on the floor before this cold grate and thrust into you?"

She smoothed his hair back from his forehead, trying to soften him. "I have a pelisse that might soften things a bit."

He growled and turned away from her. "I have no bed to offer you, Fiona. Not even a room that belongs to me. We are locked up in a workroom in your father's shop because I have nothing. Do you understand?"

She thought she did, so she took his hand and uncurled it from its hard fist shape and placed it on her chest, just above her beating heart. He did not speak of the current moment only. He spoke of all his moments, his every day before he met her and all the days he expected in the future. And that made what she wanted seem less scandalous, less wrong. Because she did not want him for what he could provide her outside of their two bodies together. She had no need for a man who owned a home but who would never understand why she had done the things she'd done in her past. She would never marry because she'd have to confess her sins, have to burden her husband with them, mark him.

But she was a woman awakening, and she finally understood what she would lose by giving up on the marriage bed. Strong arms and a chest to sleep on, soft kisses on the forehead, and hard eyes glittering with lust. More important, he knew her, knew her sins and her failures, knew her quirks and her flaws. And he still wanted to treasure her like he did that bit of broken glass in his pocket.

Lips could say more when not speaking, so she pressed hers against his and whispered into the kiss, "Please. Wherever you take me, just take all of me."

He hesitated to meet her lips fully, breathing hard, staring down at her, his arms like steel, binding her close, strong ribs holding in his heart. "I shouldn't."

Such hard words, but they held such hope with their unspoken *but*.

Another growl, then he showed her what he would do in spite of what he shouldn't, closing the distance between them, turning the hesitant hovering of his lips over hers into a hard claiming of her mouth.

Then he ripped away from her, stood, and dropped her into the warm hollow of the chair. He used the tinderbox to light the fire, and once it was roaring, he found her pelisse where it had dropped beside the worktable and stretched it out before the flames at a safe enough distance so it—they?—wouldn't get scorched.

Too late. Watching his long, lean body work efficiently and with speed to carry out what he clearly saw as practical necessities fired her, having him take care of her comfort, as he saw it, reassured her. She'd made the right decision. She would never regret what happened tonight.

Finished with his tasks, he knelt before her, head bowed, big hands rubbing up and down her thighs. "I will not do anything to get you with child."

"As my mother tells it, you must be inside me for that to happen."

"Your mother is an informative woman."

Fiona outlined his ear and pinched his earlobe. Still, he kept his head bowed. "She is," Fiona said. "Thankfully. But ... Zander ... I want it all. All of you. That means I want—"

His hands curled into fists on top of her legs. "Yes." A hiss of a word. "But I'll guard against a babe." Finally, he lifted his head and met her gaze.

She offered him a smile, small but confident, and he swept an arm under her legs, placed the other behind her back, and lifted her, carried her to the thin pelisse stretched before the flames and laid her down. His knees hit the floor on either side of her legs, and she sat up to meet him, to tug the buttons of his waistcoat loose, to push it off his shoulders, to lick her lips as she reached for the band of his trousers and fisted her hand into the linen tucked tight there. Up. A good direction for a shirt to go, for his shirt to go, revealing skin pulled taut against hard planes of muscle, dark hair lightly dusted across abdomen, and high across this chest.

He lifted his arms to allow her to do as she wished—toss the shirt over his head. He caught it, though, at the last moment, and bundled it up, reached behind her and settled it on the floor. A makeshift pillow? Her comfort his focus? The man knew how to wrench her heart from her chest without even trying.

Her focus? Him. She outlined the contours of his muscles, the dips and cliffs, and marveled at discovering a love for the texture of the hair around his navel, the hair that arrowed lower toward parts yet unseen. Quite ... crisp. She wanted to paint him. Felt inspired. She might have found the one thing she could render with any passion on her own—Lysander Bromley's body. So much better than a still life composed of fruit. So much more enticing than copying a dead man's work. If she could paint Zander, she might actually enjoy painting.

Where was her reticence? She should have some, yes? But she seemed to lack it entirely. A thought, a desire, popped into her head, and her fingers answered the call, tracing the narrow shape of his waist, smoothing over his ribs, admiring the slabs of muscle at his chest, the hard rounds of his shoulders. Marble come to life, more beautiful than any art she'd ever seen.

His hands, hot and gentle, wrapped around her shoulders. "Have you changed your mind? You can, you know. Just say the word at any time, and I'll—"

"No!" She lunged for him, wrapped her arms around his bare middle. "No." That one a whisper against his skin. "I have not changed my mind, and I will not change it. It is only that I've never seen a male form before. Well ... one made of real flesh and bone. I was taking my time. Admiring. Savoring."

"Minx," he chuckled. Then his hands cupped her face and tilted it up for another kiss. May there always be other kisses.

There likely would not be. A thought to break her heart, and she had no time for heartbreak this night. It was not part of the tale she was weaving for herself. So she kissed him back hard, shoving away the shadows, and hooked her hands in the band of his trousers.

Those, oh yes, those were next. He had her all but naked under him, and she wanted reciprocity. One button and one slightly trembling hand and one corner of his fall loosed. And she almost lost focus because he had pulled the neck of her shift down over her shoulder and had begun a seduction there with his mouth.

"I love the way you taste," he said, nipping her collarbone.

She swallowed and took care of another button.

He licked his way up her neck.

She flicked open another.

He tilted her head to the side and tugged her earlobe between his teeth.

Enough. No more. Buttons all done, she shoved his trousers down his lean hips and looked her fill.

"Change your mind yet?" he grumbled near her ear.

"No. Never."

Then the sight of him, long and thick—and frankly a bit unnerving—disappeared because he bound his arms around her like iron, and the length of him pressed into her belly, only the thin cotton of her shift between them. She liked the feel of that, though she'd missed her chance to touch.

She broke their kiss to look up at him, to hold his face still and meet his gaze. "Have you changed your mind? I want everything you can give me, but I do not want you to regret any of it."

He shook his head, an almost imperceptible action that punctuated the slow rise and fall of his chest. Something clever and quick was happening behind his eyes, and when he spoke, he did so without hesitation. "I will regret nothing. And I will give you everything."

He laid her down then, slowly lowering her to the pelisse, positioning her head on his balled-up shirt. He kissed down her neck, down the length of one arm. He placed a kiss on her navel, then dipped a thumb inside and dragged that thumb down, down, to the place already needing him between her legs. Then he kissed some more, over the sharp point of one hip and down her thigh. He lingered at her knee before making his way down her shin and placing a long, slow, sweet kiss over the thin bones of her foot.

She shivered and arched, and now that he'd touched her to transformation twice, she suspected what was to come.

He dragged his lips back up the length of her body, taking an alternate route between her breasts, which he stopped to play with—puckered, licked, and teased—until she arched and moaned and tangled her hands in his hair. Then he moved on, not to her lips for another kiss, but to the shell of her ear to whisper, "I know you are a dragon and like to have things your way, but this once, *this once*, let me have mine. Let me show you gentle and slow. Let me show how to make the best of a hard floor and hurried night. Let me show you what I want for you, what you are worth."

Hard floor? She'd not noticed. Not with him so hard above her. She grasped his hair at the nape of his neck and held him still, caught his gaze. "Only listen to me about what I want, only believe me that I want this, hard floor and all, only trust I am bright enough to understand what it is I am doing, risks and all, and that I choose to do it anyway."

He ripped out of her hold and kissed her hard, his body pressing against her. "I know," he said between stone-hard and coal-hot kisses, "I know. But still ... I wish. Shall I show you what I wish?"

She bit his bottom lip.

"Close your eyes," he said, "and let's put that brilliant imagination to good use."

She closed her eyes. In the darkness, every sensation magnified.

His voice, dark and deep near her ear, said, "Small home, cozy but lovely. A bed almost as big as the room." His voice descended into silent darkness. "No. A small bed so you can't roll too far away from me. Even in sleep. Then a fire roaring nearby, as now, so I can see every freckle. Did you know you have a constellation of them right here?" His lips soft on her shoulder pressing a kiss before returning to her ear. "God, they're amazing. Where was I? Ah. Pillows to spread your pretty hair out against, curtains drawn tight against the world. Your paintings on the wall. Your designs in a sketchbook nearby. And you. Nothing on, of course."

His hand appeared at her waist, and she felt it clench there, felt the thin material of her shift shimmy up her body, over her shoulders. Then off.

"Yes," he breathed. "Like this. Nothing better than *this*." His hands squeezed her waist. "Just you." His voice took on a hypnotic lilt. "You need no adornment." A soft chuckle. "He says to the jeweler's daughter in a shop brimming with valuable jewelry. But if I could break into a case and put any of these baubles around your neck, your wrists, your ankles ... if I could pool diamonds in your naval, sprinkle emeralds along your collarbone ... I would not. What good would they do? You have all the beauty you need already. They would merely get in the way."

Then his mouth disappeared from her ear, and a slight air blew between their bodies. "Do you want diamonds? And jewels?"

Something in his voice—unsure, wavering.

She opened her eyes, found him staring down at her, flames flickering shadows across his face.

"I can never give you diamonds."

Silly man. She'd lived her life with shiny things, and they had never tempted her much. She shook her head and cupped his cheek. "I prefer broken buttons and discarded wire. I prefer you."

She stroked her hands down his body as if he were the most precious of gems. Perhaps he was. To her. He hissed with the trailing touch, and she did what she'd not been able to do earlier, grasped him. A brazen thing for an innocent like her to

197

do? Was she even supposed to touch him as she was doing? She almost laughed. If she'd listened to *supposed tos*, she'd never have copied this man's paintings, never have met him.

His hiss became a clenched jaw, his hips rolling against her.

"Should I ... let go?"

"No." His hand cupped the space between her legs, and she found herself rolling against him. He stroked her as he had before, and as before, the sensation built an ache within her. Mimicking him, she stroked his shaft, and he buried his head in the curve of her shoulder, seeming to hold so very still.

She did it again, and he slipped a finger inside her in response, letting his thumb move in magic circles around the sweet throbbing bit of her body.

"Slow," he said, soft and low, as if to himself. "Slow, slow, slow." One hand at her core, he let the other roam up and down her body, lingering in places that bloomed beneath his touch. Each pathway he stroked seemed a thing of high art, of genius, the Rubens of her pleasure.

In comparison, she felt like a clunky novice. She was a clunky novice, with no idea of what to do, only of what pleased her and, according to his little sounds and the rhythms of his body, what he liked as well. So she let her hands roam as his did, one growing a fire between them and the other becoming a wanderer, a pilgrim over the hills and valleys of Lord Lysander Bromley. Shoulder, spine, and—oh, yes—a lovely backside she could linger on. Thighs like rock. Lovely too.

Sunlight. She wanted to do this in sunlight so she could see what freckles he had, what scars from childhood, so she could see how life had painted him like a canvas. The touching, even lacking sunlight, made her body glow. Every time she made him hiss, made his fingers work faster in her, on her, her pleasure doubled until she was clawing at his shoulders, biting at his neck, pleading, "Lysander. Lysander."

"Shh, my dragon," he said, kissing her softly, trying to tame her, failing, "I will. I will. But it might hurt."

"Lysander," she said again, tugging at his shoulders, biting his bottom lip. She was about to fall apart as she had on the table, as she had in the alcove. "Please."

Then he was between her legs, and his manhood replaced his hand, and poised above her, hands on either side of her body, he slid slowly into her.

"More," she demanded. It felt tight, but still, she needed to know more.

So he showed her, gritting his teeth, closing his eyes.

She rolled her hips, meeting his last thrust and gave a little cry. It felt tight. So very tight. He'd promised pain, and this was not the lovely building ache from before. Her clinging hands became bands hugging his body to hers.

"Breathe," he said. "I think. I've never done this with an innocent before."

She grunted.

"Breathe."

She tried to. Then she did, slowly but strongly. Then she remembered the glowing and how touching him had helped, so she did that, sliding her hands over his rear. "Touch me," she whispered, pressing her chest into his.

His hand came to her breast, his thumb flicking over her nipple.

And the spike of pleasure washed her in a wave of relaxation. The tightness stayed but the discomfort did not, and she lifted her hips to tell him all was well.

He kissed her cheek, her forehead, the tip of her nose. And began to move, long thrusts at first then faster, kissing, touching, making her glow all over again until the two of them made a sun on the floor of the workroom of Frampton and Son's, her own body the brightest diamond the walls had ever seen, fractured into sparkling multicolored rays of light. She cried out as that little earthquake she was fast coming to love shook her again and again, shook him, too, until her limbs went weak and wiggly, and she sank into the floor, and he went limp and became a lovely, heavy weight atop her.

She set her frantic breaths to the pace of his own, and he gathered her into his arms, rolled until she rested atop him, a contoured mattress only slightly softer than the floor but leagues more comforting. He'd not wanted to take her on the floor of a shop. He wanted to give her more. Silly man. Darling man. She focused on that as she drifted in a haze of satiated pleasure and not of the end of their adventures soon to come, not of the day he'd never set foot again in the shop or leave her a note or pull some bit or bob from his pocket to toss around as he thought.

But the focus provided no joy because though he said he wanted to give her more, he could not, and he had made that plain enough. She expected nothing. He'd lain with her only to— She frowned. He'd said he would protect against a child, but he had been inside her the entire time. The detail banished the fog of happy that had turned her muscles and limbs into slow, lazy rivers. She'd not even thought of it in the moment, not considered the implications. All she knew, even now, was that he must be inside her to create a child, and he had been. The entire time.

Until now. But surely now, after the act had come and gone did not matter. At least not to biology. It must be admitted it mattered rather a lot to the heart. His arms holding her tight, his heart beating beneath her ear, his lips whispering over her temples, his fingers drawing lazy shapes all over her body. *Now* mattered quite a bit. But did it *matter*? She suspected not. She suspected something had been forgotten. Should she speak of it?

She bit her bottom lip. No. To speak of it would be to ruin

this important *now*, and that she would not do, no matter the consequences of their unplanned actions.

But was it unplanned? Or had something in him shifted during the act, his plans changed without a word. And did those new plans include a future with her? Preposterous ruminations. She'd let her fancy run away with her again, but since she liked the direction in which it ran, she gave the thought, the wish, its head and grinned into the reckless winds of dreaming sleep.

Nineteen

Z ander stood on the street outside Fiona's home and
watched the black square of her bedroom window.
Not even a candle flame illuminated her form,
though she would have arrived by now. Perhaps she was
crawling into bed in the darkness. It would be cold and
narrow, softer—he hoped—than the table where he'd laid her
bare and made her scream his name, than the floor before the
fire where he'd taken her fully.

And forgotten in his panic of lust, the maelstrom of
emotion, to pull out of her, to do as he'd promised and
prevent a pregnancy.

Not a gentlemanly thing to do. Stand outside a woman's
window, watching.

Not a gentlemanly thing to do. Bring a woman not your
own to climax and force on her the risk of a child. He'd
promised her he would not. Promised her.

And he'd failed. Too dark a night inside himself, despite
the promise of dawn at the edges of the city, for even a bitter
laugh.

Of course he'd failed her.

And now he'd marry her. When she didn't want it. Another failure, that.

His boots should march him straight home. Well, to Theo's home. Or Maggie's. But he stood there, watching the nothing inside her window, which was as close to her as he could get, refusing to imagine what it might be like to share a bed with her night after night, wide and warm and full of laughter. And failing not to imagine it.

When pink dawn edged the city skyline, his boots finally lost their boulder weight and let his feet carry him away. Theo's or Maggie's? He had a room at Maggie's rather than a couch, so he made his way there and planned. He'd send a letter to Raph this morning, then visit Mr. Frampton this afternoon.

But hell, where would they live? A muddle, and even worse, a part of him clutched tight in the center of his heart celebrated this turn of events, beating with bursts of exultation, forgetting that Zander was a scoundrel who didn't deserve Miss Fiona Frampton. Not only did he swindle trusting old ladies out of valuable pieces of art in order to line rich men's walls, he'd come inside an innocent, damn the consequences.

But with Fiona, consequences seemed very much like miracles, like what he'd wish for if the bit of broken locket in his pocket granted wishes. *Bah.* Let that little bit of him be happy as it pleased, the rest of him knew ... he'd failed Raph again. Failed him the first time when he realized he couldn't go into the church. Then when he'd rented the paintings and had them copied. And now he'd ruined the best woman he'd ever known and would marry her and—

He stopped, backtracking several steps at the sight of an old black coach waiting outside Maggie's townhome like a squat spider. Odd, but not odd enough to rip him from the much-needed sleep beckoning to him from inside. Sleep first.

Before he wrote to Raph, before he paid Mr. Frampton a visit to tell him he'd doomed his daughter to a lifetime of need and deprivation. Hell. Hopefully a few hours sleep would help him see the matter in a less bitter light. He trudged toward the door.

"Lord Lysander."

He stilled, hand mere inches from the handle, and turned. "I am he."

Lord Balantine stepped down from the spider. "May I have a word with you?"

"Why?" Zander stepped forward, hunching his hands into his pockets. "I can assure you we meant your mother no harm. Both Miss Frampton and I are quite fond of her and—"

"It's about the Rubens you have for sale."

"Oh." He'd quite forgotten about that little intrigue in the intervening hours. "Yes, um, I'm exhausted, actually." And he couldn't take advantage of the dowager's son. "Come back this afternoon, and we can talk then." By that time, he'd have a plan made up, a justification for why he couldn't sell the nonexistent painting to the man.

"I'm busy this afternoon. I cannot come back." He stepped closer, his arms folded behind his back.

"Then tomorrow. I am in no place to discuss business matters at the moment. I have had an eventful twenty-four hours and am in need of rest. You understand." He yawned and nodded. "I bid you good day, and I look forward to our conversation. Later." He turned.

The swift snap of footsteps on the ground behind him warned him, but his body and brain were too sluggish to do much about it. He turned in just enough time to see the baron raise a heavy-looking marble statue above his head and crash it down onto Zander's temple.

Zander stumbled, and the man hit him again.

"Hell," Zander hissed, clutching his skull. The ground

rose up quickly to meet his falling body, and he had but one thought. *Felled by a baron wielding a statue of a man, cock out for all the world to see. The statue, not the baron.*

He couldn't taste defeat like that. He struck out his leg with every bit of force in his body, despite the blinding pain in his head, despite the blood flooding his vision, and he heard the *oof* followed by the thud of a body hitting the ground, a statue breaking.

Hoped that damned cock had broken off.

He dragged himself toward the door, but the world blanked around him, and before he could touch it, grasp its handle, darkness swallowed him whole, an oil painting gone up in flames, singed black around the edges first ... then nothing.

When Zander woke, the world swayed around him, and his head felt like it had been bludgeoned with a heavy object.

Ah. Wait ... memory flooded back. It had been. Well, at least he had a reasonable explanation for the pain, but what about the swaying?

He peeked open one eye and slammed it closed once more, lifting a hand to his head where his fingers met not soft hair but the crust of tangled blood.

"Hell," he hissed.

"Not Hell, Lord Lysander. Kent. Nearing one of my estates."

Zander pushed himself upright and forced himself awake, forced his eyes wide open. "Lord Balantine. Was this truly necessary? The Rubens could have waited." He kept his tone light, though every muscle in him raged to fly across the coach and show this man the fury of his fists. In time. In time, he would break that man's nose in at least five different places.

The man sat on the opposite side of the coach, and he leaned into the shadows, his long, lanky frame folding out from them at uncomfortable angles until he pulled his heels in and leaned forward into the dusty sunlight streaming into the space between them.

"I don't want the Rubens," Balantine said, "I want you."

"I am sorry, old chap, but I'm not for sale. Can't say I blame you, though." He swept his hand the length of his body and gave the cocky grin that curled the ladies' toes. "I'm exceptional."

Balantine flushed but kept his forward leaning position without flinching. "I want your skill."

"Skill? Don't have any of those. Who told you I had skill? Liar, they are. Fed you a right bouncer. I'm a worthless fourth son."

The corner of Balantine's thin lips quivered upward. "You're the most skilled forger I've ever seen."

What in Hell?

Zander quirked a smile, gave a laugh, tried to puzzle it out. "I can't paint my way out of a fully lit, unlocked house."

"That made no sense."

"See." Zander held his palms up flat, empty. "I don't even have a talent for verbal communication."

"You can prattle all day, but it doesn't make false what my mother told me when you left her home yesterday."

Dread pooled low in Zander's stomach and increased the pounding at his temples. *No, no, no.*

"'There goes,' dear Mama said, 'that talented forger I told you about.'" Balantine sneered. "My mother is a useless stream of nonstop gibberish, but she is no liar. And you are caught. I'll alert the authorities of your activities. Unless you help me."

There did not exist a curse word strong enough to express Zander's current emotional state. More practical thoughts crowded out the echoing cursing, and one in particular rang like a church bell through crisp winter air. *Protect Fiona.*

Because if the man had considered for one moment that a woman could be a skilled forger, Fiona would be in this coach going to Kent instead of himself. And he'd die before that happened, die to protect the woman he was bloody well going to marry when he got back to London because ... well because he had no other option. And not because he was a scoundrel who'd touched an innocent.

He'd learned anger from his father. And futility. But he'd also learned the value of love, and even though his father's scheme to will them paintings he knew to be fakes was a daily thorn in Zander's arse, without it, he would never have found Fiona.

Would never have fallen in love.

That was it. Not infatuation. Not some vague "something more." Not obligation because of what they'd done, but love ... pure and sweet, clear and inevitable. And no damn milksop of a baron would keep Zander from it.

"I admit nothing," Zander said, leaning back into the squabs and folding his hands over his stomach. He would admit nothing but deny nothing either. Keep the man's interest off Fiona without implicating himself past the point of no return.

"You do not have to admit anything. You just have to paint."

Ah. That would be the point of no return. Zander could not paint a single stroke.

"What do you want with a forger, anyhow? From what your mother has said, I thought you hated art."

"I do," Balantine snapped, leaning back with a dusty huff. "It's only good because others find it valuable."

Ah. That, Zander understood. Balantine wanted paintings, forgeries, for money.

Balantine's lips twitched. "Who knew my mother had so much of value in her possession?"

Zander stopped breathing. *Triple hell. All the hells ever.* He'd be dried up of them after this because ...

He forced the words out through a chest tight as an iron maiden. "Did ... you ... steal your mother's pieces?"

Balantine snorted. "What's hers is mine. Wasn't stealing. I reallocated all those funds gathering dust on walls and pedestals and put them to better use."

"Lining your pockets?"

"Feeding my family." Each word hard. "I have two small children and a wife and close to nothing left."

They hit Zander harder than the cursed statue had. What do you know? He had at least one more *Hell* left in him, but he kept to himself. Who knew what revelations were yet come?

"I understand," he said, as his chest loosened a bit. "Believe it or not, I understand."

"You? An arrogant bachelor and criminal?"

"Oy! Who are you to call me a criminal? You stole and sold off your mother's art." Had he? Or did he, by some miracle, still have the Rubens?

"Not all of it. I've had ... troubles." Balantine rapped his knuckles on the glass. "You'll soon see. That's why I'm taking you to my house in Kent. A dilapidated thing. More curse than inheritance." He turned his head like it was a cog on a pike and speared Zander with a hard gaze. "How is it fair that a man inherits his father's debt and the man's wife keeps all her own possessions. I'll tell you how. No one knew the wife had those possessions."

"You inherited massive debt, then?"

Balantine reddened. "No. Not as such. But keeping everything running costs money, and investing is not as easy as it seems." He wouldn't look Zander in the eye.

And no wonder. He'd inherited a flush estate and ruined it himself. At least he had the decency to know it even if he wouldn't say it.

"Perhaps," Zander said, wincing as the coach wheel hit a rut, "you should have asked your mother for help. I'm sure she would have—"

"No. She would not have. She loves that art more than she ever loved me."

Hell. There it was. The man's words could have come from Zander's own lips.

"Listen," Zander said, leaning forward and bracing his elbows on his knees. "I can see, thievery and abduction aside, you're a decent chap." A bit of a lie never hurt anyone. "I'd hate for you to get in trouble with the law. Let me go and—"

"And I'll tell everyone of your great artistic expertise."

Zander swallowed his growl and raked his fingers through his hair, yelped, then remembered too late not to touch anything above his eyebrow line. "What do you expect from me?"

"I expect you to paint exclusively for me."

And this charade would last only until Zander had to make his first brush stroke. Then, when Lord Balanbonkers realized Zander couldn't draw a straight line if his life depended on it, the memory of his mother's words—*there goes that talented forger I told you about*—would rearrange itself, focusing on the pretty little blonde with green eyes and lithe fingers who had walked at Zander's side that day.

Zander would kill the man sharing the coach with him before it came to that.

But he'd really rather not have to.

So he turned sideways on the bench, leaned against the side of the coach, and, stretching his legs out before him, crossed them at the ankle. He closed his eyes and spoke into the darkness. "Well, then, boss, what should I paint first?"

Much could come of this little subterfuge. Once he arrived at the man's crumbling estate, he'd have access to whatever art the man had hoarded there. Perhaps he would find the originals, his long-sought-after Rubens, collecting dust and waiting to be saved.

A new urgency settled around that goal now, and not simply because he had nearly accomplished it, nearly found them (if they'd not been sold), but because if he had his inheritance, perhaps he'd have a reason to create a piece of art that would win it for him. And he'd keep this money for himself.

To build a home for himself and his dragon.

Twenty

T he eardrops taking shape beneath Fiona's charcoal
pencil looked suspiciously like lips. Male lips of the
kind she had lately become familiar with.

Lately?

It had been almost a week since he'd walked her home, and
she'd heard nothing from him since. Had he been so mortified
by their dalliance, by her inexperience, he'd run off? To the
Continent likely. Farther afield possibly. To Africa? He was,
even now, on the prow of a ship (was that the right word?)
telling a tale of the pitiful spinster who kissed like a toothless
dog and knew not how to touch a man. Or he'd hid himself
away at the ancestral home, begging his marquess of a brother
to put him to work in the fields till he was so exhausted he
could no longer remember their nightmare of a night. Or—

No. She slammed her pencil down and slammed her eyes
closed. Enough. Her body knew them for lies, even if her heart
wasn't convinced. He'd been satisfied with her. He had never
pretended with her, and she believed him. He wanted her,
liked her touch, unskilled though it was.

Besides, five days was not an overly long time to have gone

without contacting her. He'd gone longer. His work required long stretches of time away from home, and he had no obligation to keep her abreast of his movements. He was likely on a trip for a client, and he would show up in a week's time with a devil-may-care grin and a tweak of one of her curls and news on the paintings they searched for.

Yes, the most likely scenario, that.

She opened her eyes and returned to her design, trying to block out the chatter from the front of the shop. They were busy today. With shoppers and with merchants. Mama was even about, viewing the gems their supplier had brought. Later, she'd tell Papa which she wanted, he'd purchase those. If they'd let Fiona design, she would get to partake in that conversation as well. Instead, she sat in the candlelit dark in the workshop, sketching when she should be, according to her parents—

"Fee, why aren't you painting?" Her mother rested in the doorway, Lillian pushing her chair from behind.

Fiona slammed her sketchbook closed. Mama would only scoff, tell her not to waste her time. "I needed to sit for a bit."

"You do not have to come here every day, you know," Mama said. "We can set up a room for you to paint in the back parlor."

Fiona tapped the top of her sketchbook with a single fingertip. "But everyone else is here. Papa's sketching, and Posey is dealing with customers, and you're doing sums and such. Why should I be anywhere else?"

"You should be at home to accept gentleman callers."

Fiona flattened her hand on the sketchbook and looked up, mouth open. "What gentleman callers?"

"There might be some if you stayed home now and then."

Fiona stood and came round the back of her mother's chair. She nodded her thanks to Lillian and took her place, moving her mother toward the fireplace. "You want me to marry?"

"That would be lovely."

"And what of Posey?"

Her mother frowned. "If she finds a fellow who tolerates her work, yes, that would be nice as well. You have no such limitations, though." She frowned. "Unless ..." She licked her lips and turned to peer up at Fiona. "Have you heard anything? From that Lord Lysander? From the dowager? Your father will not speak of it, and—"

"I have. Lord Lysander has, I mean." She sat in the chair across from Mama.

"Excellent! As soon as that business is taken care of, I'd like to introduce you to the haberdasher's son. He's a lovely, tall fellow training to be a surgeon. You two will prove perfect for one another, I'm convinced. You can paint all day and line his home with your work. His clients will value him more because of you and your accomplishments. And as he is a man of sense and intellect, you won't have to worry about your wandering mind. He'll take care of every detail for you."

Fiona dropped her face into her hands, near tears. She did not want that life at all, but no one would listen to her.

"Fiona." Posey's voice.

Fiona straightened and turned to the door where her sister stood, her eyebrows furrowed, her hands smoothing her skirts. "There's a man and woman here to see you. Will you speak to them?"

Fiona stood and tidied her hair in the small oval mirror near the fireplace. "Yes. Of course." She pushed her mother to follow her sister into the front of the shop and stopped when she saw the man and woman.

He looked like Lysander, only ... different. His hair lighter, his body slightly shorter, and bunched with muscle where Lysander's limbs were lean and tough. He did not have

Lysander's light grin, nor the twinkle in his eye that spoke of good humor. This man looked on the world not with amusement, but with bitterness.

The woman beside him had hair the color of a Titian painting, uncontrollably curly, and her face—perfectly proportioned to Fiona's painter's eye—wore a look of worry.

Other than them, the only other person in the shop was Papa, standing curious behind the counter. The jewel supplier must have left.

Posey pushed Fiona forward and replaced her behind Mama. "This is Lord Theodore and his companion Lady Cordelia."

Fiona blinked out of her stare and dropped a curtsy. "I am sorry to stare so. You look like someone I know." Someone she missed, even with so little time parting them.

Lord Theodore's grim mouth gave a little. "You do know someone who looks like me. My brother, Lord Lysander. I am afraid I know you better than you know me. I was leaving my sister's house the day you visited her and peeked in at you. And I've seen you with my brother at … other times, though your face was partially hidden." He dropped his voice with that last, as if he meant his words for her alone.

He'd been at the auction, too. "It is wonderful to meet you." He would know where Lysander had scurried off to, surely.

"It is lovely to meet you as well," Lord Theodore said. "But I am afraid I am not here for a social call."

Fiona's gut knotted. "Oh?"

"My brother is missing.

The knot became stone. Fiona's hand fluttered to her chest and circles of light danced before her eyes. Posey appeared at her side and held her tight with one arm round her waist.

Fiona pushed her away. "No, Posey. Thank you. I am

fine." She turned to Lysander's brother. "He's not traveling for a client?"

"No. He tells us where he goes and when, and he always returns to Maggie's house or to Briarcliff, our brother's estate. But Maggie says she's not seen him in almost a week, and he's not been at my rooms for longer. A letter to our brother at Briarcliff produced no Zander, and neither did a letter to our other brother in Manchester. He's ... gone. Unless you can produce him."

"I hope you do not mind," Lady Cordelia said, "our inquiring."

"I did not think it worth bothering you," Lord Theodore admitted.

"But I know better." Lady Cordelia reached out a hand toward Fiona. And lacking anything better to do, Fiona took it, found it squeezed hard between long, strong fingers. "I insisted on him visiting you and on my accompanying him. First because, well, he can be intimidating, and I hoped my presence might soften things a bit."

Lord Theodore snorted.

Lady Cordelia ignored him. "What Lord Theodore cannot comprehend is the way Lord Lysander looked at you when you appeared at the top of the staircase at the auction. And I saw you dancing together. I understood well what language that passed between you, even though I could not hear your voices."

"The *what*?" Posey's voice rose high and startled. "What auction?"

"What dancing?" Mama demanded.

"What *looking*?" Papa shouted, spittle flying.

"Confound it, woman," Lord Theodore hissed. "I was trying to save her from being found out."

Lady Cordelia winced. "Ah. Yes. I do apologize. I was rather ... overeager."

"What auction?" Posey repeated, her voice more heated than before.

Papa and Mama repeated their questions at the same time.

Found out. She'd have to spill all now, but she hadn't the time, not with Zander missing.

"I'll tell you about that later," Fiona promised.

"I'm positive," Cordelia continued, "that you are dear to Lord Lysander, and that he would not let you worry about him long. If anyone will have heard from him, it will be you."

Fiona shook her head. "I have not seen him since—" She glued her lips together before details slipped out that shouldn't. He did not wish to marry her, and if his very stern-looking brother knew that the last time she'd seen him had been after midnight, and that they'd been alone, and that she'd been scantily dressed, and that they'd lain with one another, shattered around each other … Well, he would demand Zander do the correct thing, the thing Zander did not want to do.

She shook her head again, this time slowly. "I have not seen him in days. I am sorry."

"Days?" Papa stormed around the counter and rushed toward them.

"Better to say weeks, daughter!" Mama clasped at her chest, as if to soothe her madly beating heart. "It's been weeks since he barged into our home and turned everything topsy-turvy. Answers, Fiona. Now."

Fiona faced her family, looking on each beloved but frustrating face one at a time. They wore worry like heavy cloaks, for her, for themselves, and she'd dressed them in those cloaks. She should divest them of those as well. But Zander was missing.

"I will explain all, I swear it," she finally said, "but Zander is more important at the moment." She set her lips firm and turned back to Lord Theodore. "What else, my lord?"

"Do you know anything about this?" Lord Theodore

pulled a piece of marble statuary from his greatcoat pocket and held it up to her.

She took it. "It's broken." A nude man, about the size of her forearm, heavy, one arm as well as its ... manhood ... missing. And stained a deep, violent red. "No, I cannot say I know it." And yet ... it seemed familiar, tried to spark a memory deep inside her mind. She could not place it, though, so she shook her head. "It is familiar ... but I do not know from where."

Lord Theodore took the statue back. "My sister found it outside her home almost a week ago, around the time Zander seems to have disappeared."

"Is that ... blood?" Posey's voice shook.

Almost a week ago. Around the time he disappeared. Could it have been the morning he left her, the morning after their night? Was that Lysander's blood?

Fiona shook her head over and over and over. "No. I know nothing." All she could say.

He bowed, stiff and curt. "Thank you, Miss Frampton. If you hear from him or discover any detail, please contact my sister. You know her address, yes?"

Fiona nodded, and they turned to leave.

First the dowager goes missing. Then the paintings. And now Zander. That last blow the worst, even if a swinging rope came with the other two.

"Wait!" She fled toward them. "There's one more person we should speak with about him who might know something." When three related things went missing, perhaps there was a connection no one yet saw. "Lady Balantine. We have been helping her locate her paintings." Fiona lowered her voice as Lord Theodore and Lady Cordelia turned back toward her. "*Your* paintings, my lord."

Lord Theodore inhaled sharply. "I see. Where is she?"

"I'll show you. Wait for me." Fiona rushed for the back room to don her pelisse, but her father stepped into her path.

"No, Fiona. You are not to leave this shop. In fact, you will return home this instant." Papa's hands were hard like diamonds. His face, too.

She swallowed hard. "I have to go."

"You have to do what your father says." Her mother's voice was calm, like always; but like always, it told Fiona what to do. *Sit still, focus, paint, stay home, marry a future surgeon.*

"No!" Fiona swept past her father and snatched up her pelisse, shoving her arms into it. "No, no, no." She stood tall before her family. "I love you. I love all of you. So very much." Ah, now the tears would fall, just one, a lone sign of her inner weeping. "I would not have done anything I've done if I did not, but I am not who you want me to be. And I cannot be that person. Mother befriends a duchess, and Posey is your apprentice, Papa. They live lives that suit them despite what the world might think of them. And I'm supposed to make up for their refusal to fit in by doing just that? No!" She'd said that word now more times than she'd ever said it to them before.

She paused, giving her family time to speak, to react to her long-coming rebellion.

They did not speak. Just remained frozen with mouths slightly parted and eyes wide, and thank goodness, because she still had plenty more to say. And the bloody statue in Lord Theodore's pocket gave her courage to say it all.

"I will not shrink myself to the accomplishments others think suitable, and I will not marry a man I do not know, and I *will* go find Lord Lysander because ... because he does not think me silly." Her voice had reached new heights, so loud the glass cases almost shook, their shiny wares inside them, too.

Posey reached out a hand, a statue coming to halting life. "Fiona—"

Fiona swiped the hand away. "No." It felt good to say. Again and again and again. "I have made mistakes. Of that I am well aware. And I am trying to rectify them. My mistakes are my duty to—"

Her father took a single step forward. "Nonsense!"

Mama nodded in agreement. "Your father is absolutely right, Fiona. Your mistakes came when you thought to do something we did not approve of, nor even knew of. Don't you see you do not have the brain to—"

"No!" She screamed it. She'd raise her voice as loud as it took for them to listen to her, to hear her finally. "I knew it was wrong, but I did it anyway, and you cannot comprehend the good it did us at the time. Or you are not willing to admit it. You would let me help in no other way. I have sketchbook after sketchbook filled to brimming with designs, and surely one of them will put that old Foggy to shame. But my helping seems to be most shameful to all of you. I am not ignorant. I am not useless. But I am willing to take risks for those I love, and despite your insistence on calling me silly and worse, I love you. And Lord Lysander needs me. So ..." She swallowed hard and stepped backward away from her family. "I'm going with Lord Theodore, and I will be gone as long as it takes to find his brother."

Mama held out a hand, a gesture of reconciliation. "Consider the propriety of it all, what it looks like. You cannot understand—"

"I do understand, yet I make this choice anyway." She took another backward step toward the two bodies waiting with held breath and averted eyes near the front door of the shop.

She turned on her toe and made a steady path toward them. Lord Theodore pushed the door open, and Lady Cordelia stepped onto the street.

A hand clasped Fiona's wrist. "Fiona," Posey, squeezing her hand. "I do not think you silly. I promise I do not. I love you, too, but ... a missing man, a mysterious auction ... why aren't you speaking with me?"

"I will," Fiona promised. "I'll tell you everything. But I must go now. He's *missing*, Posey. And my heart feels like it might bleed forever if we don't find him, if he's ..." She dashed at a tear rolling down her cheek and looked at her sister over her shoulder. "Will you please let me do this? It is what I must do, what I need and want to do. Because I ... I ... well, we have no time right now for me to explain how I feel about him, but—"

Posey released her only to push her toward the door. "Go. Be safe. And know I'm rummaging through your sketchbooks while you're gone."

Fiona smiled and stepped into the crowded street with Lord Theodore, then climbed into a hack with him and Lady Cordelia.

One short, tension-filled ride later, she was knocking on Lady Balantine's door, the others standing behind her like personal guards.

When the butler swept the door open, Fiona demanded, "I must speak with Lady Balantine."

"She's unwell, Miss Frampton." He eyed the two behind her. "And you are?"

"This is Lord Lysander's brother and his companion." No idea what else to call her. His friend? His ... mistress? But she couldn't say that out loud. His betrothed? Didn't matter. "May we come in and speak to Lady Balantine?"

"Now might not be the time for a chat," the butler said.

"Please." Her inflection made it sound like a question, as if she asked permission, but she edged her way inside, ducked beneath the butler's arm, and darted down the hall. "My lady!" She ran for the small downstairs parlor she knew to be the baroness's favorite that had been stripped bare. The paintings gone from the walls, the rugs missing, the statues—

Fiona gasped, the memory she'd been reaching for earlier slammed into her like a carriage at full speed. A statue of a naked man, about the size of her forearm used to live on the back corner of the mantel. It no longer did, and its absence almost brought her to her knees. She whirled in a circle and fisted her hands in her skirts, trying to gather her thoughts. But with her ladyship sunk lifeless and dull eyed in a chair near the window, and Lord Theodore and Lady Cordelia running down the hall toward them, she had no time for thinking.

She sank to knees beside Lady Balantine and grasped her hands. "My lady, what has happened here?"

Lady Balantine pulled up tall, the ire of a goddess in her eyes. "My son took everything. He said he needed it, that it would catch a pretty penny, and that I owed him."

"Your son took the statue? That used to be just there?" She pointed at the mantel.

"That and more."

Lord Theodore and Lady Cordelia entered the room, gazes flying everywhere. Did they notice what was missing though they'd never seen the room?

"Who are they?" Lady Balantine demanded.

"Lysander's brother, Lord Theodore, and Lord Theodore's ..."

"Friend," Lady Cordelia supplied. "I do not like being called his companion, as if he's an eighty-year-old dowager."

The real dowager in the room barked a laugh. "I like you, and I can't like much right now, so you're welcome to stay, the both of you." She patted Fiona's hand. "As well as you, my darling. But where is your beau, your Lysander?"

"That's why we've come. We don't know. He's been missing for nearly a week." She looked over her shoulder at

Lord Theodore. "Do you still have the statue? In your pocket?"

He pulled it forth, held it out to Lady Balantine. "We found this outside my sister's house. I have no particular reason to think it's related to his disappearance, but he was often traveling with valuable art, and it's not far-fetched to think someone might have—"

The dowager screamed. "That's mine! Is that ... is that *blood*?"

"She looks like she might swoon," Lady Cordelia said, looking at Lord Theodore.

"What do you wish me to do?" he asked. He looked sternly at the older woman. "Don't swoon. It's not helpful."

She broke off mid wail and blinked at him. "Perhaps you're right."

"That worked?" Lady Cordelia said..

"Of course it worked," Lord Theodore snapped. "Don't sound so shocked."

Never mind them. Fiona turned to the now calm but sniffling Lady Balantine who turned the broken statue over and over in her hands. "My lady, you say your son took this statue?"

"He did. He took it all. Loaded it into a coach and told me I'd served my purpose well." Lady Balantine dropped the statue to the cushion beside her and hid her face in her hands. No wails broke the wall of skin and bone, but her shoulder shook and near-silent cries filled the air around her.

Fiona wrapped her in a hug. "I'm sorry. So terribly sorry."

"If your son had the statue," Lord Theodore said, "and the statue was found bloody outside my sister's house—"

"It cannot be that Lord Balantine has Lysander, can it?" Lady Cordelia asked. "That he's ... harmed him in any way?"

Lady Balantine continued crying.

Fiona continued rubbing her back.

A pair of heavy footsteps, then Lord Theodore's deep voice. "Lady Balantine, do you have any idea where your son has gone?"

She lifted her face to them and spoke steadily. "No. But he was in the coach with the family seal on the side, painted in blue. It's quite distinctive. Please." She grabbed at Lord Theodore's hand and pulled him closer. "Please find him. If he has harmed Lord Lysander, I will never forgive myself."

Lord Theodore pulled his hand from her embrace. "I'll follow up on this information, Lady Balantine. Thank you for your help. And I'm sorry for your sorrow. I'll let you know as soon as I know anything."

She patted Fiona on the hand. "You are distressed, too, my love, and you must go home and rest." She pushed Fiona to her feet, then wavered and sank back down, hiding her face in the arm of the chair, her shoulders heaving though she made no sound.

"I must return you to your sister," Lord Theodore said, turning to her and sweeping her toward the door.

"No." Fiona anchored her feet to the floor. "I want to help, and I cannot sit still. I cannot go home when Lysander may be far from his. And hurt."

Lord Theodore's shoulders stiffened. "I must inquire around town about the coach Lady Balantine described. If I discover anything, I'll send word. I swear. I may have to hie after him. My lady"—he turned toward the dowager—"where is his estate?"

"Oh! He would not have bludgeoned and abducted a man and taken him to his wife and children. Surely he has that much sense. But ... he has another house. In Kent. Less than a half day's ride from London. He does not visit it. It was a favorite haunt of my husband's. Good hunting."

"I will start my questioning along the roads to Kent, then," Lord Theodore said.

Fiona stepped forward. "And I'll come with you."

"No."

"Yes." She marched up to him and pressed her finger to his chest. "Your brother learned quickly enough that I do as I please when something is important to me. Nothing could be more important to me than Lysander's life. I'm coming, even if it comes to leaving town." She'd not have stood up to her parents only to be sent back with her tail between her legs.

"And with what chaperone?" he demanded.

"Me." Lady Balantine stood on steady legs, her voice strong as steel despite the wavering tracks the tears had drawn down her wrinkle-lined face. "I agree with Miss Fiona. She has a right to save the man who holds her heart. If she needs a chaperone to do so, then I will accompany her."

"See?" Fiona held an arm out to the older woman who had as much a right to this hunt as Fiona did, as Lysander's brother did. "I am well-equipped with whatever you require to make this proper."

"Can I stop you?" he growled.

"I'm afraid not."

He swept from the room with a wave of his hand. "I'll return when I know something. Better safe with me than wandering off on your own, I suppose."

Lady Cordelia grinned at Fiona and the dowager then hurried after Lord Theodore.

Fiona and Lady Balantine stood tall together, one weeping for the betrayal of her son, the other weeping for the man she loved.

Twenty-One

Z ander paced the long gallery, stepping from sunshine to shadow as he passed by each window. A large room, empty and filled with light. Excellent for painting. If Zander painted. The entire house was empty and large. Reminded him of Briarcliff at its worst moments, when Raph sold off anything he could grab as soon as their father turned his back for a breath. And that suspicious patch of roof in the corner, drooping and cracking? That reminded him of Briarcliff, too. The sale of Raph's inherited Rubens was supposed to have gone to fixing the roof, but that had gone south quickly, and here was the result of the entire intrigue— Zander abducted and shuffled off to an abandoned property somewhere east of London. Zander holding his fists close instead of letting them fly because doing so might put attention where he refused to have it.

On Fiona.

He'd been here for five days and hadn't painted a thing yet. Thankfully. Because as soon as he did, the trick would be done, and the baron would know the truth. Or he would shoot Zander. Neither optimal possibilities.

Did he have a gun? He'd not shown one yet, but Zander operated as if he might. Safer to assume. He must figure out a means of escape quickly, though. The baron grew angrier by the hour.

Good thing artists had reputations for being difficult in regards to their art.

Good thing Zander had plenty of time observing artists and their ways.

He'd considered running last night as the baron slept. But then what would happen? He might get back to London in enough time to warn Fiona, get her on a ship to who knew where. Somewhere safe. But the baron would be close behind him, would scream forgery to the very tip of London's rooftops, and even if Zander cried abduction and thievery to cover it up, the damage would be done. The art would be inspected.

Fiona's life would be at risk.

So Zander remained. Only to bide his time, to find a way to escape that wouldn't cost Fiona her life, cost her family their reputation, their livelihood.

The door to the gallery slammed open, hitting the wall, and Lord Balantine crashed in. "Nothing? Nothing! You've had hours. I've had enough." He pointed to a pile of painting supplies in the corner. "You've not even set anything up!"

Zander pretended calm, clasped his hands behind his back, and tamed his face into a somber expression. "There are so many things currently wrong. I could never paint." He sighed loud and long. "Where do I even begin to explain?"

"What else is wrong?" the baron screamed. "You've rejected every room in the house, demanded specific types of supplies, and insisted on eastern light that only lasts an hour. You are delaying!"

Zander shrugged. "You do not understand the artistic temperament, my lord. You cannot make demands of the muse. She'll never listen. She'll go fluttering away. Besides, what if I do paint and it rains?" He held a hand toward the sagging corner of the roof, palm up. "It could be ruined in a single night while we sleep. And another thing"—he stepped closer—"you have not provided me with a painting to copy." That was the main point, the point he kept trying to strike through the man's head. Because if he did, perhaps he would be shown Lord Balantine's hidden stash of art, and hopefully that stash would include Zander's paintings.

"No. I've told you. You must create an entirely new scene in the style of another painter. That seems the safest bet. I already ran into trouble with one of my mother's pieces. Didn't know it was a forgery, did I? But the man I tried to sell it to did. Do you want to know why?"

Zander shrugged. "I don't really care."

"He knew because he owned the original!" His voice nearly shook down the cracking roof. "No more copies. Only originals good enough to pass for pieces by a dead painter's hand."

Could Fiona do that? He'd only seen the copies she'd made for him, not the ones that had been stolen by this buffoon.

Zander stood at the window and considered the tangled landscape beyond the glass. Worse than Briarcliff out there. Raph, at least, had learned the work of the gardener when they'd had to let theirs go, had tried his best to keep the estate as tidy and profitable as possible. This man had simply ... done nothing it seemed, had let everything rot. He understood Balantine's desperation, but he didn't understand him in other ways.

He swung back around to face him, lifting his arms wide. "Bring me something. I must have a painting to understand the style to paint in. The thickness of the paint, the composition. I can't create it out of my imagination. I need an example to work from. I admit the light in here is passable, but without the proper tools"—he scoffed—"you'll have nothing from me."

Balantine's hands balled into fists, and his face turned apple red. "You have been abducted, and you dare to—"

"*You* should not have abducted an artist. You clearly have little experience with them. We have very little control over our muse. She comes and goes as she pleases, and really only comes when we seduce her a bit. A stretched canvas here, a proper paint bladder there. An example to work from." He tried to loosen his jaw so his frustration did not grind out between his words. He observed Balantine with as cool a gaze as he could manage

The man might explode. His cheeks puffed out and he fairly vibrated. He stamped a foot into the floor, and the sound vibrated across the empty space. "Very well. I'll bring you a painting." He stomped out of the room.

Zander yelled after him, "A Rubens, if you have one! I'm particularly good at those!" Then he melted against the door-frame. Odds of the man returning with one of his family's paintings was low, but perhaps he'd not wish to risk scaring off Zander's muse by bringing something other than requested.

The ruse would soon be over. He wouldn't be able to pass himself off as the forger much longer. He needed another plan, but escape to London was not an option if he wished to protect Fiona, and he had little at his disposal. He slid back into the room, ruffling his hair. "Think. What would Raph do?" How had his brother kept an estate running with so little? All Zander needed to do was get his own feet running before the man discovered he could not paint a fluffy cloud let alone mimic a masterpiece.

He paced the length of the gallery again. What did he have at his disposal? An empty house. No one to hear the other man scream. Good. The clothes on his body. Cravats could be deadly if given the chance. Yes, something he could work with. A coach and team rested in the dilapidated stables, but Balantine would notice him missing before he had them harnessed. Perhaps if he took just one of the horses. And Balantine would take the other, and Zander would lead him straight to Fiona. No good.

His only other resources were the art supplies in the corner. Better to wield them as weapons than to attempt to use them for their intended purpose. He knelt near the piles of canvases—stretched and unstretched, paint bladders, watercolor cakes, crayon, and brushes. The man had been thorough. Some colorman had profited well, but where had Balantine gotten the funds for it, if he was so hard up? Anger cracked Zander's bones as surely as a hammer would. It was common practice in the ton to accumulate debts, but when those debts would never be paid ... there was the crime. And against people who worked hard and did not deserve it.

He picked up a canvas in each hand and snuck into the hallway. He left them both at the top of the stairs, just below the landing to obscure their presence. A tumble down the stairs might kill the man, but Zander didn't particularly care at the moment. His work done, he returned to the gallery and gingerly stuffed one paint bladder into his half unbuttoned waistcoat. He'd seen too many of the things explode to take risks, but that's exactly what would make the volatile little things so useful. He held the other like a precious jewel shaped by Fiona's hand and waited.

But not long.

Balantine kicked the door open again and entered holding a painting. A small one, but one that made Zander's heart slam against his ribs.

"There you are. A Rubens." Balantine tossed the painting to the floor.

Zander dove for it and caught it, but not before the corner

bounced against the wood. "What the hell do you think you're doing?" Zander stood, holding the painting with trembling fingers. He had to calm himself. He could not give away the true meaning of the paintings, how important it was. "You want to sell it, yes? You'll decrease its value by at least half if you damage it."

Balantine's brows shot toward his hairline. Had he really not known? Worse and worse. If he had no sense of how to care for valuable artworks ... where was he keeping them? And how?

Zander swallowed a groan and focused on the painting. He'd never really liked it. But in this moment, he wanted to hug it. "This will do. Thank you. The style is easy to view and should be easy to imitate." For Fiona perhaps. For him?

He took a steady breath.

Now or never. He placed the painting on the floor behind him, leaned it against the wall. Felt wrong. Every muscle screamed not to do it, but he couldn't risk damaging it. And now he knew where it was, he would come back. For it and for the others. Hopefully Balantine had not had the opportunity to sell any of them yet. That his attempt to sell one thing had ended up in the discovery of one of the baronesses forged pieces gave Zander hope. Perhaps that had been his first attempt, and he'd not moved past that complication yet. The art world was close knit and difficult to break into.

Balantine turned on his heel and made for the door.

Zander trotted after him. "Wait."

"What is it now?" He didn't even turn to look at Zander.

Damn. That was exactly what Zander needed. He'd have to be flexible with this plan. He passed the other man, holding his upper body steady, hoping Balantine did not notice the giant bulge by his left ribs.

"I was just wondering," Zander said, "whether or not

you'd prepared for us to eat?" They'd had nothing but crusty bread brought from London.

"No. Paint or starve," Balantine sneered.

"Hm." Zander held the paint bladder he'd been cradling in his hands up between them. "Not filled with wine, you know, and neither brain nor body can exist without sustenance." He flattened his palm, curling his fingertips toward the floor, and let the bladder balance there. "It's a precarious thing, the artistic temperament. Unless it's well-fed ..." He took a half step back, rocking onto his heels, and let the bladder fall.

An explosion of paint sprayed upward, but Zander had closed his eyes, and he ran now, counting the steps toward the staircase and keeping on the side of the wall to avoid the canvases he'd dropped there earlier.

From the top of the hallway, Balantine screamed. Paint burned a bit when you got it in the eyes. The scream turned into a gurgle, punctuated by a volley of footsteps down the hall behind Zander. Then one step sounded off. Softer. He'd found the canvas.

A crash. Another scream.

Zander risked a glance behind him. Balantine lay still, sprawled across the top several steps, the entire front of his body covered in deep-green paint.

Zander grinned, wiping the paint off his face. Green and goopy and covering his legs and his chest as well as his cheeks. He might have just killed a man, but the thought didn't kill his grin. He'd need to consider that when he had more time. Spoke to some deep moral failing he'd always known was there but hadn't known went so ... dark.

He yanked at his cravat, remembering the last time it had been loosened, Fiona's fingers, long and strong and fluttering against his skin. He raced around the corner, yanking the length of linen completely off and ducking into the first room off the hallway. He held his breath and listened.

Heavy breathing. A groan. Not dead yet, then. Footsteps, uneven, plodding, getting closer to the bottom of the stairs, then echoing down the dark hallway. Zander wrapped the cravat's ends tight around both fists and held his breath, waited until he saw a flash of movement past the doorway. Then he lunged.

Twenty-Two

It would be truer to say Fiona bounced the coach with her shaking feet than that the coach bounced her. And, all captives of their own thoughts, none of the other passengers in the conveyance seemed to notice. Lord Theodore stared out the window as if he saw nothing but horrors there, tight-lipped and white-knuckled. Lady Balantine gabbed away as if anyone was listening. Thankfully, she did not need another participant to have a full conversation.

She'd kept her head turned to one side so she did not have to contemplate Lord Theodore's gloom or the dowager's nerves. Her neck hurt now. But it would be worth it if they found Lysander, saved him. And they would. They had to.

"How much longer?" Fiona asked, whipping her head around to face the dowager.

Lady Balantine pressed her nose against the glass window. "Oh! We're turning into the drive."

Fiona exhaled, deflating into the seat. "Thank heavens."

"The drive is so very rutted," Lady Balantine exclaimed. "How remiss of Herbert to neglect it."

Perhaps that explained the increased jolting Fiona had

experienced. It hadn't been her at all. It had been neglect. She sat on her hands to keep from flinging open the door and throwing herself from it. Surely she could move faster than the coach currently traveled.

Lord Theodore blinked out of his focused state and turned his death stare out the window. He'd asked few questions about her on the journey here, given nothing but a tight nod. How had the same family produced two such different men, one all frowns and the other always with easy grins? Perhaps they'd produced Zander because they'd needed him, needed his quips and fancy to combat his brother's grimness. No. Wait. Was not Lord Theodore Zander's younger brother?

No matter. If they did not need his teasing nature, she did. She knew that well enough. Had known it before the discovery that he'd been bashed over the head with a statue and shoved into a traveling coach last seen rambling east out of London.

The coach lurched to a stop, and Fiona jumped from her seat, flew herself out and onto the ground below quicker than either other occupant could straighten their bent knees and leave their seats. She hiked her skirts high and felt an iron band clamp around her elbow.

"Miss Frampton."

She turned slowly, craning her head back to look up, up at Lord Theodore.

His eyes were kind, at the very least, and he loosened his grip on her, though he did not draw it away entirely. "We do not know what is in there. Or whom. I've allowed you to make this journey because it seems it's yours to make, but I'll not let you throw yourself at danger. Besides, if what Cordelia says is true, Zander would not appreciate my letting you fling yourself around when I could prevent it.

"Zander calls me a dragon. I'm not afraid."

That stern mouth of his broke, curved into a tender smile

she would have called impossible had she not seen it, and the resemblance between the brothers appeared, suddenly, like a new star in the night sky. "I can see you are not afraid." Yet he pulled her back toward the coach anyway. "I admire that, but you will stay here until I have determined there is no danger." His grip tightened, and he all but lifted her up into the coach, slammed the door shut, and turned toward the house.

"Unacceptable!" Fiona cried with a huff.

"I agree," Lady Balantine said. "Just look at the bricks. Falling right off. Piles of them circling the house like a fairy ring." She clucked her tongue into the roof of her mouth. "He's let the place fall apart. It used to be so lovely."

"I wish I could have seen it," Fiona said without attending to what she actually said. The house had appeared quite old and almost ... funereal. She lowered to the seat, but her rear met the cushion only for a moment before she bounced back up and pushed the door on the opposite side open.

"Whatever are you doing, darling?" the dowager asked, leaning forward.

Fiona crouched behind the conveyance, her skirts billowing around her bent knees.

"Miss," the driver said from his perch, "is there anything you need of me?"

She pressed a finger to her lips. "Your silence is all." Half standing, she waddled toward the back of the coach, peered around its bulk.

Lord Theodore tried the door handle, found it unlocked, and swung the door open wide. As soon as he disappeared into the black night of the inside air, Fiona bolted. Straight for the house, around the side of it. She picked her way over tangled roots and skirted overgrown bushes. She almost tripped over a large pile of bricks that had fallen from the walls. She yelped, hopping to a halt, then jumped over the pile and jolted into a run once more.

Doors. More than one. Leading inside, yes, but where inside? Didn't matter as long as she avoided Lord Theodore. And whatever nefarious villains likely scurried round the place like ants after the crumbs of a picnic lunch.

Any door. Didn't matter. She ran for one, found it open, and then she, too, rushed into the darkness. And the dust.

She covered her mouth to muffle the sound of her cough. No one here. And two more doors to choose from. She ran for the one to her side, not the one across the room, and found herself inside another room. A library? Books on every surface. Likely ruined, covers curled, the smell of rotting paper in the air. Empty, too. She ran for the first door she saw, grasped the handle, turned—

And froze. Voices on the other side. One particularly familiar and … jovial? That boded well. Yet, Fiona would not push forward too quickly. Best to take a peek first. The handle already turned, she nudged the door open, just a slice, and peered through.

A man was tied to a chair. First thing she saw. With a rope of some sort, white and green in color. He snarled. At Zander, who leaned against a large desk, his clothes and face smattered with something green. Dirt? Paint? And … what was that he held in one hand?

She cracked the door open wider to better see, and when she recognized it, she pushed the door open completely, quite forgetting herself. "Is that a paint bladder, Lord Lysander Bromley?"

His grin disappeared. "Bloody hell. What are *you* doing here?" He carefully placed the bladder on a nearby table.

The captured man swung his head toward her. "You're the woman who was with him at my mother's house."

Fiona gasped. "You! I knew it!" She rushed to Zander's side, reaching for his head. His hair was matted with a dark, crusty substance, and she recoiled right before her fingers tangled with it. "You're hurt. We found the statue. When your brother appears—"

"My brother?" His eyes flew wide, and his words came out with a choked cough. "Which one? Why? Bloody hell ... what plague have you brought upon us, Fiona?"

"What *rescue*, you mean."

"Same thing, apparently."

"What have you done to him?" She bobbed her head toward the captured baron.

Zander grinned, wily and wicked and slow.

"He tried to kill me!" the baron cried.

"Hardly," Zander said. "A paint bladder exploded in your face. Hardly my fault you don't understand art materials. The things are highly volatile. And you did not watch where you were stepping, now did you?" Zander clucked his tongue. "Poor fellow stepped on a canvas carelessly left on the stairs and had a bit of a tumble."

"Did you perhaps aid in the placement of the canvas?"

"No one can prove it." His face lost its light, and his hands wrapped around her shoulders. "Hell, Fee, you have to leave." He turned her and pushed her toward an exit. "This is a bloody nightmare."

"Not like any nightmare I've ever had." Lord Theodore stood in the door, arms crossed over his chest. With a placid face, he took in every detail of the room before his gaze settled on the man tied to a chair. "Is that ... paint?"

"It is." Zander strode forward, fury in his tight fists. "And have you brought her"—he shoved a finger in Fiona's direction—"here? Why in hell would you do that, Theo?"

"I have brought her, though she was ordered to remain in the coach."

"Ordered. Precisely the best way to get her to do what you asked her *not* to do." Zander shoved his fingers through his hair and began to pace the length of the room. "What now?" he said to himself. "What the hell now?"

"Now you're going to damn well untie me!" the baron bellowed.

"No," Zander and his brother said together.

Lord Theodore stepped forward to stand before the baron. He pulled the statue from his pocket, still dark with Zander's blood. "Do you recognize this?"

"I do." Zander snatched it from his brother's hand. "He bashed me over the head with it." He huffed. "At least it lost its cock." He slammed the statue on the nearest drop-cloth-covered table.

"Why did you violently injure and abduct a marquess's brother?" Theo asked, his tone hard as rock, sharp as a knife's edge ... dangerous.

"You can't prove it," the baron insisted. "My word against his. He's the one that violently attacked me. And tied me up!"

"In order to escape you," Zander added with a growl. "I'm taking you back to the coach." He grasped her arm and steered her toward the door. Where they bumped into the dowager.

"Here you all are," Lady Balantine said, blinking in the gloomy light. "I'm so glad I found you."

"What fresh hell?" Zander wove his arm through hers and pulled them both from the room, found a door down the hall and pulled them into it. "Sit."

Fiona sat in a cloth-covered chair. The room, sparsely furnished, all visible surfaces dusty beneath the gray sunlight flooding through dirty, curtainless windows, seemed ghostly, and it reminded her of the first time Fiona had followed Zander into a house where she'd not been invited. The dowager's house had also been draped in dust cloths that day. So similar, but so much had changed.

What had not changed was her determination to steer her own future, to be included in the decisions about her life. And he was part of her life now. But ... perhaps she'd ... missed the mark. She'd come to save her helpless love only to find him rather in control of the situation and terribly angry with her. She tugged on Lady Balantine's skirts, encouraging her to sit. She didn't.

Zander pinched the bridge of his nose with one hand and stuffed the other into his pocket. Did he have a trinket there? Something discarded and bent with age, painted with rust? Something he found valuable enough to keep on him and protect during his own abduction?

Finally, he stopped and let his head fall back, his arms collapsing to his sides. "I was trying to *protect you*, Fiona." He dropped his chin to his chest. "The baron thinks I am the forger. Has it in his mind to keep me hidden away in order to make a fortune he seems to have lost. And as long as he thinks I'm the one who can make that happen"—his gaze flew to Fiona's face—"you are safe. Unfortunately, that state of affairs can last only until I put paint to canvas. I half killed the man in an attempt to get things under control, find some means of bribing him or controlling him. But then in you waltz! The actual forger." His voice, which had been calm and steady before, turned low as a snake's hiss with those last three words, which wobbled out of his control. "But I do not intend for him to discover that."

Fiona's brain stopped working.

"Herbert ... knows?" Lady Balantine sank slowly, clumsily into a nearby chair.

"Yes, he does. It would be nice if you could hold your tongue now and then, Lady Balantine."

She sniffed. "I realize emotions are running high right now. But that is no reason for rudeness. If you stretch your memory back a bit, you'll remember that I told not a soul for years. Not even when your father—" She snapped her lips together and turned from him.

"My ... father? What about him?"

She waved her hand. "Nothing. Nothing."

"Tell me."

Now she fell into a chair, her shoulders slumping forward. "I suppose I must tell you now. He's dead and you've come for the paintings. I would have had to tell you eventually."

"Tell. Me. What?"

She finally met his gaze. "Your father visited me. He knew I had the paintings. I don't know how. Perhaps he followed you, had you followed. He sat in front of the six paintings you gave me very quietly for a very long time. Then he asked me if he could hide letters in each one." She swallowed. "They will still be there if my son has not lost them, between the canvas and the frame backing. I was worried he would be angry with me, but he said not a single recriminating thing. Just sat before the paintings. Quiet."

"Letters," Zander said, barely a breath. "Hell."

"I never told him about Fiona. Not a bit, and he even asked. I think he was impressed with her work. Likely he wished to support her art career."

Zander snorted, and the sound rippled relief through Fiona. If he could snort, he would not shatter, and he looked more fragile than a porcelain cup at the moment.

"I would have gone to my grave with Fiona's secret, I swear." Lady Balantine wrung her hands. "But he's my son. And he came back into my life wanting a relationship. Didn't know he was a scoundrel. An outright nefarious villain. I thought ... I thought he wanted me, not my collection." She collapsed into violent sobs.

Fiona crossed the distance between them to wrap her in a hug once more.

Zander winced, his only sign of sympathy before he pushed onward. "He's not a very clever villain. He tried to sell that statue of yours, the one he bashed me over the head with, only to discover it a fake. Then when you announced that one of the two of us was the most excellent forger of your acquaintance, he assumed it was *me*."

"He tried to sell poor Richard? That piece was never even meant to replace an original."

"You call the statue Richard?" Fiona asked.

She hiccuped, but her crying lightened. "After my husband. It was a clever joke, his gift to me. Shame it seems Herbert is foolish as well as a scoundrel." Another hiccup. "I'm a failure as a mother."

"You sound more upset over the foolish bit."

"I have my priorities, darling."

Fiona's brain snapped back on, trundling forward over the rocky road of information. "Zander, you are letting him think you are the forger?"

"Yes. Of course I am."

"No *of course*! You could hang if he tells anyone."

"I don't care!" he roared. "I'd rather die than have a hair on your adorable head plucked. Do you understand? I love you, and—"

Lady Balantine gasped, and she flew from the room. "Oh! Love. It *is* love. I *knew* it. He'll not ruin it. I won't let him!"

They ran after her. Zander pulled Fiona back, trying to force distance between her and the others even as he tried to hurry after the baroness. Not an easy dual task to accomplish, and Fiona fought him handily, gained the lead, and hurried after Lady Balantine.

"He will not get away with this," Lady Balantine muttered. "This, every bit of this, is my fault, and I will fix it. Easy enough to do." She slammed into the room. "You!" She pointed a wavering finger at her tied-up offspring as she rounded the chair to stand straight and tall before him. "Explain yourself."

"Don't see what there is to explain," Herbert said.

241

"Oh, I see many things. House that should not be falling down around our heads, and yet it is. A man covered in paint tied to a chair. And why? Because he abducted another man, bashing him over the head with a piece of his mother's favorite art."

"It's worthless," Herbert growled. "Better off broken into pieces."

"No, you fool," she shouted. "It might not have any value to you or whomever you tried to sell it to, but Richard meant much to me."

"Who's Richard?" Lord Theodore asked.

"The statue used to conk me on the head," Zander said.

"Ah." Lord Theodore's gaze flew to the statue on the table, now missing a particular appendage. "Pity."

Lady Balantine nodded tightly, water shimmering in her eyes. "He was cast after your father's figure. A very good likeness in *every* way. And he was posed in the style of the *David*. It was our favorite, you see, the *David*. And the statue meant your father was *my David*. Now it's ruined. Broken and bloody."

Herbert growled.

The baroness made a *tsking* sound in her throat as she waltzed toward him, wagging her finger in his face. He turned his head to the side, and she had to wag at his cheek. They looked the very picture of a recalcitrant boy and his lecturing mama.

"You've wasted your inheritance," she said.

"I should have had more," Herbert snarled, "but father left you the lion's share."

"Me? You received two estates, lands, farms, three thousand a year, everything that comes with the title. I received the townhouse in London, the remainder of my own dowry that I brought into my marriage, as well as what it had earned through investments. And all the art, which you never wanted, which you hated. Your father was responsible with his money, made wise investments. You, it appears, are not. I was struck bereft when I first learned of your perfidy and could do nothing but cry, but now that I have had an entire coach trip to think it over, I believe I shall go gather your children and your wife and bring them to live with me in London if they so wish. No need for them to suffer for your mistakes."

"I have made no mistakes!" the baron shouted, jerking at his binding so that the chair jumped off the floor. "And I'll not suffer for your crimes. That man there is a criminal, a forger." He jerked his head toward Zander. "And he tried to kill me. And if he does not paint for me what I tell him, what will sell, then I will tell whoever will listen what he's done."

"Him? An art forger?" Lady Balantine laughed, putting her hand over her belly as if the mirth made her stomach ache. When she finally quieted, she wiped a tear from her eye and pinned him with a pitying gaze. "Oh darling, the art forger is *me*." She closed the distance between herself and her son and leaned forward to wrap her hands around the arms of his chair. She went nose to nose with him, and, without blinking, said, "You may tell the world about my crimes, but you will bring yourself down with me. Do you understand? What connections you still retain will be lost. What gazes view you with respect will soon shift to sneers. There will likely be some publicity that comes with hanging a dowager baroness. And then you will be questioned as well. For haven't you lately dipped your toes in the art world you insisted on separating me from? And if your mother is a crook ... why ... they often say that children drink the sins of their mothers with their milk."

She stood and shrugged, then walked toward Zander. "Any word against this man will open my own mouth and release a flood of guilty confessions. I am, indeed, sorry for my crimes, and the slightest notion that someone else might suffer from them will simply tip me over the edge of my grief, spill out all those words, and then you are over as well as I. I have lived a long life, though. I am glad to give it if it means a free conscience."

She strode to the window and pressed a palm against the glass. One finger *tap, tap, tapped* in the silence around them.

Zander cleared his throat. "The things he stole. They're somewhere in this house. I saw one. It's upstairs in the portrait gallery."

Lady Balantine's head turned slowly, and she smiled at him over her shoulder. "Ah. A good thing to come from today. A blessing. Go find the pilfered items, darlings."

Zander nodded. "He's already sold some. But I don't know what."

"I'll get the information from him." Lady Balantine turned back around, and the gaze she pinned to her son did not bode well for him.

Zander wrapped an arm around Fiona's shoulder and guided her into the hallway. Theo followed them out, and shut the door to let the mother handle her progeny in private.

"I must admit things have not turned out as I expected them to," Theo said, staring at the arm Zander used to pull Fiona safely to his side.

At least it should have felt safe. Right now, with his recent confession and his brother's calm face hiding what must be a storm of pointed thoughts, she felt a little raw, a little vulnerable, a little lost.

Lord Theodore blinked and looked away from them. "Let us spread out to look for the paintings. I'll retrieve the one from upstairs first. Give a yell if you find anything. I suppose we'll need to cart it all back to London and to Lady Balantine's home once we discover it?"

"We'll put that question to her," Zander said. "She's the kind of woman to have opinions."

Theo rolled his eyes and turned to trudge down the hall toward the front of the house. "I'm rather tired of that sort."

Zander turned them without a word, and with steps that seemed quite heavy, he ushered her in the opposite direction. "I do not think they will have been hidden upstairs. I can't imagine old Herbert going to that trouble."

Fiona fit her strides to his. "Looking at the state of this place, I'm a bit concerned. What if they were not well protected?" Better to focus on the practical, even though that word—his confession of *love*—bounced around inside her, begging for attention.

She would not admit the possibility of the paintings having been ruined. If it had been her copies, she would not have cared. She would have celebrated. In fact, she planned to ask Zander to burn the copies she'd made of his paintings as soon as he returned to his home. But these were his originals, the paintings that would allow him and his brothers to release some of the weight of their father's irresponsibility.

"I wish my own father had been as responsible as Herbert's," Zander said. His mind must have been moving in the same direction as Fiona's.

"Then you would not have ended up as responsible as you are," she said. "You see, a responsible father formed an ungrateful son. A wastrel. And you were shaped to be a different sort of man."

"A different sort of scoundrel, you mean."

She poked him in the ribs, and he yelped and jumped away but quickly returned to her side, the corner of his mouth tugged up.

"You do not have to be a scoundrel, swindling people out of their art. I have seen how good an eye you have for fakes and forgeries. What if instead of helping rich people acquire art at low prices, you help everyone determine whether what they have is of value. Let them know exactly what they have, so they cannot be swindled. As you did at the auction."

"Value is in the eye of the beholder." He slipped his hand into his pocket and pulled out half of a bent locket. "Trash to everyone, but a reminder to me."

And that was why she loved him.

She stopped right there in the hall, turned to him, and cupped his jaw in both hands. She bit her bottom lip and shook her head as she stared at him. His usually clean-shaven face had several days' worth of scruff growing on it, and he was covered in green paint. She needed to tell him. Right this very moment. But ... his glassy gaze could not focus. It kept journeying from her to somewhere else.

"What are you thinking?" she asked.

"About the letters. Do you think they truly exist? They must." He straightened, pulling out of her grasp, and the rough stubble on his cheeks scraped against her palms.

She curled her fingernails in, welcoming the sharp bite.

He paced away from her, then spun around, arms spread out wide. "But what would the man have to say? Why did he *know* and never reprimand me? Where were his tears of betrayal? His tirades about ungrateful sons?"

She tiptoed toward him. "Did your father often descend into tirades?"

Zander deflated, curving in on himself with slumped shoulders. "No. Before we discovered the state of the coffers, I ... I loved him very much." His words ripped from a raw throat. "He was kind and ... and he's the one who taught me to spot a fake. Said it was a good thing to know for everyone but the forger."

She rolled her lips between her teeth. "He would not have liked me." And ... what if ... Zander liked her only because his father would not have? She smoothed the wrinkles in her skirt to do something with her mind other than cry out, other than demand from him the truth.

He decimated the distance between them and tilted her chin up, kissed her softly. His lips offered more than a caress. They offered a silent answer to her unknowns. She believed the truth of that kiss more than she'd ever believe any speech. When he pulled away, he took her hand in his and pulled her toward a door.

"First, we will find the missing art. Then, we will return to London. And if there are letters ... I suppose Raph and Maggie should read theirs. He clearly meant only the inheritor of the painting to find them." His steps slowed. "I'll never be able to read mine."

She stopped, yanking on his arm to stop him too. "Whyever not?"

"I've told you. I'll never be able to create a work of art valuable enough for my mother to grant me my inheritance." He snorted. "She offered to just ... give them to us after Raph almost refused to marry his wife. But I can't. It seems ... wrong, even though I know I shouldn't have to do anything. It was my father's final wish, and in the end, I must respect it."

She cupped his cheek. So much pride in this man who called himself a scoundrel.

"Found 'em!" Lord Theodore yelled.

They ran, hand in hand, Zander's longer stride forcing Fiona to fist her skirts in her free hand and pull them high so she didn't trip as she rushed to keep up. They ran toward a room near the front of the house, the direction Zander's brothers had set off in.

The door was open, and Lord Theodore's head and shoulders popped out. "In here. I don't know what we're looking for exactly. Something like this one, I suppose." He nodded to a painting leaned against the doorframe at his feet. "It's the one you told me about from the gallery."

The room was piled high, every wall with paintings of every size leaned against them. Statues picnicking together on drop cloths, the frames of some smaller works digging into the paint-covered canvases of other larger ones.

"Hell," Zander hissed.

"Double hell," Fiona agreed. "He's no idea how to care for any of it. Who knows what damage has been done."

"She knows art, too, then?" Lord Theodore said. "Good. I've no idea what's what. You an artist yourself?"

Her gaze swept the room as she bounced on her toes and fisted her hands in her skirts. Where? So much to look for, and —oh! She covered her mouth on a gasp. *There*—familiar colors and brush strokes. She ran for a stack of paintings and gingerly peeled them away from one another to release a small one partially hidden.

Zander appeared beside her. "Is that one of …?"

He left the word *yours* unsaid, but she heard it anyway.

"Yes."

"This will take hours," he said, "to properly sort everything."

Lord Theodore grunted, pointed toward a corner. "That looks familiar."

Zander strode toward the direction the finger pointed in. "By Jove, it does look familiar." He picked it up and laughed. "It is. It's *ours*."

And it hadn't taken hours. The cartoonist who claimed to not know art had set out a roaming eye and landed on it immediately.

Fiona laughed, too. If one of his paintings was here, the others might be, too. And all of hers as well. The baron had not known what to do, after all. Hope and joy threaded together in her like the silver and gold wires Zander had stolen from her shop floor—discarded once, but full of beauty—and she hugged it to her as she did Zander's promises for a bed and a life. The missing could be found, and mistakes could be erased, an old painting covered with a new one.

Zander carefully flipped the painting he held over, his gaze and fingers roving over the brown backing. Looking for the outline of a letter? If mistakes could be erased, perhaps misunderstanding could be, too. Perhaps forgiveness could be found in dusty corners as well as masterpieces.

Twenty-Three

Z ander had never experienced a more torturous carriage
ride than the one that came after his rescue. They had
two coaches at their disposal, yet they'd had to all pile
into one so that they could store Herbert's pilfered artwork in the
other. Still, it did not all fit, and they had to prioritize which to
bring back to Lady Balantine's house and which to leave for later.

Six paintings (and six hidden letters), however, were
nestled between their legs, wrapped carefully in dusty drop
cloths, and with each bump of a frame against Zander's shin,
he felt his shame. And his relief. They'd found them all. So he
took each bump that bruised his leg as penance, a necessary
part of this difficult ride.

The other difficulty came not just from being squished
between three full-grown men to a single bench but from
being squished next to the odious Herbert. Theo sat on the
thief's other side, looking steadily with a cold eye at the baron,
making him squirm. A squirming thief covered in paint
offered no good companionship.

So Zander lightened his discomfort by seeking out more

delightful views. Fiona sat across from him. So close but so very far away. What the hell was he going to do with her? They'd found the paintings. All bloody six of them. But he could not earn his inheritance. His father had known that when he'd set his children this task. He'd known Zander had no talent. He'd also known Zander had replaced the paintings with fakes. A rather poetic situation for the old man.

What had he written in his letters? He'd seen no sign of them when he'd inspected the backs of the paintings, but that meant nothing. What did they say? What could they say to make it better? Nothing. And Zander would never know the words written for him, never be able to earn them.

At least he had Fiona to look at, the sweet plump curve of her cheek, the pink bow of her mouth, those shoulders straight strong, and little bits of paint dotting her gown, her cheeks, her fingers clutched in her lap.

The paintings bumped against his shin. The letters bumped against his mind.

Her gaze slipped from the sights outside the window to him, and she smiled, a slight thing, a mere turnup of the corner of her mouth, and he returned it.

"You're a bloody clever woman," he said, pushing back the growing cadence in his head—*letters, letters, letters.*

She blinked, clearly startled, and blushed. "Me? Clever?" The question in her voice seemed pleased, and that sly turnup of her lips curved even more.

He nodded slowly. His grin grew wicked as his gaze slid to the paintings. She blushed, but she did not turn away from him.

From the other side of the baron, Theo groaned. "Could you please save the lovemaking until you're well in private? Bloody Lady Cordelia was right. The two of you *are* in love." He scoffed.

"Lord Theodore," Lady Balantine said, "do you scoff at the name of love?"

"Everyone should," he assured her.

Zander let them bicker and continued gazing into his dragon's green eyes. And she gazed right back, and who knew how many hours brought them to the edge of London. He spent every one of them looking at her, fighting back the urge to rip off the drop cloth and rip into the backs of the paintings. Only when the carriage rolled to a stop outside of a row of terrace homes he now recognized, did she break the gaze-held chain between them as she stepped out of the carriage.

He moved to stand. "I'll escort you inside."

"No." She waved him away and shut the door between them. "I must face them alone. They are not best pleased with me."

"I understand why," he grumbled. He had been upset with her, too. He wanted to kiss her cheek to tell her he would clean himself up and visit later because he did, after all, need to talk to her father, but he could barely form the words because his body was so tired. And painted green, his head still pounding. And the letters. The letters still pounded in his brain, making thoughts of much else close to impossible.

So he did as she wished and retook his seat before the carriage set off again. It did not take them long to bring him to Maggie's door.

"Why are we here?" Zander asked. "We must help her ladyship unload our cargo."

"And I'll do so," Theo said. "You, however, must clean yourself up. I will take Lady Balantine and her son back to her place and help her unload there. I'll hire a couple of runners, too, to keep this one straight." He elbowed Herbert.

Herbert elbowed him back. Theo merely glowered at him, not even flinching or blinking when the man's elbow hit his ribs. Herbert shrank away from him.

"Lady Balantine needs guarding. Just in case."

Zander did not disagree.

"Not going to hurt my mother," Herbert mumbled.

"You hurt my brother." Theo crossed his arms over his chest. "I don't trust you. Nobody should, and until I'm quite certain you're going to keep your mouth shut—"

"I will," Herbert insisted. "My mother says she will ruin me if I don't."

"And you won't hurt her for that?" Zander asked.

"I'm a thief, not a murderer."

"Slippery slope, dear fellow," Theo said.

Zander had no doubt Theo had some sort of cartoon in mind, something to blackmail the man with. He also had no doubt Theo knew someone, a group of nefarious someones, who would guard the dowager closely. Zander might be something akin to a thief, but his brother was unscrupulous, rather close to not having a heart.

"I'll clean up, then. Make sure the paintings are safe." His hand rested on the top of the largest one's frame. "Then I'll come help you." He gave Lady Balantine a reassuring smile and left the coach, one painting under each arm. He entered the townhouse and shut the door with his entire body, resting his forehead against the cool wood with closed eyes.

"Lord Lysander." Maggie and Tobias's butler had a voice like a squeaky hinge.

Zander jumped. "Ah, Barnett. Could you retrieve some paintings for me from the coach outside? There are three more."

"'Tis for the best, my lord." He cleared his throat. "You've a visitor in the parlor."

"Tell whoever it is to wait. I've had a bit of a day." He put the two paintings down, leaning them against the wall. "I need rest."

"He says he's here about a Rubens, and you told me I was

not to send anyone away if that was their reason for visiting. In fact, Lord Lysander, you told me to keep them here by any means necessary excluding death."

"Right." He pinched the bridge of his nose. "Bloody hell. Very well." Let the man meet with him as he was—paint-splattered, blood-matted, and rather odiferous. Barnett marched outside, and Zander marched into the parlor.

A man stood from a low couch like a released spring, his arms folded behind his back. "Are you Lord Lysander Bromley?"

Lysander rocked back two steps, almost into the hallway again. "Could you, eh, show me your hands? The last time a man asked me that question, he smashed me in the back of the head with a statue, and I'd rather not repeat that experience."

The man slowly, and with a perplexed brow, unfolded his arms and showed Zander his hands. Empty.

"Excellent," Zander said, striding into the room and falling into a cushioned chair. "Excellent. Yes, I am Lord Lysander Bromley, and I'm told you came about a Rubens?"

"Yes, I have." The man sat slowly with a straight back.

"There are no bloody Rubens here or with anyone in my family," a deep voice said from behind Zander.

Zander jumped to his feet and turned. "Raph! What are you doing here?"

"What are *you* doing here?" He left the frame of the doorway and sauntered more fully into the room, his large frame filling it. "I was told you were missing."

"Is that why you're here? Found out I'd mucked it all up again and came to ring a peal over my head?"

"No, I did not come because of any perceived fault of your own. I came because my brother is—was—*missing*." He flicked a blue-eyed glance at the other man. "You may leave."

"I think not," the other man said with a sniff. "You may save your family spats for later. I came to inquire about a—"

"And as I already said," Raph snapped, "we have none. I need to speak with my brother alone, and you will leave."

The man rose slowly to his feet, thrusting his shoulders back and his chest forward. "Who are you to—"

Raph's eyes glinted menace. "The Marquess of Waneborough." He nodded at Zander without taking his gaze from the other man. "His brother."

Zander rolled his eyes. Raph liked throwing fists, liked a little drama at times, and he'd had enough drama for the day. "Ah, Raph." Zander lifted a finger. "We do, actually. Have a Rubens. Six of them. You could sell yours right now if you'd like."

Raph snapped his gaze toward Zander, eyes wide, and Zander pushed himself to standing, legs almost refusing to do so. He took the other man's shoulders and pushed him into the hallway. "Come back tomorrow, sir. If you insist on staying, my brother over there will likely physically kick you from the house, and as someone who's so recently been manhandled himself, I'd like to save you that ignominy."

The man scowled and brushed Zander's hands off his shoulders, but he left, and Zander slammed the parlor door shut, fell onto a nearby couch with such a heavy thud the thing shuddered and creaked.

"Explain. Were you really about to sell that man a *fake*?"

Zander found just enough strength to grit his teeth. "No. Never." He scrubbed his hands over his face, wishing he could scrub away his brother's justified distrust. "I was missing. That's why you're here. And the fellow who bashed me over the head with a statue and abducted me"—he sighed, loud and long—"is the same fellow who stole the original paintings Lady Balantine had been keeping for us." In a halting rhythm, he completed the story.

At first, Raph paced, hands clasped behind his back, boots thudding on the floor. Then he sank into a chair, slumped over, fingers scratching through hair as dark as Zander's, the heavy weight he always wore across his shoulders ... lifted. Just a bit.

Or was that merely Zander's imagination? His hope? It made him feel lighter, too, though.

When Zander finally stopped his narration, Raph said, "How much does the baroness want? To get them back?"

"Nothing. She feels bad they were stolen to begin with. Claims it was her fault, and that she owes us."

"We should not allow it."

"We should allow it." There was pride, and then there was stupidity.

Raph fell into the back of the chair. "We will."

Zander pushed to sitting, draping his arms along the back of the couch, letting the sculpted wood jab into his flesh and muscle. He leaned his head back, closed his eyes, and spoke into the darkness above his head. "I have, I hope, finally atoned for my sins. We have the paintings, and you and Maggie can sell yours. Put it toward whatever you like."

"You don't sound pleased."

"There are letters, supposedly. Father not only knew what I'd done, he'd apparently followed me. All the way to Lady Balantine's home. He spoke with her, convinced her to let him hide letters behind each of the paintings that were to become our inheritances."

"Letters? What about?" Raph's voice sounded bright, alert.

Zander shrugged. "You can see for yourself."

A silence in the darkness, the pause of Raph thinking, no doubt. "Yes. And this forger you spoke of, the one you lied to save ..."

"What about her?"

"Why? You put yourself at risk. And for what?"

Zander laughed, a hard bark that bounced off the walls

then fell flat and heavy to the floor at his feet. "For love, I suppose."

"Love?" A caress of a word for a man with a wife he adored. "Do you plan to ... marry her?"

Zander fell forward, eyes still closed, braced his elbows on his knees and hung his head. "I'm damn sorry, Raph. I didn't even try to do things the right way."

"Right way? You never have done anything the right way. I haven't expected you to in an age." His voice held a chuckle that Zander ignored.

"You're missing the point." He opened his eyes but kept his gaze trained downward on the rug, thick and busy with curling vines, the shapes of elegant white flowers. Fiona would look best with red flowers in her hair. "I love Miss Frampton. And I can't stop myself, and I have no idea how I'm going to manage with a wife. How will I support her? But I can't *not* marry her." He looked up at his brother. "I've mucked up. Again."

Raph's brow furrowed. "As always? I can count at least three times you've brought the world to ruination." He stuck out a finger. "When you rented out the paintings." He added a second finger to the first. "When you had the paintings forged and tried to pass them off as real to Papa who, *of course*, would know in a breath they were fakes." He added a third finger. "And that time you poured glue all over poor Typhus Macmillan's latest watercolor."

"I was six."

"And he was the Queen's favorite watercolorist, and we were all punished for it."

"It was not solely my idea, if you remember."

Raph chuckled. "I do." He pushed out of his chair with a sigh and joined Zander on the couch so they sat elbow to elbow. "The point is you've done much to help our family. Your art curation for your clients has helped fill the larder and made it so we did not have to sell off the common lands. I know it appears at times as if we are barely surviving, but it would be worse—so much worse—if you did not do what you do. If you did not put your family's need before your pride and sell your talents out to greedy men. I have likely never thanked you for that. I am sorry. And I am grateful."

Hell. How did Zander respond? His brother's speech quite melted his own linguistic capabilities away. "I would like to meet Miss Frampton," Raph continued. "Though I must say, I hope she plans to use her talents for good in the future."

Zander laughed, feeling more joy than before. "She hates painting. Never wants to do it again."

"Excellent. I may have found a kindred soul in her, then." Raph chuckled. "Does ... she love you?"

Hell. He didn't know. She hadn't said so, and she'd left the coach earlier so willing to be rid of his helping hand when, in previous days and weeks, she'd pursued him, chased him down, and always, always showed him exactly what she wanted. Wasn't a woman to keep silent when she wanted something. At least she never had with him. If she loved him, she would have ...

Hell.

"Zander," Raph said, caution in his tone, "I don't think falling in love can be classified as mucking things up."

Zander flipped his hands so his palms were open to the ceiling, empty and soft. "I have nothing to give her. I slouch from Maggie's home to Theo's rooms. And I do not think I can continue doing what I've been doing. Swindling the vulnerable out of the very things that could bring them relief. And doing so for men who already have everything." He scratched the back of his neck. It felt red and burning. Shame spreading across his skin like a rash.

"Do something different, then. You're clever. Work for

those people you've swindled in the past, so they can't be swindled moving forward."

Zander laughed, a hard bark that relieved the scratch of shame a bit. "That's what Fiona said."

"I knew I'd like her. Matilda will, too. Mother will likely adore her to distraction. Bring her to Briarcliff while you're working it all out. We don't have much, but we have rooms, and we will share what we have with those we love. Besides, despite what the entailments say, Briarcliff is as much yours as it is mine. You can never say you have no home. It is your home."

"How can I return after what I did? After selling our inheritance, then—"

"Finding it? Near killing a man to find it and to keep the woman you love safe? Ha. Well, after all that, you'll return as a conquering hero. Would you like a parade in your honor?"

Zander shook his head lightly. Difficult to admit such a possibility. Him? A hero. Ha. Finally, he lifted his gaze to Raph's. "Would you like to see it? Your inheritance? The letter …?"

Raph's jaw tightened, but he nodded. They stood together and found their way to the entrance hall. Six covered paintings leaned against the wall.

"Which one?" Raph asked.

Zander knelt, lifted a small one, and handed it over. Raph didn't even spare a single glance for the painting. He immediately turned it over and tore at the back.

"Careful!" Zander cried. Too late. The damage to the backing was done and a small piece of parchment found, Raph's name scrawled across it.

"Bollocks," Raph whispered.

"Hell," Zander hissed.

Raph's hands shook, but he held the parchment gently and looked toward the stairs. "Maggie must know."

"Naturally." Zander yawned, exhaustion stealing over even the shaking excitement of their find.

Raph clapped him on his back, winced, then pulled his hand away, inspecting the palm and wiping it on his trousers. "Why don't you go upstairs and clean up, yes?"

"Yes. Don't wait for me." He gave a weak grin and retreated. Don't wait for him because he had no place in the triumphant conversation. He'd never earn his inheritance or his letter. But ... he'd found the paintings, and hell, that felt good. He'd finally helped. It was all he'd ever wanted—to be useful, not a burden.

Miracle of miracles, Raph did not consider him a burden, a stone, a nuisance, or a failure. All those things Zander had always thought himself. Tilted the world a bit, it did. The light outside the window turned gray as he savored his brother's words. Everything he'd always wanted.

Except now ... now he wanted something else. Someone else. But did she want him?

She'd chased him once. Did she run from him now?

Perhaps it was his time to give chase, to show her how much he loved her, needed her, to be the sort of knight his dragon needed.

Twenty-Four

F iona had lost track of the number of times she'd walked around the square and meandered through the small garden at its center. Every time she passed close to her home's front door she paused, pondered going in, retreated, needing more time to gather her thoughts.

There would never be enough time, and cowardice made her wiggly. What she'd said to her parents that morning ... she'd meant it, and she would not regret having said it. She must face them. So, with resolute steps, she made her way to the door and pushed inside. The same warmth as every other time before, the same glow. Her home, at least, still welcomed her. But would her family?

She took steady breaths as she approached the parlor from which firelight flickered, shadowed on the opposite hallway wall. They were always there of an evening. They would be there now.

And they were. Mama and Papa playing cards by the fire, Posey curled up with a book near the window. When she cleared her throat, they turned and looked. Mama dropped her cards, and Papa knocked over a wineglass as he jolted to his feet. Posey froze entirely, eyes wide, book forgotten.

Then they were on her, arms folding round her, exclamations so close to her ear they deafened her.

"You're home."

"You're safe."

"Did you find him?"

Who said what she could not say? They all spoke at the same time, warm hands pulling her farther in the room, pressing her down onto the same settee Zander had draped her across when she'd pretended to faint weeks earlier.

She looked up at their concerned faces and cried, hiding her face and wetting her palms.

A heavy thud made her jump, and she looked up, sniffling, to see her father's face in front of her own, misery-etched with swimming eyes. "I am so sorry, my dear." He held his palms up to her, open and curved and ... offering. "It was all my fault. I have not listened to you. I have not taken you seriously. Your paintings for that woman. Your taking up with that lord ... it is all my fault."

She wrapped his hands in her own and shook them. "I ... I forgive you. As long as you do not make me pick up another paintbrush ever again."

His gaze dropped to their hands crushed tight between them. "No. Not if you do not want."

She looked up at her mother, at Posey. "I understand. I do. That we must walk a careful line, as careful as any of the ton in order to keep their patronage. I am not as silly or clueless as you all think."

"No!" Posey sank to the settee beside her. "I do not think you silly. I think you see the world in a different way than most. I think that is a strength. And I looked at your sketches."

"So did I," Mama said.

"And they are brilliant." Posey hugged her hard, but not hard enough to dislodge the hold Papa had on Fiona's hands.

Fiona felt smothered, but not unhappy about it. She'd imagined a chasm between herself and those she loved, imagined she'd have to sever herself from them in order to be herself. But perhaps not. *Perhaps not.*

She laughed. "I am sorry. So sorry for doing things I should not have."

Her mother patted the arm of her bath chair. "We all benefited from it."

"I wish I had been able to provide better," her father said, "so you would not have found yourself in such a position. It is one of the reasons I have been so angry. I think your painting was, to me, a sign I was not failing as a father. It is terrifying having two daughters and no son. Who will look out for you after I'm gone?"

"I thought," Mama added, "a marriage might fix things. Give you a husband and us a son who would mind the shop without revealing the truth of Posey's involvement. But"—she shook her head—"it was a poor idea. Especially if it drives you away."

"I've not gone anywhere. A day's jaunt out of London is all, but—oh!" She met all their gazes with bright eyes. "We found the copies. We found my work, and they are now back where they are supposed to be, but tomorrow I will visit Lady Balantine. And I will burn them all. You are safe. Frampton's is safe."

"And you are safe." Her father's shoulders slumped, and he breathed easy, long breaths, his hands tightening on hers. "You are safe."

"Did you find Lord Lysander?" her mother asked. "Is he well?"

"We did. And he is."

"And is that ..." Posey brushed her thumb over Fiona's cheek. "Paint?"

Fiona laughed and told them all, too relieved they'd welcomed her home with open arms to care about much more. When finally the story was told and yawns echoed through the room, she took herself upstairs and paused outside her chamber, resting her head on the door. She should not feel so heavy. Everyone safe, and all paintings accounted for. Her own involvement in the situation was hidden for now. For as long as Baron Balantine would keep his mouth shut. And even then, safe because Zander had lied. To save her.

That did not feel safe at all. Felt like him at risk or every breath he took for the rest of his life. She clutched at her heart, constricted in a vice, and slipped into her room. She found the tinderbox in the dark and soon had the room blazing with light.

"Good evening, dragon."

She yelped and jumped as she spun around. "Zander?"

He laid across her bed, legs crossed at the ankles, hands folded over his chest. He was clean now and neatly dressed, missing only his boots and his jacket. "I hope you do not mind I doffed my boots." He nodded toward the end of the bed. "Didn't want to get London muck on your lovely little bed."

"What are you doing here?" she hissed, rushing toward him. "How did you get in?"

"I have my ways. As you well know." He patted the mattress next to him.

What did this mean? She hesitated, but his lazy, beckoning gaze shattered her hesitations, and she joined him on the bed, his arms welcoming her as she laid her body alongside his. He tightened his hold on her, bringing her home against his beating heart.

"Why are you here?" she asked. "You should be resting."

He kissed the top of her head. "I am resting. Right here."

"Your paint is gone," she said, reaching up to his temple. "Do you still hurt?

He winced and gave her another kiss. "A bit. Just don't poke around near the back of my head, yes?"

"Why are you here?" Repeating it because he'd still not answered her. Another kiss for another nonanswer. She tried to find insult, but the kisses wore her down, made her snuggle deeper into his embrace. "Zander." A note of caution for him there.

"I am here because I've dreamt of holding you like this. In a bed."

She kissed his chest.

"And I'm here because I missed you."

Another kiss for his admission.

"And because I have a key, of course."

"Of course." A kiss rumbling with laughter this time.

"And I'm here because … I need to know." He tipped her chin up with his knuckles, and the gaze he raked her with was rawer than any he'd given her before. "I need to know if you're done with me." He looked away, let loose her chin. "We have found what we set out to find, after all. And though you might be with child, you also might not be, and me being me, I would not wonder if you wished to … part ways."

She sat up right, slapping her palms on his chest to do so and keeping one hand there to pin him while the other forced his chin center, forced his gaze back to hers. "Part ways?"

He nodded, closed his eyes. "It's best for you, naturally. After we're sure there's no child. But I confess I am having a difficult time reconciling with the idea. I keep finding ways we can make do. Live with Raph at Briarcliff. You designing and I traveling a bit to authenticate pieces. It might be safer for us as well, in the country. Closer to the ocean too if we have to make a dramatic getaway because Baron Balantine's lips have loosened. And who knows. Perhaps one day, I'll accidently create something of value and earn my inheritance. But, Fiona ..." His eyes opened.

"Yes?" The only word she could muster, her brain so full of his little speech, his words building a story so like the ones her imagination so constantly spun.

"I am here because I realized you've chased and chased after me."

"I'm not so sure that's complimentary."

He laughed and wrapped his hand around her hip. "It is. I needed chasing. Wanted you but didn't feel I could do the chasing myself. And there you were, always telling me exactly what you want, never hesitating to ask for it. And I've given in because I want it, too. But you shouldn't have to do all the chasing. And I don't want to run from you, no matter how difficult life might get. I want to love you, and I do love you, and maybe if I chase you long enough, I might convince you to love me back."

She gave a little huff. "I do not think you'll have to chase me very long." Not long at all, in fact. She let her body melt, meld to his, and she kissed the tip of his chin. "Just out of curiosity, do you have any qualms against a woman secretly running a jewelry shop?"

"No, not particularly. Wait ... does she dislike it? Because if she'd rather be doing something else, then—"

"No." She kissed his neck this time. "It's her dream."

"Are we talking about you?"

"No. My sister. Seems we need a business-minded fellow so Posey, and I of course, can continue doing as we please at Frampton's. Someone who can provide a male face of propriety."

"Do you mean you need a husband to pretend to be a jeweler so you and your sister can actually be the jewelers?"

"Pricisely."

"Sounds diverting. Are you accepting applications? I'm in the market for a new position, and—"

She kissed him, stopping all sound but those sounds of hunger for one another.

He returned the kiss, hard, and stroked his knuckles down her cheek then flipped them. Her belly erupted into the tiny flutters of hundreds of butterfly wings, and he kissed her again as his big body rested on top of hers, and he braced his weight above her on his elbows, using his hands to clear the hair away from her face, to stroke the soft skin at her temples, to rub a thumb over her winged eyebrows. He dipped and kissed the very tip of her nose. "Make love to me."

"Finally, *you* ask *me*," she breathed, parting his lips with her tongue. She arched her back to press her breasts against his chest.

He let his hand trail down her neck and over her shoulders, pulled at the neckline of her bodice, while his other hand stretched lower to lift up the hem of her skirts. When he had them pooled above her hips, she sat up, forcing him upright onto his knees. She tugged at the hem of his shirt, freeing it so her fingers could slip beneath it, could rake down his warm skin and taut muscle. She traced the lines of his abdomen and felt other parts harden. Ah, yes. Other parts of him beckoned, and she reached with curious fingers for his fall, hearing an unfamiliar squeak from her own throat, an odd little sound of desire.

He rubbed his hands over her shoulders and kissed her neck, a small chuckle rumbling through him and into her. "God, you amuse me to no end. I want to hear little squeaks like that the rest of my life."

She wanted to hear words like that for the rest of hers. The buttons of his fall proved numerous but trifling, and she flicked them all open with little difficulty. When he sprang free, she took him in hand, as she had with such boldness their first night together, and rubbed her thumb across the tip of his shaft. He groaned and caught her up in his arms once more, stroking his fingernails up and down her back before he slid palms flat against her ribs, then cupped her breasts in his hands and squeezed. Her head fell back with a moan.

"You are perfect," he said. "Every inch perfect. The only perfect thing in my life I've ever coveted."

She scattered kisses along his neck and jaw as her hand, between their bodies, played with him still. She loved holding the pulsing length of him, looked forward to learning in more detail what to do with it. She'd tell him what she wanted, listen to his desires, too.

"Will this differ from what we've done before?" she asked. "Making love?"

"There is a bed this time. Other than a bit more softness, no. Did you not know," he whispered into her ear, "that it was love then, too? I did not want it to be, but that does not stop it. Does not make it any less dangerous."

"Dangerous?" Her fingertips made indentations in his back.

"It damn well is. No one runs from something that is not dangerous, and nothing is as dangerous to a hardheaded man as love. You, my dragon, have always been a danger."

That pleased her, so she kissed him to show him, pressing her lips to the heavy muscle of his chest above his beating heart. "That *is* a compliment."

His dark eyes glinted wicked in the firelight, and he slid a hand over her thigh between her legs, and inside of her.

She gasped, arched against him.

"I should play the part of the proper gentleman," he groaned. "Speak with your father first."

"I did not fall in love with a proper gentleman," she breathed. "I fell in love with you, so you'd better ravish me right here and now, Lysander."

He stilled then slammed her backward into the bed, stopping his body from falling on hers with taut arms, the tip of his nose almost brushing the tip of hers. "Say it again," he growled. "If it is true, say it again."

"Ravish me."

"Not that."

"Lysander."

"Not. That."

She tapped her nose against his and closed her eyes. "I love you."

He nudged her legs apart and thrust into her in one smooth move, making her gasp, making her clutch at his shoulder, his back. She wrapped her fingers around steel-hard arms, which made her want more though he gave her everything. Her hips rolled against him, as a welcome tide of pleasure rolled through her, and she dove her fingers into the hair at his nape and pulled him down for a kiss that shook her like a roll of thunder across the sky.

He thrust into her over and over again and laid his voice close to her ear, heating her, driving her higher. "Marry me. Marry me. I can give you nothing but myself, love, but dear God, marry me."

"Yes," she cried before her body shattered around him.

He came seconds later, pumping harder and faster and collapsing beside her. He rolled, clasping his arms tight around her and taking her with him so they could end the interlude, the consummation, as they had begun it—her resting atop his chest, his arms pulling her close, his lips resting in her hair.

When her heart slowed, and she could think once more, she slipped curious fingers inside his pocket, found the twined wire there and held it up for him to see, twirling it between her forefinger and thumb so it sparked in the dim light.

He took it and bent it, coiled the ends around each other

and slipped the little ring onto her finger. "There. I cannot afford much better, but—"

"There is no better." She kissed the ring and kissed his chest and knew without a doubt— because who better than a forger to know these things—that the ring he looped about her heart was real and more valuable than anything she could hope to forge from diamonds and gold.

Epilogue

Zander read the letter once more before tossing it to the desk and standing. He strode across his bedroom and looked out onto the garden below. Briarcliff had always been beautiful in late summer, and this year proved no different. He'd have to leave in a few days, though, to meet with a Mr. Harding, who had been approached by a buyer to sell a family heirloom. An icon of Russian origin. Zander smelled rubbish in the man's description of the icon, doubted it was as old as the man claimed. He scratched his chin and tapped the glass. But it might not be as old as the buyer claimed. Why else would the buyer want it? Unless it was valuable.

Matilda, his sister-in-law, strolled outside—bounced, really, backward—calling to someone, her bonnet falling to hang at her back.

Fiona appeared, laughing, running, her bonnet a tangled, forgotten mess as well. Zander's heart knocked about his ribs, and he flattened a palm against the glass. He loved his wife. Married but a fortnight, and he hated letting her go for a moment. But he'd had correspondence to go through, and she'd needed sport beyond their bedroom. She'd needed sunshine, so he'd sent her out to play with the women of the house.

A knock on his door took him across the room in a few steps, and he opened it. "Mother. Good afternoon." He looked over his shoulder at the window, the garden beyond. "I thought you were romping with Matilda and Fee. What brings you to the top of the house?"

She beamed up at him, her hands folded behind her back, a position he still found terribly suspicious. He took a wary step back and eyed her. "Lysander, oh my dear son."

"Ye-es?" He took another step back.

She bounced up and down, her arms still behind her. "You've won your inheritance! Though I would have given it to you before now, if you'd asked."

His slow retreat stopped, and his feet took root in the rug as he tried to order his thoughts. "I know you would have but ... Father's final wish." He shook his head. "I'm confused. Is this a joke? I've not painted a thing."

"I just spoke with Fiona."

"What's she to do with it?"

"I already knew, of course, all about your harrowing adventure with that dreadful baron, how you bested him, and how they found you both covered in paint." She unfolded her arms from behind her back and held out a roll of something or other to him. No. Not something. A canvas. "Take it."

He did, unrolling it, not recognizing the beaten canvas spread haphazardly with green paint. "What is this?"

"It's the canvas, taken off its frame, that you propped on the stairs to stop the baron in his tracks. After, of course, you exploded a paint bladder all over him."

Fully unrolled, he held it out before him. Ugly. Blobs of green paint, a speck of red that might be blood. "Where did you get this?"

"Fiona had it, saved it from the sight of that man's crimes, brought it to me. Said it was a secret wedding present for you, just arrived by way of Lady Balantine."

"Why would Fiona want this? It's ugly. It's a trap for a silly man, not a work of art."

"I disagree. I adore it. I'm going to have it framed. And I'm going to give you your inheritance. You've won it nicely with that." She nodded at the canvas.

"This?"

"Is your hearing well, Lysander?"

He shook his head, rolled up the canvas, and handed it back to his mother. "This is absurd."

"Not at all. You boys are always accusing me of absurdity, but you're wrong. You created this out of love for your wife. You were willing to do anything to save her. That sentiment should be framed and cherished. And, frankly, you did one better than just paint me a work of art. You brought me an entire artist, Lysander. She's designing me a necklace, you know, made to look like rose thorns." She hugged him. "Thank you." Then her arms disappeared, and so did she, bouncing down the hall, and soon, returning to the window, he saw her with Matilda, saw them wander in the direction of the lake. Where had Fiona gone?

Zander rolled up the green-stained canvas and put it on the desk. Then, with numb legs, he turned his steps toward the long gallery on the house's second floor. He stood before the Rubens hanging there. The real ones. They'd burned the copies weeks ago. He considered them all but stood longer before the one that was now ... his. Bewilderingly *his*.

"Hell," he whispered, pulling it from the wall. He sat in the middle of the floor, legs crossed, and held it backside up in his lap, running his fingers across the brown paper there.

Raph had found a letter. Words of pride. Words of grief. Words of love.

Maggie had found one, too. Full of sun-filled memories

from childhood and reminders to always remember she was her name—magnificent.

Hands trembling, Zander poked a hole in the bottom right-hand corner of the paper, right where the other letters had been but went no farther.

Footsteps in the hall.

He looked up.

Fiona stood in the doorway, leaning on the frame. "It worked, then? I was not sure if it would, but if you've poked behind that painting, I gather"—she took two halting steps toward him—"it's worked."

He reached out for her, needing her by him. She came to him on swift feet, floating to the floor beside him, lavender skirts spilling over her legs, her knees brushing against his thighs, her body leaning into his as she placed her chin on his shoulder, kissed him on the jaw.

He turned from her, set his gaze upon that small hole he'd made. "Thank you. I'm not sure ... how in the hell you—" He closed his eyes and shook his head. "No matter. It worked. Somehow a green blob of a backside on a canvas worked." But it hadn't been the blob. It had been the love.

She kissed his jaw again. "Sorry my gift is late. I didn't think about it until after I'd met your mother and heard her story about Raph and Matilda's winning of their painting. Once I knew it was gone with the bathwater, I knew this would work. I knew she'd see that green blob of a backside for what it's worth. She is, after all, your mother, Zander, and knows the correct value of things."

Raph had painted a heart on Matilda's arm, and their mother had seen it, awarded him his inheritance.

Zander chuckled. "I should have thought of it. You're brilliant, you know that?"

"That's what you keep telling me." She kissed his jaw again, and this time nipped his earlobe, too. "I'm just glad it was still lying on the stairs of that estate, untouched, and that Lady Balantine found it so quickly. Now you can do as you wish. Use the funds from the sale of this painting for whatever you like."

"I'll speak with Raph. See what needs to be done." He did not feel so useless living here as he'd thought he would. Fiona and Matilda were thick as thieves, and Mother adored them both. Fiona had time and encouragement to make her designs and sent batches of them to London where Posey was busy bringing them to life. Life here was good. He had purpose and happiness, but ... "Perhaps we can put some money back, or invest it, for a home in London."

"I would like that." He would, too. "Are you going to see?" She nodded at the painting, the hole.

He took a deep breath and stabbed the paper again, made the gap wider and let in light, revealing a square of creamy white. The letter. His letter. He lifted it up and studied his name scrawled across one side in his father's loopy, familiar hand.

"Would you like to be alone?"

He shook his head, put his free hand on her knee, and squeezed. "Stay. Please."

She leaned into him, clasped his free hand in both of hers, and rested her head on his shoulder. "As long as you need."

He opened it. Read it. Such a short note, such a small thing to wreck him like the angry stream of a flooding river, carrying him away like a broken bridge. He let the silence and the tides around them gather as he read it a second time, a third.

Finally, she squeezed his hand and whispered, "What does it say?"

He swallowed hard and pressed the heel of his hand into his eye. "Thank you. He says thank you for being stronger than him, for doing what he could not do and selling the paintings. He says … he says I am a better man than him, and that …" His throat clogged with emotion, but he pushed the words out anyway. They'd somehow gotten easier to say since meeting Fiona. "He says that he loves me."

"Oh, Zander." She hugged him tight.

He hugged her back, the letter floating to the floor to lay crisp against the painting's brown back, slightly bumped up by the wire that held the painting on the wall. Ink splatters marred the paper. Tear stains, too. Uneven script made almost illegible. Imperfect. Like Zander. Like his father.

But Zander had always loved imperfect things best.

When he finally pocketed the letter and replaced the painting on the wall, he pulled Fiona close to his side, with one arm slung over her shoulders, and led her into the gardens where his family had gathered. Raph in a grumpy mood because of some farming thing or other. Matilda teasing him. Mother demanding to know if anyone had heard from Theo, and if he was going to let her languish without word from him for the rest of her life.

Imperfect, all of them, but the love that held them tight together, that bound him to Fiona like the gold and silver wires bound gently round her finger, was the only thing of value in the world.

Sneak Peek

HIS MISTRESS, HIS MUSE, AND OTHER MADNESS

May 1822

The solicitor had told Lord Theodore Bromley what the woman looked like—orange hair, freckles, young and slender. The woman framed in the window of the house on Drury Lane must be her, both like and unlike her description, with hair more of a deep copper than orange. And beautiful. The solicitor had not mentioned that.

She seemed a perfect picture, a medieval lady of the castle, more goddess than woman. Her thick, curly hair, a medusa's nest of snakes, coiled high, ringlets escaping to frame her face. Her gown, a spring green muslin affair, high necked and long-sleeved, encased a straight spine, confident shoulders, and a slim but lush figure. If not a Guinevere, she could, easily, be taken for a proper miss, a barrister's daughter, sought-after and beloved. Or, perhaps, one might mistake her for a newly-wed wife, innocent yet beguiling, waiting for her husband's arrival after a long day of separation.

She was none of those things.

She was a thorn in Lord Theodore Bromley's backside. And he'd pluck her out and stomp her under his heel in less time than it had taken him to walk from his sister's home here. A quarter of an hour and he'd be done. His part of fulfilling his father's cursed will completed.

Theo ripped his gaze away from the window and the woman framed within it and glared up at the row house. Nice and neat and well-positioned. He'd only just learned of the house's existence at the same time as he'd learned about the lady. A nice house, too, and likely stocked with servants when Briarcliff, the family's country seat, was falling down around their heads.

He snorted and strode for the door. His father had taken better care of her, one of the artistic leeches who'd drained his family's coffers over the last decade or more, than he had his own family. But his father was dead, and once Theo found this woman new coffers to rob, he and his family would be rid of her.

"S'cuse me, mister," a voice said from behind.

He didn't turn around. "Yes?"

"You're blocking my way into the house."

Theo did turn, then, narrowing his attention on the slender man standing in the street. "You've come to visit Lady Cordelia?"

The slender man with golden hair, queued at the back of his neck, nodded.

"Go away. She's no time for visitors today."

"I was paid to come here!" The man's face flushed a mottled pink.

She paid lovers, then, did she? With what money? He almost growled.

"Leave." He did growl, a warning that sent the other man scurrying away.

Good. Theo knocked on the door. Lady Cordelia would have no pleasure today. Only pain.

The door flew open, and a woman with a wide mouth, hooked nose, and frizzy gray hair entered. "Good day. May I ask who's calling?"

"I wish to speak with Lady Cordelia Trent." Better to keep his identity a secret lest the woman run for a backdoor.

The housekeeper, for that's what she must be, dragged her gaze down the length of Theo's body then back up. "Ah, yes. She's expecting you. I'll show you where to go." She pulled Theo into the house and pushed him down the hallway, stealing his hat and gloves and greatcoat before tucking her hands beneath the lapels of his jacket and tugging the garment off from behind.

Theo jerked out of the woman's reach. "What are you about, madam? Give that back!"

The housekeeper chuckled. "Shy? Very well. You may do the rest yourself. Just trying to be helpful."

"You're not my valet!" He'd never even had a valet. No funds for it.

The housekeeper shrugged but did not give Theo's jacket back. She led him deeper into the house, stopping at a door in the shadows at the very end of the hallway. She pushed it open and ushered Theo inside.

Six women, sitting in a circle, easels stationed before them, pencils nestled between fingers, looked up at him. They were of various ages and two wore unrelieved black. They stared at him unabashedly with clear interest in their eyes, which roamed down the length of his body. Then back up. Some of them at least. A few lost their way somewhere round his midsection. A tad lower, actually. Their gazes... hovered. As if glued there. They'd stripped him to his skin without lifting a finger.

"What the hell is happening here?" he demanded. He tugged at his waistcoat, the cuffs of his shirt sleeves, feeling naked without his jacket to pull over that region where their collective interest paused.

"Very nice," a young woman with mischievous blue eyes said, tugging at her bottom lip with her teeth. "The agency has not sent so burly a specimen as *this* before."

Another woman, gray streaked in her dark hair, jumped to her feet. "Let me help you with your waistcoat, sir." She reached for his abdomen, tickled the buttons lined up there.

He swatted her hands away. "Hands off, woman!" Hell. He'd inadvertently entered a heretofore unknown level of hell where randy women and *helpful* housekeepers stripped you bare and—

"You're not the model I hired." A voice, low and rich and rather like a good wine, snapped out the observation.

Theo looked to the doorway. There she stood. The woman from the window—Lady Cordelia Trent. The thorn in his backside. His prey.

She stood with absolutely composure, and her voice hid no trembling fear. "Mrs. Barkley? Who is this?"

"The ... model?" supplied the housekeeper, Mrs. Barkley it appeared, her arms full of Theo's stolen clothing.

"He most assuredly is not. I chose the model myself." She returned her attention to Theo, head tilted to the side. "I apologize for the confusion, sir. But ... who are you?"

Theo moved to snap his jacket tight but found no jacket so crossed his arms over his chest instead.

Several women sighed.

He scowled. "I am Lord Theodore Bromley, your late patron's youngest son. And you are Lady Cordelia Trent."

The tilt of her head righted, revealing a strong column of creamy throat. Her pale brown eyes softened. "I am. I ... I heard of your father's passing. It was a blow. But howsoever it pained me, it must have distressed you so much more. My condolences. He was a good man. My savior."

"He was a fool. Now, will you tell these women to leave, or shall I?" He wouldn't even ask what hijinks occupied them, prompting them to undress strange men upon entering rooms. He would not ask because he could guess well enough. Models. Agencies. Easels and chalk and pencils. Now he had a breath or two to think on it, he knew. He'd spent his childhood in a home where nearly-naked human models were common. The better to study and paint anatomy, his father had always said. The body is a beautiful thing, almost divine, his mother had sighed, the perfect subject for the artist.

Lady Cordelia's pink lips parted with a gasp, but she recovered quickly, clapping her hands and facing the riveted women. "I am deeply sorry for this confusion. It appears we'll have to cancel our class for the day. I'll speak with the agency and find out what's become of Trevor."

"The shivering fellow with the slender build?" Theo asked. "I sent him packing."

Lady Cordelia sucked her cheeks in, and for a moment, her heart-shaped face grew gaunt. Then she let out a frustrated breath, short and staccato. "At least I know he's safe." She forced a smile for the women and ushered them toward the door.

As the women gathered their belongings and exchanged parting words with their hostess, Theo walked the edges of the room, studying it. New-ish wallpaper, thick rugs. Fine art on the walls. Naturally. In all, a better room than any in his one-room apartment. A better room than any in his family's country estate, Briarcliff Manor.

Better. He'd hoped to find composure through his observations of his surroundings. He'd found rage instead. Nothing new, that. It always bubbled close beneath his skin.

When the room quieted, he whirled on his toes to face her. "You're teaching a class for women to paint nude men?"

She stood calm, hands folded together before her. "I facilitate it. They are all widows in need of diversion, wishing to learn a new skill. I do not have the skill to teach such a thing. Lady Fordham—the woman who attempted to relieve you of your waistcoat—teaches it."

What a farce he had walked in on. But at least it would make an excellent print for the Ackerman's next week. He'd give the women in the sketch greedy eyes and draw his own frame as slabs of ham and chicken legs. He'd title it something like "Widows Take Solace in Learning New Skills." He'd make it clear the solace they actually sought had nothing to do with the application of art.

She walked toward him calmly and with the precision of a soldier. "Who are you to come into my home, send my guests away, walk about as if you own the place, and—"

"I *do* own the place." At least his brother did.

Lady Cordelia rocked back a step, her body going rigid. But not for long. She flowed into movement once more until she stood right before him, her chin held high, her hands fisted tight in the green muslin of her skirts. "No. It is *my* home."

"For now. But it was my father's property. And now it is my brother's." And the only thing that kept his brother Raph from selling the house was its current occupant.

"Then why is your brother not here?" she demanded.

"Because he is in the country trying to avoid selling off all our lands and to keep the manor house from falling into complete ruin." And being an alarmingly content newlywed. Though that was not her business. "Attempting, in short, to right our father's many wrongs. Of which *you* are one."

Her gaze dragged over him as the other women's had, from his beaver hat to his muddy boots, stopping for a moment on the practical and simple knot of his cravat before popping up to his face, and she raked that, too, trying, it seemed, to learn or understand every inch of his visage. She stepped back, her hands loosening on her skirts, revealing the wrinkled inroads she'd made in the muslin. "Lord Theodore. I see him in you. Your father. Same nose, if you don't mind me saying. Same eyes."

Theo grinned, and he knew it showed teeth. Sharp teeth. "I'm nothing like the old man. As far from him as you can imagine. To begin, he bought you a house, kept you here like a little doll because he thought your art special—"

She opened her mouth and raised an arm to interrupt him.

He barreled forward. "But I am going to kick you out."

Her hands became fists again. "You can't."

He raised a brow. "Pretty, but no brains. Pity. Look, if you need proof of the situation, you're welcome to visit the family solicitor. I'll give you his name and address."

Her eyes narrowed. She would have hissed, spit poison at him if she could. "You are a devil."

He bowed, a concession. "At your service."

She blinked, shook her head. "You're not joking."

"I never joke."

"I believe that." She groped for a nearby chair and fell into it, her eyes glassing over. She clutched the scrolled arm of the charm with one hand and waved the other hand at him. "Your face is too stony."

"The stony nature of my face is neither here nor there." He sat across from her. "Now, tell me what sort of art you produce so I can find a suitable patron for you, one interested in your talents." Then they could sell the damn house and be part way to solvency.

She squared her shoulders, met him with chin high. "Nothing."

"I'm in no mood for games, Lady Cordelia. Your housekeeper stripped me to my shirtsleeves. Do not play with me. Tell me now what your medium is."

She laughed, falling forward and burying her face in her palms, her shoulders shaking. Had she gone mad? Hell. Should he leave? Call a doctor? The housekeeper at least. Did she need ... tea? Just when he parted his lips to call for some (it was better than nothing at least), she breathed deep and stood.

"Follow me, Lord Theodore. I will show you my masterpieces." She swept into the hallway, and he followed her up the stairs and to a tiny room nestled at the back of the third story of the house. Its walls were lined with paintings and shelves, on which rested various statuary, silhouettes, and pieces of jewelry.

She held an arm out wide, inviting him in. "Take a look, my lord. Behold my many talents."

He studied the paintings first. "You did these?"

She stood beside him. "Oh yes. Delightful, aren't they?"

The watercolors were of a ... street? With horses, no ... dogs? Pulling carriages?

"They look as if a child drew them," he said.

"And by that you mean they have an air of irresistible innocence about them, yes? A polite man would say so."

"I'm not polite, and no I do not mean that. I mean they show no understanding of perspective or anatomy or, even, of how watercolors *work*."

"I'm aware." She strode to the shelves. "Would you like to view my ceramics?"

He joined her. Hell. Worse and worse. "Is that a ..."

"Soldier riding a horse? Yes, of course it is."

"I meant to ask if it was a likeness of a giant pile of horse sh—"

"No."

He tapped the top of the ceramic. "If so, it's remarkably like it."

"I wish I could say it was. Now come see my silhouettes." She nodded to a nearby shelf and stepped to the side to allow him to better see its contents. "Here's one of your dear father. And one of the King."

They looked like pigs, the both of them, with snouts where noses should be and hair turned up at the top like floppy, pointy ears. What odd hell was this?

"What do you think?" She batted her lashes at him, all innocence.

"I think you're playing some elaborate joke. My father would not have taken you on had you no talent. All the artists he supported were geniuses, had already won fame. I assumed the only reason your name is not a household one is because you're a woman."

"You do not mince words, Lord Theodore."

"Why should I?"

She made her way toward the only window in the room, a small one, no curtains hanging over it. She leaned her body into the frame and stared outside. "He hoped I would develop a talent." She looked at him over her shoulder. "Do you really know nothing of my story? Your mother knew. She visited several times, first to help me settle into the house and then to visit. Once."

"I knew nothing at all of your existence until our solicitor gave me a list of the artists my father named in his will."

"He named me? To deed me this house?"

"No. To ensure my brother did not stop funds flowing to you until we'd found a suitable patron to replace his support."

She slumped against the window. "He said the house would be mine. Promised me."

"Ha. He made many promises he didn't keep." He surveyed the room, his stomach sinking. "How the hell am I supposed to find you a patron when you can't do a damn thing—" He snapped his teeth together and crossed the room. "Why did he do this?"

She lifted her gaze to him, and he expected to find it watery but found it strong and clear instead. "Do you mean why did he save my life?"

"No. I mean why did he give part of our family's fortune to house and feed and clothe a young lady as if she were a bastard daughter or a mistress when our own pantry remained empty at home? Tell me."

"Such accusations." She paced toward him until their chests almost bumped. Close enough to smell her. Tea and mint. "I'm not his daughter." A snap of passion in her voice. She wagged a finger in his face and marched forward, forcing him to retreat until his back hit the shelves behind him. "Nor his mistress."

"I know that bit. I said *as if you were*."

"My father is—"

"The Earl of Crossly. Dead."

She flinched, her hand wavering up to a small, gold chain necklace at her throat, a tiny golden bird dangling from it, resting between the folds of her fichu. The movement brought his attention to the hidden swell of her bosom, and he refocused on her face before speaking.

"The last of his line but for a daughter. You. No cousins, even, to speak of." A brittle bit of wall around his heart cracked a bit. She appeared so very alone. His father had been a charitable soul, and despite the woman's lack of artistic talent, he could well understand why she'd pluck on his father's heart strings. The woman had no one. Not even her title could help her. "Why aren't you with friends? Do you have none?"

"I did. Your father." Her words, hard as the bricks he built walls for himself of, said clearly she would say no more. "It is enough for you to know your father found me a home when I most needed it. And he brought the marchioness to meet me and comfort me. And he sent tutor after tutor to me every month, trying to help me find my talent. Only ... I do not have one."

Slowly, recognizing the wild animal in her eyes and not wishing to scare it, he lifted an arm between their close bodies and nudged her hand to the side until that wagging finger in his face went limp and hit her skirts. Her other hand covered her eyes, and she swayed forward as if she might sway into him, lean on him for support as she had done his father four years ago.

But he wasn't his father, so he cupped his hands around her shoulders and set her aside. "Do you expect sympathy from me?"

She peered into his eyes. "No."

"Good. You'll find none." He took a step forward, walking her backward as she had him. "When my father died, he left us with debts and everything in ruins. He left the only thing of value—his art collection—to the Royal Society but for six paintings and a will demanding we continue to pay for the lives of three artists until we found patrons to replace him. The man, you see, continues to penury us from the grave. But not for long. I've found two of these artistic hangers-on already, resituated them—one with a duke with more money than sense and the other with a wealthy merchant of equally substandard reasoning skills. You are last on my list, and I thought it would be an easy matter to rid ourselves of you." Two more steps brought her up against the window once more, a barrier of only a few inches of air between them. "This complicates matters. *You* complicate matters."

She threw her head back and laughed. "A complication, yes. I've often been told so. I have been for a long while now, I suppose."

"I can't find you a patron if you've no talent. And I can't

stop payments to your account unless you find a new patron." And he couldn't do his part to save the estate, to rebuild the family, if didn't do those things. And they couldn't sell the house until she left it. Not because of any will stipulation but because he and his brothers, oddly raised as they had been, *were* gentlemen at the very base of everything.

"I'll figure something out," he muttered.

She sauntered toward him, her body swaying but her face a brittle mask. "I could always become your mistress, Lord Theodore. Since your father's death, I have contemplated a life in the demimonde. If I run out of options. And with no talent and no one to care for me, I'm already low on those." Her fingers traced the buttons of his waistcoat.

Elegant fingers, long, like those of a pianist. Her nails were rounded and smooth. The hands of a pampered woman. As they trailed, her eyes softened, her lips, too, as they parted slightly.

Theo's cock tightened. She was beautiful—delicate and strong, fiery yet soft—and her touch scorched him, stole breath and warped bones. And she touched him, gazed at him with those soft eyes, as if he were wanted, *needed*. So damn beautiful he had to squeeze his fingernails into his palms, cutting, biting, to keep from reaching for her. Those pinpricks of pain reminded him well—beauty lied. Beauty was false, an illusion that entranced, ruined.

He snorted and turned from her, stopping in the doorway. "You may seek a man's bed in exchange for stability, Lady Cordelia, but it won't be mine. I'll be back." He left the house, never pausing to look back. His father hadn't left him an artist to foist off on someone else, he'd left Theo a moral dilemma. They couldn't continue supporting this woman and her house and her servants and her gowns and frippery. But he couldn't toss her out. He'd investigated her connections. She had none, at least none interested in accepting a woman with a murky past into the bosom of their family. What then?

He stopped cold on the street. Hell. He'd left his clothes.

~

His Mistress, His Muse, and Other Madness will be available October 2023!

Also by Charlie Lane

The Cavendish Family

Leave a Widow Wanting More

Teach a Rogue New Tricks

Bring a Boxer to His Knees

Love a Lady at Midnight

Scandalizing the Scoundrel

London Secrets

The Secret Seduction

A Secret Desire

Sinning in Secret

Keep No Secrets

Secrets Between Lovers

The Debutante Dares (with WOLF Press)

Daring the Duke

A Dare Too Far

Kiss or Dare

Don't You Dare, My Dear

Only Rakes Would Dare

Daring Done Right

About the Author

CHARLIE LANE traded in academic databases and scholarly journals for writing steamy Regency romcoms like the ones she's always loved to read. When she's not writing humorous conversations, dramatic confrontations, or sexy times, she's flying high in the air as a circus-obsessed acrobat.

Visit my website with the QR code and your phone!

Made in the USA
Monee, IL
04 December 2023

48172360R00176